OLIVIA MANNING

(1908-1980) was born in Portsmouth. The daughter of a naval officer and an Ulster-Irish mother, she described her childhood as 'middle class and uneventful'. She came to London in her early twenties, after art-school training. She advanced from typing vanlists at Peter Jones for 15s a week to painting furniture, and then moved to book production at the Medici Society. Her friendship with Stevie Smith, bridesmaid at her wedding, dates from these times. Her first novel, *The Wind Changes* (1937), was published when she was twenty-nine.

A few days before war was declared she married R.D. Smith, then a British Council lecturer, later a distinguished radio producer, and Professor first at the New University of Ulster and then at Surrey University. Olivia accompanied him to his post in Bucharest: from there they moved to Greece, and were evacuated to Egypt from Athens two days before the Germans put up their swastika on the Acropolis. Olivia was Press Officer to the United States Embassy in Cairo, and from 1941-45 worked in Jerusalem as Press Assistant at the Public Information Office in Jerusalem, and for the British Council.

After the war Olivia Manning established herself as one of Britain's foremost novelists. *Artist Among the Missing* was published in 1949, followed by *School for Love* (1951); *A Different Face* (1953); *The Doves of Venus* (1955, also published by Virago); the Balkan Trilogy: *The Great Fortune* (1960), *The Spoilt City* (1962), *Friends and Heroes* (1965); *The Play Room* (1969, also published by Virago); *The Rain Forest* (1974); and the Levant Trilogy: *The Danger Tree* (1977), *The Battle Lost and Won* (1978), and *The Sum of Things* (1980). She also published two volumes of short stories, a travel book on Ireland, a biographical study of Stanley in Africa, and a book on her much-loved Siamese and Bur᎐᎐᎐ cats.

Olivia Mannir᎐᎐᎐᎐᎐᎐᎐᎐᎐᎐᎐᎐᎐᎐᎐᎐᎐᎐᎐᎐n's Wood, North London᎐᎐᎐᎐᎐᎐᎐᎐᎐᎐᎐᎐᎐᎐᎐᎐᎐᎐on Trust Award in 1949᎐᎐᎐᎐᎐᎐᎐᎐᎐᎐᎐᎐᎐᎐6.

VIRAGO
MODERN
CLASSIC

NUMBER
302

OLIVIA MANNING

THE
WIND CHANGES

**WITH A NEW INTRODUCTION BY
ISOBEL ENGLISH**

Published by VIRAGO PRESS Limited 1988
20-23 Mandela Street, Camden Town, London NW1 0HQ

First published in Great Britain by Jonathan Cape Limited 1937
Copyright Olivia Manning 1937
Introduction Copyright © Isobel English 1988

British Cataloguing in Publication Data

Printed in Great Britain by Cox and Wyman Ltd., Reading, Berks

INTRODUCTION

Olivia Manning was twenty-nine when
Jonathan Cape published *The Wind Changes* in
the spring of 1937. It was her first book and her
only novel to deal with 'the troubles' in Ireland.
Set in June 1921, shortly before the Anglo-Irish
truce, it provides an ironic commentary on
partition. In the opening chapter there is a scene
where the Black and Tans burn down an old
woman's cottage because she has not warned
them of a Sinn Fein ambush. But had she done
so, the Sinn Feiners would almost certainly
have taken her out and shot her.

At Olivia's home in Laburnum Grove in
Portsmouth, where she and her younger
brother grew up, such events were often talked
about by their parents. Their mother was an
Ulster Presbyterian, who never lost her Co.
Down accent and abhorred strong drink: she
was by way of being a scold, and when her
husband gave Olivia a copy of *Adam Bede* she
took it away on the grounds that it was not 'a
nice book' for a young girl to have. Commander
Manning, who had risen from the ranks in the
Royal Navy, had been born in Clerkenwell in
1869. This made him appear, in the eyes of his

children, almost a historical figure, and sometimes they thought of him more as a grandfather than a father. Olivia used to say that he looked like Edward VII and once on the royal yacht he had been mistaken for the King. He had been brought up in the great days of Empire, and would recount thrilling tales about the sabre battle in which he had fought at Tel-el-Kebir in 1892 and the raiding party which he had led during the Boxer Rebellion in 1900.

During the long stretches when he was on active service, Mrs Manning used to take the children to stay with relations in Bangor in Northern Ireland. She also had cousins in the South in Galway and Co. Clare. When the family returned home after these visits—sometimes they lasted for more than a year—Olivia and her brother would be teased and made fun of in the school playground. 'They used to shout at us and call us half foreigners,' Olivia told me, 'and we suffered an identity crisis at a young age.' This is reflected in an early semi-autobiographical short story where the narrator describes herself as 'a sort of mongrel ... [who does] not seem to belong anywhere'; she maintains, too, that not only does friction and hatred exist between the North and South of Ireland, but also between the Ulster people and the English.

The story, in which these remarks are made,

is called 'Portrait of a Hungarian Doctor' and was first published in the November-December 1935 issue of the little magazine *New Stories*: it was her first story to appear under her full name. During her early twenties she had brought out three mystery serials under the name of Jacob Morrow—her mother was a Miss Morrow—and later she had contributed articles and short stories to local Portsmouth papers under the name of O.M. Manning. In 1948 she was to tell a BBC reporter: 'I chose initials because of a prejudice against women writers at the time.' It was Hamish Miles, one of the editors of *New Stories*, who persuaded her to change her mind. 'Olivia Manning is a beautiful name,' he told her. 'It is a half hexametre.'

Since the early 1930s Hamish Miles had been Edward Garnett's chief assistant at Cape. He was both shy and gregarious, and much liked by rising authors such as Malcolm Lowry, Sean O'Faolain and Stevie Smith. In 1938 he was about to become the editor of the *Times Literary Supplement*, when he was struck down by a brain tumour and died shortly afterwards.

When Olivia had first gone up to London to see him, on a cheap day return from Portsmouth, she had had a presentiment that the day would be of momentous importance to her future as a writer. In rejecting a manuscript of hers, he had included both a note of encouragement and an open invitation to call at his office in Bedford Square. He also asked her if she had ever tried her hand at a short story, and went on to tell her about the magazine with which he was connected.

To begin with their relationship was very much that of teacher and pupil. On one occasion when she showed him a story in manuscript, he had gone through it with a toothcomb cutting out every superfluous adjective. It was a lesson that she never forgot. She confided in him her future hopes and plans, and he in turn entertained her with gossip about the Bloomsbury group. But when she asked him to introduce her to Virginia Woolf, he absolutely refused to do so. 'Virginia would tear you to pieces,' he warned her. 'She hates young women writers.'

Hamish liked to keep his friends in watertight compartments. The same could be said about his domestic life—as Olivia was to discover. He was a married man, but his wife was an invalid, he explained, who could no longer tolerate sexual intercourse. They were Roman Catholics and divorce was out of the question. Not surprisingly he had strayed—and there had been an affair with a neighbour's wife. This was now over and had become instead an intense friendship. Olivia was of the opinion that she and Hamish might achieve something similar.

viii

One evening, however, the inevitable happened. Sitting over the gas fire in her room in Margaretta Terrace in Chelsea, he suddenly scooped her up and carried her to the bed . . .

Many years later Olivia was to recall the scene: 'Like Madame Bovary, I could say "I have a lover."' She was to remember nostalgically too how one of Hamish's ambitions had been to translate *Madame Bovary*. But at the crucial moment in her bedsitting room, all she said was: 'I knew from the beginning that it would end like this.' To which he had replied: 'Yes, when you first came into my office there was a flash—like lightning.'

Their love affair, cut short by his death, was to last exactly three years, and during that time Hamish gave her a copy of Joyce's *Ulysses*. He had bought it at Sylvia Beach's bookshop in Paris, and on the title page he had written: 'From Ulysses, the Wanderer and the Deceiver.'

When Olivia was working on *The Wind Changes*, she and Hamish had a holiday in Ireland, visiting Dublin, Galway and the Aran Islands. All three feature in the novel—though the islands are unnamed. Olivia regarded this book as an exercise in learning how to sustain a long narrative. The Jacob Morrow serials had been produced to a formula, with each chapter limited to a precise number of words. In *The*

Wind Changes there are chapters of fifty pages and more. Strictly speaking, however, this is not her first novel. There had been several earlier attempts, one of which had been about a painter born in a dull provincial town, who had run away to Paris and later died there of consumption.

Commander Manning had had eleven brothers, ten of whom had died of consumption, and in *The Wind Changes* Sean Murtough, one of the central characters, has two brothers and a grandfather who have died of it. His third brother has been shot by the English after the Easter Week Rising of 1916. Sean suspects that he himself has consumption and feels both doomed and isolated.

Living in Portsmouth in her parents' house and working away each evening in her chilly bedroom, Olivia felt unreal and cut off. The dull thud on the mat of homing manuscripts would elicit remarks such as 'Poor old Olivia' from her well-meaning father. Her wages as a typist were fifteen shillings a week, out of which she gave her mother ten for her keep. 'I existed in a limbo of loneliness' was how she recalled her life at the time. In *The Wind Changes* Elizabeth Dearborn, who is slightly better off than Olivia, tells Sean when they are out walking: 'I am doomed to loneliness.'

Portsmouth—the hated town as Olivia refers

to it in 'The Balkan Trilogy'—held only the bleakest memories for her. When her mother died in the early 1950s, Olivia went down to clear up the house and made a pile of her unpublished novels and stories; then, much against her husband Reggie Smith's advice, she threw nearly all of them on the fire. 'They were too embarrassing to preserve,' she told me.

The Wind Changes is written with a noticeable masculine impersonality, which was to become a hallmark of her work. For instance, in the final chapter, when Elizabeth is getting ready to return to Galway from the Aran Islands, she takes a long last look at the clouds, fields and cattle and sees them 'as though she were Adam and this the first morning of creation'. The identification with Adam is significant.

Olivia Manning disliked the term woman novelist, preferring to regard herself as a novelist who happened to be a woman. In most of her novels the number of male characters far exceed the female, and when a woman appears in a role of importance, it is generally a self-portrait. Elizabeth Dearborn is no exception. Olivia, during the 1920s, had attended art schools in Portsmouth and Dublin, and galleries in Portsmouth had exhibited some of her work. But she had reasons for not wanting to go on painting. Her parents were hard-up, she herself earned very little, and a painter's materials were much more expensive than a writer's. More importantly though she had a genuine fear that her work as a painter was becoming facile. 'I simply had to find another medium.' Yet even as a writer there were pitfalls. After completing *The Wind Changes* she told an interviewer: 'A novel should not be written too easily.' Forty years later she was to elaborate on this in a letter which she sent me when she began work on 'The Levant Trilogy': 'My novel drags slowly on . . . as though I were digging it out of complete darkness . . . It is better to write out of darkness than ignorance.'

But Olivia never lost her painter's vision. When Elizabeth watches the salmon swimming down the River Corrib towards the open sea, she knows that 'in a month or two she [will] be able to remember them in every detail'. Olivia too had such a memory. The passage of time was unimportant—and a month or twenty years could pass and she would still be able to recall right down to the smallest detail a scene in Galway, England or the Middle East. Here is a description of the beach at Bangor, called 'Carrickmoy' in the novel, where she and her younger brother used to play:

Here the children found the bodies of the whip-tailed skate and of devil fish . . . Amongst the stones they found coins worn thinner than paper and the marvellous, fine vertebrae bones of great cod, and sometimes lifebelts and wreckage bearing the names of ships long ago lost and forogotten. Once they found a sailor's tunic and once a plait of yellow hair.

In this first novel of Olivia's, there are various themes running through it which she was to take up in her later books. Elizabeth is torn in her affections between Sean, the Irish patriot and a potential liberator of the country, and Arion, the middle-aged English novelist with pro-Republican sympathies. She sleeps with both, but is aware that neither can provide the solution to her lonely life. Sean, who is not yet twenty-one and mortally ill, is too preoccupied with plans and dreams of an united Ireland to take her seriously. Arion, who has left his wife and has a son at Eton and two daughters, is beginning to lose interest in reporting 'the troubles' for his paper in London. He is anxious to move on, since he is by nature both a wanderer and a deceiver. Behind Elizabeth's back he has fixed up a meeting with an old flame—an M.P's wife—at the Belfast docks.

Elizabeth's dilemmas are ones which perennially face the woman artist. Can she be sufficient unto herself? What is it in women that makes them so dependent for their happiness on men? Why should marriage always be made to appear the ultimate goal? These are questions that Olivia continued to ask herself. Her conclusion reached in her last book *The Sum of Things* (1980), but anticipated in her first, was: 'In an imperfect world marriage was a matter of making do with what one had chosen.' Of course to some extent the phrase 'an imperfect world' begs the question, carrying with it suggestions of original sin and the fallen nature of man—both subjects which Olivia liked to discuss with her friends.

When *The Wind Changes* first came out, the reviewer in the *Times Literary Supplement* (April 24 1937) summed it up as an account of an attempt in 1921 to bring back one of the Easter Week leaders to reunite the country; the attempt was referred to in the review as 'a wild-goose chase'. Today, half a century after the publication of the book, another reading is possible.

There should be a time-lapse, Olivia believed, between an actual event and the chronicling of it. Fiction written too close to contemporary events she dismissed as no more than journalism. Over fifteen years were to pass before she began to write about the Black and Tans and the Anglo-Irish truce of 1921; and in the case of her experiences during the Second World War, she allowed even longer to pass before she began to chronicle them in the

'Balkan' and 'Levant' trilogies. Tolstoy, she would point out, did not begin *War and Peace* until some thirty years after the Napoleonic Wars were over.

Olivia loved her father, but thought of him as a terrible old Tory. Hamish Miles too was a conservative. At Cape he once said of his partnership with Edward Garnett: 'I am the Right—and Garnett is the Left.' Politically Olivia was to move slowly from the Left towards the Right, subscribing in her youth to a form of Fabian socialism. Shaw's attack on the establishment and the petty bureaucrats of provincial life had won her support from the moment that she had begun reading his plays as a young girl. But running parallel with her radicalism, however inconsistent it might be, was a marked admiration for imperialism, and a belief that in an imperfect world Britain's rule in her colonies had been for the most part a beneficent one. But this, in her view, did not apply to Ireland.

In one sense Olivia Manning is a historical novelist, and just as the 'Balkan' and 'Levant' trilogies have now come to be regarded as historical novels, so too can *The Wind Changes* be placed in the same category. The acts of terrorism and religious fanaticism which the novel depicts are still part of the scene, both North and South. There seems, then as now, no solution. When Elizabeth watches three great Georgian houses burning against the dark skyline outside Dublin, she asks: 'What is to be gained by doing that?' Her question, though, is unimportant to those like Sean and his co-liberators, who have set their sights on a future rising. In fact, towards the end of the book, when she meets one of the 1916 leaders, who has been in hiding for five years, he puts into words the paradox which is Irish history. 'Nothing fails in Ireland,' he tells her. 'It is only that the victory is delayed.'

Isobel English, Cowes, 1988

CONTENTS

SUNDAY

As soon as the car came to a standstill Arion jumped out. Before Elizabeth could switch off the engine and follow him, he had disappeared into the mist. She hurried. He reappeared — small, slenderly built, rather elegant, looking crooked with his left arm inside his heavy black overcoat and the sleeve swinging free. She followed him up the length of the pier until the end, abruptly coming into view, brought them up sharply. He did not turn, but stood thrusting down his right-hand pocket with his right fist. His left hand lay expressionlessly in its sling. He was cold, tired, irritable and hungry. They had been driving most of the night.

He said: 'He'll lose his way in the mist.'

Elizabeth, not caring, shrugged her shoulders. After a few minutes she wandered back to the car. The nervous excitement of the journey had sustained her until, at daybreak, Costello was reached. Then the excitement failed. She was no longer necessary. She felt in the way and rather a nuisance now.

The road ran beside the shore. There was a strip of brilliant grass and a few gorse bushes with ochre-coloured flowers, then the shore. The boulders were grey, speckled black, and between them the shredded tomato-brown weed lay matted. It was high tide. A colourless wave drifted in and out. There was little to be seen, nothing to be done here. All around were the famous hills — magnificent, chameleon hills, shaped like molars and eye-teeth — but in this mist they might just as well not be there. She went back to Arion and they stood together impatiently in the cold. After some minutes she said she heard something. He nodded. But for a long time there was nothing to be seen and no sound but the sound of the oars in the rowlocks.

She said: 'He's looking for the pier.'

But Arion would not shout to guide him in case it was not Sean and he should look foolish shouting at a stranger. He stared out into the mist. Usually he had a delicate pallor that enhanced the intellectuality of his features. Now the cold had given him a peaked, reddish look and he was shivering and disagreeable. He blew his nose.

The rain struck their faces like pins and needles. At last a patch on the mist darkened and suddenly the bows of a dinghy shot into view.

The rower called out: 'Arion. Arion.'

Arion did not move or speak. Elizabeth went to the pier's edge and looked down at the young man. He stared up at her. He had a curious, crooked face with a prominent nose and thin mouth.

He said: 'Who are you?'

She answered: 'Elizabeth Dearborn. Arion is here.'

With a sullen air of displeasure he shipped the oars, made fast the boat, picked up a rucksack from the seat and jumped out to the steps. He ran up them, brushed past her without speaking, and hurried to Arion. They turned together and walked towards the car. Elizabeth, following, heard Arion's protest:

'It was necessary. I got shot in the wrist and couldn't drive myself.'

At once the younger man was all concern: 'When did it happen? Where? How?'

'A day or two ago. Some sniper on a roof near Merrion Square. It wasn't meant for me, or anyone in particular.'

'Is it serious?'

'No. Not much more than a graze.'

Elizabeth walked more and more slowly and, at last, paused in a frigid numbness of resentment. She took a deep breath and the smell of rotting weed stung her throat. She heard them start the engine. If they had driven off and left her she would have felt a morose satisfaction. But the car did not move. Arion called to her. She did not reply.

'Elizabeth.' His voice, controlled, very quiet and non-committal, now had an edge of impatience. He came out of the mist and stopped a yard from her: 'What is the matter? Why are you standing there?'

She did not answer, but looked at him. They stood and looked at one another resentfully until they were caught up in the overwhelming physical attraction that held them. He moved to her and put his hand to her waist. With the subtile, rather feminine softness that pleased her in his voice, he asked: 'What is the matter?' She put her hands to his shoulders and pulled his mouth down to her. She kissed him gently, then, with sudden passion, bit into his lips hardly, spite-fully and with anger. His hold tightened on her in response an instant before he shook her off.

At once he was as far from her as he had been before

he touched her. He swung round and she hurried after him to the car. Sean, white and pretending indifference, sat with his hands on the wheel. Arion took the seat beside him. Elizabeth sat behind. Nobody spoke as they drove along the rough coast road to Galway.

The mist hid everything. It gathered itself up into balls, then shook itself loose. It was like smoke, rolling here and there, now dense, now partly revealing a ghost shape of rock or cottage.

Having forced him to come back, forced him to consciousness of her, Elizabeth's resentment was lost in a sort of amusement. Quite suddenly she stopped regarding things seriously. She looked around her. As the country was hidden she must content herself by examining the heads of the men in front of her. Arion's neck was thin. His close-cut, greying, brown hair revealed the hollows on either side of his spine. His head was narrow and very long so that his black felt hat always looked too big for him. He sat with his usual air of detachment, quite unaware of Sean's jealousy. Perhaps he was not so much unaware of it as careless of it. Sean should have known that and kept his feelings to himself.

She began to feel indulgent towards him because, knowing so little of Arion, he was fool enough to sulk. She did not like him, but she thought him rather pathetic as he sat sulking there, so young-looking with his long, untidy, fair hair that he had probably forgotten to have cut during the whole of the six weeks he had been away. She could see the thin, bitterly set line of his jaw. He looked rather like a young actor. There

was something unconsciously dramatic about the
lines on his forehead, the width of his eyes, the long,
jutting nose with its wide nostrils; and something
dramatic about the deep pain of his ill-humour. He
watched himself, but there was reality in him. Yet —
she turned from him and looked at the materializing
roadside — she did not like him any the more for
that.

They were leaving the mist behind. Distances
became visible as they approached Galway, but the
clouds were hanging ponderously low over the gulls'
flight and the flight of the white sails in the harbour and
the white-crested flourish of the waves. It reminded
Elizabeth of washing day in her grandmother's garden
where the servants, with red, steaming hands, seemed
always to be pinning out the flapping linen under a
threatening sky. She could almost smell the acrid
perfume of the flowering currant bushes that grew
beside the kitchen door.

Across the waters a barren slope of Clare lay like the
flank of a beast. The water was black and moved up
and down in little peaks and looked bitterly chill. As
they passed a promontory Arion turned and, nodding to
it, said: 'That is one of the few places where gentians
grow in the British Isles.' Sean, reminded of her,
frowned and pressed the accelerator so her reply was
lost in uproar.

A few small boys in long, loose, cotton bathing
dresses stood on the shore. They were thin and exposed
looking. The wind blew round them and they put
their fingers under their armpits and looked down at
their knocking knees. The car left them behind. Large

houses, most of them closed and deserted in unkept gardens, stood back from the road. No one walked on the promenade or sat on the iron seats. No one gave a thought to holiday-making in this troubled Ireland. The town approached bleakly, almost as forsaken as the Salthill houses. Many of the shops were shut; some, kept by Protestants and Unionists, shuttered and barricaded. The windows of those that were open were empty, or had a few poor things thrown into a corner. People moved cautiously in the streets. The war was coming westwards.

Arion said: 'Stop where we can eat something.' Sean crawled the car by the kerb looking for a place. But the hotels and tea-rooms were shut. At last they found a more friendly one facing the quay and the manageress unlocked the front room that they might eat in style. They entered and breathed dead air. It was like entering a room that had been sealed for a century. Nothing ever changed here. Let someone put two paper roses behind the mirrored, mahogany mantelpiece and there they would remain year after year, generation after generation. . . .

With an impatient thrust of his shoulder Sean prised open the window and let in the sound of the waterways that dissected the city in every direction. The waterways hurried unceasingly their useless activity with a noise like rain. It was depressing.

Arion sat down on the American leather sofa. Elizabeth went off to find a water-closet. When she came back the table was set and the men talking together. Sean seemed half won from his discontent. Now that he was out of the wind, about to eat, and

14

returning to Dublin, Arion was becoming charming again. With close interest, smiling and nodding appreciation of every point, he was watching Sean talk.

And Elizabeth watched Arion. His face never seemed familiar to her. Each time she looked at it she saw it newly and with surprise that it should be the face of her lover. Now, as he looked at Sean, his large, silver-coloured eyes half covered by heavy lids and his full lips set smilingly, he had something of the look of Gascar's painting of Rochester. Older, thinner, smaller, more subtle, less arrogant — yet he had something of the look as he sat there hiding himself beneath the perception of his attention and appreciation. She knew he was content to listen as he was listening now, and to ask questions. That was how he led you to reveal yourself. Yes, he flattered you with his appreciation until in pure delight of pride you drew the last curtain and showed him all. Even then he would not let you see you had given yourself away. He merely sighed in wonderment at you and insisted you had but doubled your mystery, and so left you content.

Sean, his face flushing as he talked, had first asked how things had gone in Dublin during his absence, but he soon ceased questioning to proclaim how things would go now he was returning. Arion nodded and smiled agreement.

He does that well, Elizabeth thought, that listening and agreeing! But if, when you had told him all, you turned and said: 'And you?' he would at once waive your interest aside. Oh no, himself was a dull country not worth exploring; but you, with your deep, mysterious valleys, your vast, uprising hills, your silences, your strange and hidden selves — how fascinating and inexplicable, how full of promise!

Sean, she could see, had capitulated long ago. Arion excited him, filled him with the sense of his own power and mystery, enhanced for him the wonder of his individuality. He did not want to probe the hidden country that was Arion, all he asked was that Arion should guide him through the darkness that was himself. It was Elizabeth who had beset Arion with: 'What are you? Tell me about yourself'. As she had made her advance he had smiled but retreated, surely, step by step, until she was forced to pause, conscious of the importunate foolishness of her intrusion. He closed his lips and would betray nothing.

'My hidden self is sacred. It is inviolable, uncommunicable and unknowable.'

'Mine too, she replied.'

So they faced one another defensively, trapped by the physical attraction that was now the more persistent because each felt the other's strangeness.

But Sean gave himself to be explored. Arion was in complete possession of his imagination. He talked happily until, glancing aside, he met Elizabeth's eyes and stopped abruptly. Arion, turning, included her in his smile.

'Sean,' he said, 'is to be the last of the liberators.'

'Oh!' She had been hearing of Sean for some time from different people. He was spoken of in Dublin as a rather mysterious young man from whom — no one knew exactly why — much might be expected. He was going to do something. Soon, quite suddenly, he would do the thing, whatever it was, that was necessary to bring victory out of all this muddled squabble and destruction. His plans and goings and comings were known only to five of his friends and that encouraged anticipation amongst those to whom they were not known. Elizabeth, now she had seen him, was unimpressed. His pale, crooked face irritated her, and, because he was five or six years her junior, it satisfied her to discredit his fame. She thought him a mixture of egoist and fool.

'But how can you be sure he will be the last?'

'Because,' replied Arion, 'there will be no need for another.'

Sean watched her suspiciously, only half unsure of her because he was still half unsure of himself. 'It is not I that will be the liberator,' he said in an irritated voice to Arion, 'but Riordan.'

That was the first time he had mentioned Riordan. Arion merely said quietly: 'So you found him?'

'Yes.'

'Where?'

Sean glanced sideways his distrust of Elizabeth and said: 'I will tell you another time.'

For a moment Arion was silent, then he said in a strangely dull voice: 'Don't tell me. It is just as well not to let anyone else know.' After a pause he added: 'And he is coming?'

'Yes. I will meet him at Costello a week from to-day.'

'Quite a lot can happen in a week.'

'I know. But we must have some time in which to prepare them.'

'And what is he going to promise them? Peace and prosperity?'

Sean lifted his eyes in which there was something at once tired and feverish: 'Peace and prosperity?' he looked from the window towards the grey stones of the windswept quay where the Spaniards had unloaded their cargoes in the days of wealth in the west, 'If there is peace and prosperity in Ireland we might become contented — and then how would our poets be inspired?'

'If not peace and prosperity, what do you want?'

The woman brought in bacon and eggs and a pot of coffee. Whilst she was placing them on the table, Arion touched distastefully the sticky knives and forks. The Irish, he decided, were a shabby people: closely acquainted with the finesse of death but living crudely. As soon as the woman was gone he cleaned his knife and fork on his napkin. Elizabeth, who came from the north, did the same. But Sean neither copied them nor noticed what they did.

Again Arion insisted his question to this bewildering and complex Sean: 'If not peace and prosperity, what do you want?'

Sean, quite willing to be bewildering and very complex, ate his eggs and bacon, and shook his head and smiled. It was not that he did not know, but that he would not tell. 'I will not tell you what I want in case you should give it to me and end everything.'

Arion clicked his tongue in appreciation. Then he said: 'I suppose Riordan wants to come?'

'I don't know. He was very quiet, but he said he was ready to come when they wanted him.'

'No more than that?'

'Not much more. He asked me about men he had known in Dublin.'

'I suppose you can rely on him?'

'Of course. Why? Do you want me to distrust him?'

'No. But you want to trust him?'

'Yes.'

'And you trust him because you want to?'

'Why should I distrust him?'

'You should ask: "Why should I *trust* him?"'

Sean, lifting a piece of bread to his mouth, paused, surprised, to look at this stranger revealed in his friend Arion. And Arion, feeling the risk of Sean's encroachment, got to his feet and went to the window.

'Raining again,' he said. Galway Bay was blotted out and the air was grey with cold. Who would believe here that spring was ending and the summer already upon them. He turned: 'Haven't you finished yet?'

'No. I'm hungry.'

'It's nearly eleven o'clock.'

'The devil!' Sean crammed the bread into his mouth and washed it down with a gulp of water. He jumped up. 'Come on.'

When Arion, by flattery, invested him with the leadership, he assumed it magnificently. Sean, the leader, the liberator, strode from the hotel. 'Come on.' Arion paid the bill. Elizabeth followed them without a word. Feeling herself excluded by their interest in one another, it pleased her to exaggerate her exclusion by silence and submission.

They found Sean trying to start the engine and, as they came up to him, he jumped out to discover why it would not go. Whilst they were eating, someone had emptied their petrol tank and filled it with sand, water and roots of grass.

Sean, in passionate anger, turned and raged at the grinning louts who lounged near by in after-mass idleness. He demanded to know who had done this thing to the car of Sean Murtough, the patriot, the leader who was giving his life to striving to save them all from the curse of the English! At once the louts stopped grinning and admitted they had done it themselves. They had heard Arion's English accent and supposed him to be some government official come to spy amongst them.

'Fools!' shouted Sean. Arion was his most loyal follower! And now they could all set to and repair the damage they had done.

With apologies and the greatest good will in the world, they crowded round to help and Sean, mollified, gave orders. But Arion, coldly irritated and impatient of delay, wandered off to the water's edge. As she followed him, Elizabeth looked back at Sean. She saw him a tall young man with pale hair falling over his pale, crooked face. He had rolled up his sleeves to his elbows and was dragging up handfuls of sand from the depths of the tank. The louts were gathered round, not doing much to help but joking admiringly at his efforts.

No fool after all! He still irritated her, but she had to admit there was about him a certain elusive but undeniable spirit. Young — too young, that was the trouble — but no fool!

Arion stood looking across at the little white houses of the Claddagh.

'Let's go round and explore,' suggested Elizabeth. But he would not go. He would not risk attack. It was not that he feared hurt but that he feared to be made to appear undignified. So they crossed the bridge over a canal, unused and clogged with American water-weed, and wandered through the old streets. Here, as on the outskirts, everything had the shuttered and deserted Sunday air. To Arion, not many months come from London, there was always something unbearably desolate about the poverty of the Irish provincial towns. There seemed to him no reason for their existence or the existence of the people living in them. The people troubled him.

'The way they slouch about,' he said. 'You'd think they hated one another.'

'But people always seem to hate one another in towns,' she said, unwilling that even the southern Irish should be criticized.

'Yes,' he nodded, 'like a lot of hedgehogs huddling together to keep warm.'

They walked in silence as though despondent. Arion was usually silent when with her, and when he spoke it was with none of those haltings that seem a fear lest some embarrassing and terrible truth should be revealed. Had he been silent from embarrassment it would have been bearable, but she knew he was silent because he had nothing to tell her. They had scarcely known one another three weeks and already they were come to a standstill, each frustrating the other's curiosity, yet not at an end. They had not even learnt very much about one another's past. He knew she had been brought up in the north and had come to Dublin to study painting. Now she lived uncomfortably on a small income left her by her mother. Before she met him, she had heard of Arion's coldly intellectual novels that left unrevealed nothing but their writer. He was married and lived apart from his wife. No one knew why he had come to Dublin, only that he was acting there as correspondent to some English paper. Visiting Sean's father, he had met Sean and, capturing him and his confidence, was soon enough in the midst of things.

This is Arion, my friend Arion! Accept him. And Arion, small, delicate-looking, with his charming appreciation of everything and his mental isolation that precluded familiarity, went in the midst of things by the side of his friend Sean.

And what, she wondered, was Arion getting out of it all? But Arion, who alone could tell her, would tell nothing.

They came to the bridge over the Corrib and stopped to look down at the salmon, marshalled like soldiers, motionless in the water. Elizabeth glanced sideways at his face as he stared down at the velvety, dark fish motionless in the purr of the transparent, shallow water. He watched them with a curiously reflective intensity. He pressed the back of his fingers to his lips.

No doubting it was real — his appreciation of things. He was one for whom the visible world had meaning. And there, she thought, was his essential difference from her. She wanted to see things; she was curious; she sought out things to see — but when she found them she looked at them a moment and the interest was gone. Few material things could absorb her interest. Give me a perpetuity of new emotions and I will be entertained though eternity. But new things . . .

She looked away from the river, eager to be moving on. She had seen enough of the salmon. At this moment she was bored with them. Yet, strangely, she knew that in a month or two she would remember them in every detail. Perhaps she would feel she must paint them — not that she would, but she might feel she must — or she would speak of them to someone as though they had held her in wonderment:

'. . . motionless, hour after hour. Dark velvety green-grey forms. . . . What did they think all the time? Nothing, of course. They existed only in consciousness of the delicious curl of the waters along their flanks. . . .'

Something like that. She never really knew what she thought about anything until she started to tell someone, and then she was surprised to find she thought so much. Yes, she would be sure to say something surprising about the salmon that at the moment were nothing but a source of impatience to her. But it wasn't good enough — this lack of genuine interest in everything but a few personal relationships. It proved her to be nothing but a silly woman. Nothing but that, after all.

Arion looked up: 'Did you see that big fellow move? He suddenly darted out into the stream and then changed his mind and darted back to his place again. There he is — the third from the white stone — feeling rather foolish and trying to look as though he hadn't moved at all.'

She looked. Why should he feel foolish? They began walking back. Surely Sean would be ready by now!

But no. He was sitting on the ground with the others round him, eating potato bread and holding forth on the great liberation that was to come.

Arion approached him quietly and spoke scarcely above a whisper: 'We must be in Dublin before the curfew.'

Sean lifted his face, flushed, very excited, like a young boy that is winning a game. 'I'll be ready in half an hour,' he said. But it was late afternoon before the last of the sand was cleared out of the tank and the petrol replaced. The young men who had done the damage waved them away with cheers and, as they left Galway behind, the sun shone.

It was evening before they reached Tullamore. Under the great arc of lavender-coloured sky, gilded at the horizon and set with long, static, gilt-edged lavender clouds, the bog-land heather quivered like creeping purple flame. Where the peat had been cut the earth was naked. It was magenta coloured and richly dark. Here and there the peats were piled like bricks of wedding cake. Some had been left there so long new grass was poking out from them in emerald pins.

Sean, still flushed, triumphant, still the leader, slowed the car and looked around and said: 'It is only in Ireland that you can find a beauty that is new and has not been spoilt by some painter or other.'

'What about Scotland?' asked Arion whose mother had been Scotch.

'A museum piece. Dusty and Victorian,' said Sean. 'Ruined for any person of taste by the worst crowd of artists ever gathered together into one century.'

Arion smiled: 'But you are so ruthless! So damning!' he marvelled in his gently delighted voice. The harmless and charming Arion paused in wonder before this ruthless, rather dangerous, young liberator. This amazing Sean!

And Sean blushed, laughing. Elizabeth could see the back of his neck turn red. 'But it is true,' he insisted rather weakly.

'Not a bit of it.' Even Arion's contradiction was a sort of flattery, 'And I was just thinking how thoughtful it was of Offaly to study self-expression under the pre-Raphaelite masters solely for our delectation.'

Sean laughed, delighted. He had forgotten Elizabeth.

The evening began to fall. Outside Ballinagar their way was barred by a crowd that flowed loosely and waveringly over the road. Men and women stood talking in twos and threes. They talked with the eager impotence of anger whilst large groups of police and Black and Tans, arm in arm for mutual protection, moved silently round the fringe. Sean blew his horn. People turned their faces whitely towards the car but did not move. The police made no attempt to clear a way. Their power was gone. Had they given an order it would have been an excuse for a riot.

Sean leant out of the car shouting to the nearest man to ask what was the matter. The man, short and fat, with a round, snub, waxen face above black clothes, stared uncertainly. The opportunity to impart his knowledge to a stranger proved too tempting. He came grudgingly forward and jerked his thumb towards the

Black and Tans: 'They're after firing the poor old woman's cottage,' he said.

The crowd stood like cattle, silent and listening now, motionless, facing the car. Above and beyond them smoke tendrils turned and diffused into the air. The men and women, pale in the evening light, silent, unmoving in arrested gestures, all faces towards the car, had a strange and poetic unreality.

'Why did they do that?'

'Sure, there was an ambush laid near her cottage, sure, and she didn't inform, so the Black and Tans fired her cottage and not one's been allowed to raise a hand for her, God help her.'

Solitary members of the crowd moved forward to hear the conversation and Sean included them all when he spoke: 'It's a poor way of fighting the English have', he said.

'Aye,' they agreed, nodding their heads. 'A poor way indeed!'

'But the Sinn Feiners won't leave it at that.'

'Sure, it's true enough they won't,' agreed a thin man, dark with the involute peasant darkness, 'they'll be out to fire Meredith Lodge because old Meredith's a Protestant; and Kirkwell's place because he's a Unionist, but it's much good that will do the poor old woman except make a blaze for her to warm herself by which she wouldn't be needing at this time of the year, anyway.'

Arion, who dared not speak in case his English accent should divert all the favour Sean's sympathy was winning, silently moved his wrist that Sean might see his watch. Sean glanced at it quickly, then leant confidentially towards the little man: 'We must get to Dublin before the curfew. Do you think you could persuade the others to move and let us pass?'

'Sure, if it's wanting to get through you are, I'll do me best.' He ran forward, then paused uncertainly and, after a moment, came back. He gave a half-glance at the aloof and English Arion, 'You're not Unionists, now, are you?'

'Unionists! I am Sean Murtough,' he spoke his name as though it were famous through Ireland, although at that time it was scarcely known outside Dublin.

'Why, is it John Wellington Murtough, the great Fenian leader, you are?'

'It is indeed,' replied Sean still indignant, and the little man ran excitedly ahead clearing the way with tremendous energy.

The car was able to crawl forward. As they came up to the burning cottage the woman wailed at them: What was she to do? The Black and Tans burnt her cottage because she had not betrayed the ambush, but if she had betrayed it the Sinn Feiners would have taken her up into the hills and shot her and thrown her body into a bog, so what was she to do?

As she stood in front of the car they were obliged to draw up and listen and, unable to suggest a satisfactory middle course for anyone in her predicament, they handed her some money with murmurs of sympathy. Bowing, smiling and blessing them, she let them past but cried after them accusingly as they sped out of earshot.

'Who is John Wellington Murtough?' asked Arion.

'God knows,' replied Sean. 'Probably some invention of his own.'

Arion was all admiration of this invulnerable and dazzling Sean! And Sean glowed with delight. At once he became a part of all that Arion declared him to be. Sean, the tutorable child, dazzled and was invulnerable. His pleasure glanced through the air. Tell me only what you believe I will achieve and I'll achieve it. He drove with skill that verged on recklessness. Then a cold wind sprang up and he began to shiver. His mouth ceased to smile and set painfully.

Arion, huddling down into his heavy coat, said to him: 'Haven't you an overcoat with you?'

'I meant to take one and forgot,' answered Sean.

'Didn't you get wet?'

'Yes, frequently.'

'It's a miracle you're still alive.'

'I hadn't time to die.'

'Didn't you catch cold?'

'No. I was too absorbed in the hunt. But I'll catch one now you've reminded me.'

Elizabeth wondered at Arion's concern. Although he would often make a great show of it when he felt it expected of him, he was usually satisfied by a first reassurance and did not worry further. She wondered if Sean had recently been ill and moved in order to see more of his face. But she could only see the delicate line of his jaw running clearly down to his chin. It looked very young and, with a sudden tremulous start, she realized he had a certain beauty. Arion's jaw was losing its contour and disappearing into a thin double chin. His age accentuated the attraction of

Sean's youth. She leant forward to look at Sean, her eyes reflective.

Yes. . . .

But almost at once she moved back into her corner, smiling at herself. Compared with Arion, the experienced sensualist, knowledgeable and unknowable, with a touch of something that might even be genius in his works, this Sean was gauche and pretty small beer. She smiled at the thought of him.

The night came slowly. There was no moon. The boglands were black and silent. Their headlights lit before them a few unaltering yards of road. Darkness enclosed them until they came to the lights of a village beyond which three great houses burnt like pyres on the hill-tops.

Once through the village Sean stopped the car and they were paused down in the roadway looking up at the conflagration of the nearest house. They watched in silence until Elizabeth, furious in spite of herself, burst out: 'What is to be gained by doing that?'

Sean turned and looked at her, his expression invisible in the darkness, and said in an excited, strange way: 'It is the pyre of the phœnix'. He spoke as though defending the incendiarists against the surrounding silence that was like the silence of regret. Neither Arion nor Elizabeth answered him.

The flat, front wall with its rows of Georgian windows stood black against the out-flying pennants of the flames. Little, imp-dark figures moved against the light. Suddenly fire leapt up in a nearby building that seemed instantly to become a blaze. From the heart of the blaze horses, mad with fright, tore free to rear, like apocalyptic beasts, against the surrounding flame.

'Ah!' breathed Sean. 'The horses are free.' And returning to the car, started it and quickened speed to make up for lost time.

'It hardly matters now,' said Arion quietly. 'It's gone ten o'clock.'

'We'll get through somehow.' Sean was willing to assume the carelessness of the natural adventurer, but now Arion seemed sunken into himself and would not speak again.

By keeping to the back streets they navigated the suburbs safely, but they were challenged as they were about to cross O'Connell Bridge.

'What shall I say?' whispered Sean, grown anxious.

'Don't speak,' said Arion and, jumping out of the car, drew the officers and men aside. They stood under the street lamp talking together for some minutes whilst Sean leant forward uneasily across the wheel. The light fell on the top of Arion's black hat so the shadow hid the top of his face. His mouth was moving slowly and, even out of hearing, Elizabeth knew with what assurance and how quietly he was speaking. It seemed to her suddenly that he was like a grown-up playing a game with children. He really made a terrific show of entering into the spirit of it all, of being one of them and caring about winning or losing, but he didn't care at all. It was as though at some time he had lived beyond this nursery of a world and now could not take it seriously. He did not belong here; he had grown up.

Then he returned and she forgot what she had been thinking and the vision of him was lost. Something he had said had made the officer laugh and salute and they parted as though they had some knowledge in common that made them natural friends. But Sean, leaning forward with his thin, jutting nose and his mouth a little open, did not lose his anxious look. Rather it seemed to darken painfully as Arion took his seat and said: 'It is all right. We can go on.'

'What did you say to them?' asked Sean.

'I told them I was a spy in the pay of the Castle and had a special permit to be out.'

'No, but . . .' Sean had to laugh, but he laughed against his will, 'but what did you say to them? It really looked as though you had some influence with them.'

'Only bluff and an English accent. Let us get on. I'm tired and want to go to bed.'

Sean was still frowning for some minutes before he left them to go to his rooms above a shop on the quay. Elizabeth took the car to a garage in Nassau Street. She and Arion lived in a boarding-house behind Trinity College. She had turned the attic there into a studio when she first came as a student to Dublin. Arion lived in rooms below her and three weeks before they had collided on the dark stairway and spoken for the first time.

The house was old. It was very dark. They paused in the shadows of Arion's landing.

'Good night.' He touched her hand, suddenly tender, suddenly aware of her. She tried to move from him but he held to her and they went together up to her room.

MONDAY

As Elizabeth stood by the window brushing her hair she heard an uproar in the road below. She looked out and saw a lean red-faced man run suddenly round the corner. His head was strained forward with the fierce passion of effort that comes of terror and increasing exhaustion. After him, the first not three yards from him, his pursuers followed. As he approached the house opposite her, the door of the house opened and a little man emerged. The foremost pursuer screamed exultantly:

'Hey, Pat Murphy! Get him. Get him. He's an informer!'

Pat Murphy, thick-set, little fury of a man, instantly taking up the quarrel as though it were his own, bristled into a provoked terrier and leapt forward to bar the thin man's way. But the thin man was panic-quickened. He turned and, with the slick agility of a long-rehearsed act, leapt to a lower window sill. In an instant, he had swung himself up to an upper one. Agile, sure-footed with fear, he reached the second floor safely before looking back to see if Murphy followed. . . .

Elizabeth put down her brush and leant from the window to watch what would happen now.

. . . Murphy was following. With the crowd aswarm beneath him, he was groping clumsily about the

first-floor window whilst two men held him from the
sill below. The two below were balancing themselves
on one foot and swinging the other foot out over the
crowd whilst they gripped the short, thick, fumbling
legs of the little Murphy, so all three looked like a set
of awkward acrobats. Above them, panting but mocking, the informer watched their progress.

It seemed that all in a moment the road was in a
tumult.

The informer turned and saw a cat sleeping on the
second-floor sill. He lifted it and with stark, un-
smiling malice, threw it down upon the face of the man
beneath him. It landed all claws on Murphy and clung
to his flesh until, in a brutal rage of agony, he threw
it off.

Bristling and indignant, it fell on its feet, and a
woman bent to it: 'That anyone could hurt a poor,
harmless beast!' But as she touched it, it sped from
her and left her snubbed.

After he had thrown it off there was a full moment's
silence whilst he clung motionless before suddenly
starting to scream as though someone had thrown
vitriol into his eyes:

'I'm blinded.'

Then, as he opened his eyes and realized he spoke the
truth, he caught his breath and sobbed stupidly: 'But
I can't see.' His sob became a wail of horrified realization: 'I tell ye I can't see. I can't . . . I can't . . .' In
his desperate horror and pain his grip slackened and
he let himself sag back as though his body had turned
to jelly. They cried to him: 'You must hold on.
You are too heavy for us.' But he did not seem to hear

them. Others put up their arms, but their arms crumpled and he fell heavily into their midst.

Meanwhile the forgotten informer had skipped away to safety across the roofs.

'What's that fellow shouting outside?' asked Arion.

Elizabeth turned and saw him sitting on the edge of the bed, naked except for his socks and suspenders. She did not think to answer him. Turning from her absorption in the agitated crowd she saw, almost with surprise, his small, white, compact body sitting there aloof, apart and self-contained. She picked up her hair-brush and came back into the centre of the room. He looked at her curiously, waiting for her answer. She thought: Impossible to imagine him ever as having been one of a mob. He would always be apart there, always aloof and self-contained, always an individual.

She knew it was his individual dignity and aloofness that held her. She felt a perverse delight in overwhelming it with her contact, carrying it down with her with perverse and furious delight into the oblivion of their sensuality. 'And however much he smiles, he hates me because of that,' she thought. And that was half vengeance for his self-sufficiency and her own persistent dissatisfaction. As she thought of him, her nerves moved to touch his hard, thin, young-looking body, but she only looked away and told him casually what she had seen.

He was interested and went to the window to look for himself, but by that time they had carried Murphy into his house and the fun was over.

'Why did you let me miss it all?' he said, disappointed. Yes, he was disappointed, just like a real

34

person. She never ceased to be surprised by his interest in things. She always experienced with new wonder his passion that at times he was incapable of controlling. Amazingly, he was real!

His wrist was still too painful to move. She had to help him dress. She liked to examine his expensive clothes. 'How much did you pay for this? What a lot of money! How extravagant you are!' In her consciousness of that inviolable individuality beyond her, she made a great show of laughing at him, of dressing him as though he were a child. He responded, laughing too, both pretending the chasm was not between them.

'Twelve and sixpence for a tie! No!' For years she had never had quite enough to eat and never bought anything without asking herself: 'Is it necessary?' With her straight, fair hair and dark, severe clothes, chosen after much thought because they would not show the dirt, or go out of fashion too soon, she still had the look of the art student. All the acquaintances that had passed through her life had shared the same penury. Frugality was a habit with them. Arion's money exaggerated for her his individuality. She was not used to people who could buy what they wanted.

As she knotted the tie, he looked round the room at her canvases: 'How long is it since you sold a picture?' he asked.

'Oh!' she considered. 'Oh! A long time. Whenever anyone in Dublin becomes rich or intelligent enough to buy pictures he goes and lives in London.' She thought perhaps Arion would offer to buy one, but he didn't seem to think of it.

'What about illustrations?' he asked.

'Publishers don't like my style.'

'Then why don't you change it?'

'I can't. When I try, it's like swimming against a current. It's so difficult to keep myself afloat I haven't time to look where I'm going.'

He went to the mirror to see how she had dressed him. After a pause he said: 'Don't try to change it. I was joking when I suggested you should. Fools that try fall between two stools. When I started to write, publishers thought my style my chief fault. Now the critics think it my only virtue.'

So charming, the charming Arion that enthralled Sean. But she felt antagonistic. She thought success had come easily to him, but she could not believe it would ever come to her. She painted with difficulty and suffering and was always dissatisfied. He came from a family of intellectuals and in him the habit of thought had been congenital. But it had come newly to her with her generation and was still embryo. It was forming in her and it seemed to her she knew the perpetual weariness of pregnancy, labour at times, but no bringing forth. She envied him the ease of his lucid and subtle prose and thought with anger of her own blundering art that seemed to her to reveal nothing but her own difficulties.

She said: 'I wish I could stop painting.' Yes, if she had half an excuse she would never paint again. 'I sometimes think it would be easier to write.'

He said: 'If you tried, you'd think it easier to paint,' and told her no more than that.

The sun was high over the houses. It was noon.

They were going to have luncheon with Sean's father. He had asked Arion to bring Elizabeth to see him.

He had said to Arion: 'Who is this girl with whom O'Rorke saw you? Bring her along.' And Arion, displeased, asked her to come.

She accepted at once, chiefly because it meant saving the price of a meal, but Arion hated her accepting. He felt that by taking her with him, by introducing her to his acquaintances, the responsibility of her was in some way thrust upon him. That was unbearable.

They drove to Merrion Square. She drove skilfully as though she gave all her attention to driving, but all the time she was conscious of Arion beside her. She found it difficult to account for his physical attraction for her. From most people she felt a revulsion. She remembered how, on Saturday, she had stopped to buy apples from a barrow near the quay. As she took her change from the man her fingers touched the palm of his hand and she felt it warm and soft against her fingers. Instinctively she had jerked away from it as from an electric shock. She could not bear to touch any woman, or a man who did not attract her.

Fur was sensually pleasant, and feathers pleasant enough with their curious rustle of bones, but human flesh was naked and meaningless and filled her with repulsion.

She glanced sideways at his hand lying on his knee. It was lean and delicately shaped like her own, but, also like her own, it was square rather than long. Its leanness and fine shape disguised its essential practicability — but there it was, the essential practicability that, in its turn, disguised human weakness.

37

'And why doesn't your friend Sean live here with his father?' she asked, looking up at the Merrion Square house in which Grattan Murtough lived.

Arion shrugged his shoulders: 'Perhaps poverty and solitude are necessary to him to preserve his self-consciousness.' He was not giving much thought to what he was saying. 'Perhaps to sharpen his senses he had to run away to hunger and a bare room.'

'What good would running away do when he knew he could always run back again?'

They had entered the house and were following a manservant up the cream-painted stairway.

At Elizabeth's question, Arion shrugged his shoulders again, a little amused. He did not take Sean seriously. No. Sean, his worshipper, had for him no more reality than had anyone else. He could say anything about him. He could give away everything Sean had given him. And Elizabeth knew he could give her away as lightly — shrugging his shoulders so, a little amused. As lightly — if he had her to give.

If he had her to give.

And now to meet Sean's father! God, how she hated strangers! But the food should be good.

They entered a room made small by its lining of books and a great cat couchant of a pianoforte.

Grattan Murtough was crippled by rheumatism. He could not rise from his chair. All the unscrupulous vice that had made his youth notorious was now concentrated in his glance. He looked at Elizabeth's thick, white neck and the outline of her rather heavy breasts and, smiling crookedly, pressed his finger tips into the soft flesh of her palm. She knew he wanted to say: 'So you lie with this Arion, this elusive and strange Arion! Tell me what he is like in bed.' But he could only say: 'My dear child, I am delighted to meet you.'

My dear child! With her pale skin and light-coloured hair she might almost have been Sean's sister. The thought amused him. He pressed his thumbnail into the base of her thumb whilst with his other hand he patted her fingers as though to say: 'My dear child, I am an old man. Just a fatherly old man.'

She did not try to withdraw her hand, but stood un-smiling, looking at him steadily. As she had entered, she had realized him with immediate comprehension, but without sympathy. She looked at his small, thin, shrunken head with its dark, wrinkled eye-sockets and large eyes, and was surprised that he should be Sean's father. Not only was he physically unlike, but, recognizing instinctively the quality of the man, she was amazed that there should be anything of him in Sean. She began to consider Sean with a new curiosity.

The old man was examining her face with interest. He was used to exciting a certain fear — and if not fear, then distrust — in the young women whom he met. But at once he knew that Elizabeth's experience of men had placed her beyond fear of them. Their recognition was mutual. He wished he might question her about Arion. He knew that the depths were not beyond her sight. She was one to whom Arion would have meaning. If only Arion were not there and he might say: 'Tell me about him. What have you discovered?'

But Arion was immovable. He lay back in his chair smiling as though he were aware of the curiosity he always raised in Murtough. He had met Murtough in London years before and they had seen one another there often enough since, yet Murtough's curiosity still remained unsatisfied.

Realizing this, Elizabeth felt a sense of triumph over the old man with whom, she knew, nothing could remain unviolated. She was silent, conceding him nothing, until at last he had to release her hand. He looked at Arion with a down-twisted smile: 'And how are you, Arion? As popular as ever amongst my son's friends?'

Arion's heavy eyelids half covered his eyes: 'If I am popular,' he said, 'it is merely because I am misunderstood.' He raised his eyelids slowly and looked across at Murtough without expression. Then he smiled a little.

They sat looking at one another, smiling across at one another as though they were enemies. Elizabeth, who had taken a chair between them, wondered what was Arion's purpose in pursuing this friendship. What interest could he have in Murtough who was probably individual enough, but only surface individual. Why did Arion come here to sit mockingly within his fortress of reservations? For his reservations were a fortress; and one might ask: 'Was the man so sure of himself after all that he must go about so fortressed?' Why did he come here as though to tease Murtough with his mystery?

And Murtough allowed himself to be teased. He sat and looked at Arion. He looked at Arion's lips that were loose and inclined to fullness, but, because of his trick of compressing them into a thin smile, gave him an air of prim malice. And Arion, unresponding and puritanical, giving nothing away, looked back at Murtough. Elizabeth knew Murtough itched to ask her: 'But what is he like in bed?' and could not because Arion sat there imperturbable.

He made her think of a Chinaman she had once seen perched on a stool beside the café counter of the big Woolworth's in Belfast. There he had sat, the little Chinaman, munching his bread with expressionless face whilst the waves of sound broke boomingly around him. Voices, the screech of a gramophone mingling with a different tune from the floor above, incessant noise — and, in the midst of it, that ancient face grown blank with the extreme wisdom that is the circle's completion and scarcely distinguishable from stupidity.

But Arion smiled.

The servants came to carry Murtough in his chair down to the dining-room. He sat at the head of a long table with his guests on either side of him. His was one of the few Dublin houses in which the grandeur of the eighteenth century remained unplundered. To his profligacy had been oddly added a shrewd business head, so, during his wild youth, his inheritance had remained well invested. Elizabeth drank from Waterford glass and fingered the old silver. Her interest in, and understanding of, his possessions pleased Murtough. Discovering she was an artist, he promised to show her the painted furniture his father had collected and, for a time, they discussed painting, neglecting Arion who had already heard all that both of them had to say about it.

At last some mention of Sean made Murtough turn

and question Arion about the journey of the day before. So they had met Sean at Costello? And he had found Riordan!

Elizabeth, watching the older man's face turned from her, saw in it a sudden startling resemblance to Sean. Her nerves quivered as though the resemblance were important to her. Yes, just as though it were important. Then he moved and there was no resemblance at all. He smiled at her, including her: 'And so you drove the car! You went through the morning mist to Costello and saw John appear like Excalibur from nowhere! And he had found Riordan, the last of the liberators? Oh, decidedly the last! When all this is over there will be nothing left to liberate. And what do you think of my son John? Do you think he will succeed?'

She did not know what to say and answered without thinking much: 'You should ask Arion. He is the instigator of it all.'

She was surprised when Murtough agreed: 'You are right. He is the instigator. He is the actuating force. He is the Holy Ghost.' He turned his mocking eyes on Arion: 'That is what you are, my dear Arion. You are the Holy Ghost, the tongue of flame mysteriously moving amongst men and inspiring them to bring about their fate. You, John and Riordan form a holy trinity. Riordan, secure and smug in some pleasantly distant heaven, is God the Father and John is God the Son.'

Arion smiled undisturbed.

'And what dark crucifixion have you planned for John, God the Holy Ghost?'

Arion shrugged his shoulders a little: 'We must first find our Judas,' he said.

'What does Judas matter? He is no more than an instrument of the Holy Ghost, no more than a body housing for a little while the force of fate.'

'Then I am Judas, too!' smiled Arion. 'From what I have heard of Riordan I am afraid he will dispossess me of my influence when he comes.'

'When does he come?'

'Sean is meeting him at Costello next Sunday.'

'And do you think this Riordan, who has kept out of sight for nearly five years, will put in an appearance?'

'Sean believes he will. And, after all, why shouldn't he?'

'Why should he? Wherever he is, he is safe enough. Why should he want to come back to this inferno? There are not many fools like Sean. It will all fall through — and better for Sean if it does.' Arion was silent. 'Don't you think so?' Arion shrugged his shoulders again. He did not say anything.

Elizabeth had been waiting to speak and now spoke quickly: 'If they are the Holy Trinity, what am I?'

Murtough turned to her, his momentarily seriousness forgotten: 'Are you the Virgin or the Magdalene?'

'And you?' she asked without answering, 'What are you?'

'Ah!' he laughed at himself, and at the others, 'I am the serpent, the old Adam. I am Satan himself. Sean will tell you that I have visited him in the wilderness.' He lent back in his chair, laughing — the voluptuary grown old, and, in an instant, she realized why his resemblance to Sean was important to her. She felt a sudden impatience to go somewhere where she might hope to find Sean. But she could not go yet and her impatience had to be forced down.

When luncheon was finished Murtough propelled himself in his wheel chair into the drawing-room where Elizabeth must admire the delicately carved, white-painted wood of the mantelpiece and the wreathed ceiling. Her pleasure in them was unaffected and she forgot Sean and no longer wanted to leave. Murtough ran his hand lovingly over a console table gilded and painted by Angelika Kauffmann with white Grecian figures and pink and blue swags and urns. He peered into it as though he were seeing it for the first time: 'Delightful,' he murmured and glanced up for Elizabeth's agreement. She was bending over the table. He saw the firm white curve of her cheek raised in her slow, infrequent smile. Her blouse had fallen forward so he could see her breasts with their prominent dark nipples. He moved to touch her and she, feeling his movement, stepped away instinctively. She glanced round quickly to make sure that Arion was there still. He was there. He was walking round the room looking at things as though he were looking for something. Arion, what are you looking for? He kept his back to her as he walked round. He was not interested in her interest in things nor listening to her conversation with Murtough. He stopped in front of a painting.

Murtough produced his keys and unlocked the glass-topped tables. He let her handle the snuff-boxes and miniatures and ivories. She looked at them, but she felt troubled and unsafe and every few minutes she looked up at Arion. He kept looking at the picture. He would not turn to her. So she thought of Sean.

She felt a physical revulsion from Murtough, yet the idea of something of him being in Sean gave a piquancy to her thought of Sean and illuminated him suddenly with possibilities. And yet she wanted to be saved from his possibility. She wanted Arion to save her from Murtough and from Sean. But Arion would not look at her.

He was looking at a painting by Pieter Brueghel that an eighteenth-century Murtough had bought in Paris for a few hundred francs. It was of a snow-covered landscape interrupted by squares of livid pewter-grey ice. All over the frozen lakes and between the dark lace skeletons of the delicately drawn trees were set tiny figures, jewel bright and detailed, scarcely paused, alert to return to their fervent activity. Above them the sky was the colour of turquoise matrix darkened by dusk as though by a film of smoke.

Murtough had once had the picture reproduced and had sent Arion a copy. It had had a peculiar fascination for him. This paused second of a life, once vividly lived and now remote in time and idiom, lost, save for this destructible record, had captured his imagination with its proof of the unreality time's passing gave to all reality. He had hung it in his study and left it behind when he left his wife. Now the people in it — the hunters with their deer in the foreground, the women around the fire, the skaters, even those diminished by distance to mere specks, were as familiar as remembered friends. Curious — this combination of familiarity and unreality! It was like redreaming a dream.

He was absorbed by the picture and his memory of it. He had forgotten Elizabeth.

Murtough was trying furtively to discover if his instinctive sense of her were right. He was puzzled by her relationship with Arion. It was outside his experience and, in the hope she would give him some clue to it, he started to speak of women. His interest above all his other interests was in women and in the complex interwoven feminine sexuality that desired to give and yet, against its will, withheld because of some century-ingrained instinct to give dearly if at all.

For what could she hope from this secret and isolated Arion? Was there no resentment in her? No bitterness?

She knew what Murtough wanted to know and she would tell him nothing. When she did not answer he was quietly insistent. Just as the insistence of the sea will disrobe a fully clad corpse and leave it to wash naked to and fro, so he tried by insistence to disrobe her of her reticence. She knew it. It was a trick she often played herself. And she smiled and told him nothing.

'Ah, well!' he laughed. 'Men and women — they're different.'

'But the world is the same place for both of them.'

'The same place for everyone and everything. The difference is always in oneself.'

'Maybe.'

'Don't you suppose you are different from other women? Consider the ordinary woman with her horror of being held cheap, and her continual, gnawing, instant-analysing fear that her gift is not appreciated! And the ordinary man with his male forgetfulness, his taking so much for granted that ravages the female need to be all things to him and the first in his thoughts!

She lets nerves and weariness destroy her reasonableness until he says: "How unreasonable!" But at the bottom she is reasonable. She will forgive anything, tolerate almost anything. It is the tiredness, the nerves, the fear of having her feeling and herself overlooked, even for an instant, that forces her to make so much of trifles.'

Elizabeth smiled, but told him nothing. All the time she was conscious of Arion in front of the picture. She was conscious of his absorbed interest in it. Whilst Murtough talked she thought of his curiosity concerning Arion and that it was roused in most people who met Arion. She remembered how, a few days before they had become lovers, he had taken her and a woman friend of her student days who had called on her, in the car to Glendalough. Elizabeth had felt content with Arion there in the damp, ferny air, but the woman had been troubled by him and was petulant and half flirtatious with him. He did not speak much but when he did he was surprisingly charming. All the time the woman felt there was something wrong somewhere. As they were leaving she said in her little, gnat-wail voice: 'Oh, but I wanted some flowers!' 'We won't have time,' said Elizabeth coldly, furious with the woman, she did not quite know why. 'I think we will,' said Arion. 'Let me help you pick some.' And he went amongst the hummocks of the old graves picking the wild flowers, charmingly spoiling the woman. But she knew there was something wrong somewhere. He had that manner of rather casual charm that is irresistible, yet she really disliked him. He gave her the flowers and she took them, still exaggeratedly flirtatious and petulant. 'Like a fool,' thought Elizabeth, but afterwards the woman said: 'He is not sincere. He is only pretending to be one of us. He is something different.' Elizabeth did not try to defend him. She would not have tried to defend him against Murtough could he have spoken his censure then.

Arion turned suddenly from the picture and came over to them. There was no telling what he had heard or understood of Murtough's talk or Elizabeth's reticence. Looking at him, she felt intensely the attraction of his sensitive, pale face that was cultured, tapering, seeming refined of all crudity of feeling. He passed his hand over his thin, light hair and smiled at them. Gentle, charming, non-committal. Ah! Non-committal! Except by his restraint, he could not hurt one. A complete restraint of all emotion, even the emotion that wrought generosity. No passionate generosity in him; only a non-committal caution.

The difficulty, of course, was in reconciling this Arion who was dignified and cynically aloof when speaking with other men, with the Arion she knew transported by the force of his own desire of her.

There he stood and smiled with his mouth primly tucked in at the corners. His mouth never opened from end to end, and never stretched into a laugh. He said: 'It is getting late. I want to put through a couple of calls to London before dinner. I have promised to go and see Sean after dinner.'

Elizabeth rose. She had not worn a hat or coat. She was ready to go. Murtough said: 'Yes, take her along to see John.'

Arion had had no intention of taking her to see Sean, but now she was determined to be taken. Sean had suddenly new meaning for her and she must see him again. As though Murtough knew this, he shook their hands and laughed them away. As they went he called after them: 'Take her to see John.'

Elizabeth left Arion at their lodging-house and went to garage the car. Then she walked to Grafton Street to buy a pork pie for her supper. Most of the shops were shut, some barricaded and some riddled with shot or gutted by fire. But those remaining were busy enough. Women went to and fro filling their baskets. Men, hatless, hands in pockets, came out in groups from their offices to have a drink. The terror was out-living itself and becoming a habit. During the day, if not at night, it was no more than a background to the easy-going routine of Dublin life.

When she returned to the house Arion was still at the telephone in the hall. As she passed him she said: 'Come up for me at eight o'clock.' He started speaking to the person at the other end of the telephone and did not answer her. She went up to her room in a nervous irritation of anxiety in case he should not come for her. She started tidying her room. She looked at her paintings and turned them face to the wall. When she became aware of them, she hated them because they were not good enough. Her art did not mean enough to her. She always neglected it to pursue the complexities of her numerous *affaires* and only returned to it for consolation when each *affaire* failed at last. Her art was only a compensation, not an end. She felt a little ashamed of it and hopeless about it.

Just before seven o'clock she heard Arion go out. He always went at that time to some restaurant for dinner. She sat on her window-sill and munched her pork pie and watched for his return. He was not gone an hour. He was back almost before she had time to fear anxiously that he would not return for her. Punctually at eight o'clock he knocked on her door and, gratefully excited, she went with him. They walked down Grafton Street to the quayside. The streets were clearing, although it was still two hours to curfew. Always, as evening approached, an apprehension crept into the air. People remembered and went home. There was not much else to do, anyway.

The sky was grey. The rain was beginning to fall a little. It would be dark early. After dark Dublin life receded until it was prisoner and only terror had access to the freedom of the streets. People lay in bed and listened to the sound of rifle fire, exploding bombs, the rumble of armoured cars, and saw waving across the night sky the white arms of the searchlights on the Crossley tenders. There was no knowing what news of death and destruction the morning would bring.

The shop on the quayside over which Sean lived, had a side door that was Sean's front door and always unlocked. They could see his light burning in his uncurtained window that looked across the river towards the ruins of the Four Courts. They went up the narrow stairs fitted between two walls and came to a small landing. Arion rapped on the second door. Sean's voice, hoarse and rather muffled, called them to enter. Sean was in bed. His face was lit by a reading lamp on the table beside him. Under the lamp a book lay face downwards. The air smelt of iodoform and was sultry as though the noonday heat had come in through the open window and had not gone out again. He sat up in bed and smiled at Arion.

He said: 'I have been lying here listening to the footsteps of people passing. I didn't recognize yours. I was surprised when they stopped. That's because you weren't alone.'

Elizabeth heard the enmity in his voice. Arion heard it too, but he would not speak of her. He had not wanted her to come and she had come. She must account for herself; he'd not account for her. He merely stood with his back to her as though she were not there and said: 'Why didn't you let me know you were ill?'

Sean said: 'It's nothing. It was only a slight haemorrhage — not from my lungs, you know. It's from my throat. I've been coughing a lot and that caused it. I must have caught a cold coming back last night. I've taken some aspirin. I'll be all right to-morrow morning. I know my body. It has amazing powers of recuperation.' He laughed, but he looked ghastly. Except for the spots of colour like grazes on his cheeks his face was blanched and gaunt. A greyish handkerchief clotted with blood and phlegm stuck out from under his pillow. His bed looked uncomfortable and dirty. His pillow was dark with grease from his hair and covered with patches of dried blood.

Elizabeth did not speak. She stood back silently in the shadow and watched the two men in the circle of lamplight. She knew they were deliberately excluding her from their consciousness — Arion with malice, Sean with anger. She should not have come. They did not invite her and did not want her. She went and sat in a chair by the fire-place and watched them, seeming tranquilly oblivious of being excluded.

Arion sat on the edge of the bed and made Sean lie down again. Sean lay and watched him with an expression of trust and deep affection. Arion said: 'I had luncheon with your father to-day. He thinks your plans will all fall through.'

Sean laughed as though he were laughing with Arion. 'They can't,' he said. 'We have had a year of war now. Neither side will give in — so something must happen and happen soon. Each side is just marking time and waiting for a force to appear that will take possession of it and drive it to victory. Riordan is that force.' He took a deep breath and continued speaking very quickly as though he feared that were he to stop he would not be able to start again. 'The English are flagging and bored with it all. They're sick of the waste of men and money. They're beginning to think the game isn't worth the candle and are wanting peace from sheer lack of interest in the war. All they need is an excuse for giving in. Confronted suddenly with a new and insurmountable force like Riordan they will give in at once. Then we will have the people with us. If they won't side with us at first, they won't be against us. They'll wait and see, and when we succeed we'll have all of them.'

It was as though something in Arion's presence gave Sean the vitality of confidence. Elizabeth watched his face flush to life. He could not lie down. As he spoke he raised himself on his elbow, the coat of his pyjamas slipped open and she saw, half with repulsion, his thin, white chest. Remembering her, he pulled the coat together quickly and held it with his hand and glanced at her with hate.

She looked away from him. She looked round the room. It was bare. It was shabby and very dirty. The grate was littered with ashes. His books were piled up along one wall. He had papered the walls himself with old copies of the *Workers' Republic* dating back to its first appearance in May 1915. Here and there paragraphs were marked with green pencil. She was not near enough to any of them to read the text but could see by the headings that they all referred to Riordan's activities before and during the Easter Week Rising.

She rose quietly and went to the window in order to read one of the passages. It was the report of a meeting that Riordan had addressed, and in every line was adulation of the great leader. Riordan, Riordan, the great leader! In Ireland a leader was indeed a leader — to be worshipped in life and canonized after death.

She leaned from the window and breathed in with the summer air the melancholy sweetness of the evening. The rain had stopped for a while. Mixed with the weedy smell of the river was a smell of leaves from the park. The grey of the sky was slit by a band of prim-rose light that threw into vivid relief the roofs and the chimneys rising from them, tall and branched and angular like organ cacti, and the broken Four Courts. The river was slow moving and dim as oil. A drift of men who had been watching some horse jumping in the Park came over the bridge towards her. In the distance they looked spectral and pale-faced through the strange, meagre light. But as they passed beneath the window she heard their voices in laughter and quick argument and felt their vibrating excitement. Some, who had seen her leaning from the window, looked up as they came beneath it and smiled and she smiled back. One or two of them laughed right at her and made her laugh too and show all her beautiful white teeth. She felt warmed and grateful to them for including her in the world.

As she stood there she could hear the voices of Sean and Arion behind her. Sean was talking excitedly. As ever, Arion's presence was intoxicating him and his voice rose with a shrill agitation. But it was a pleasant voice. It rose pleasantly like a shaken tree from the quiet and monotonous plain that was Arion's. They seemed diminished there behind her in the circle of the lamplight, as figures are diminished in a convex mirror. It was the rough and tumble of voices below that impinged itself life-size upon her consciousness. Watching the faces of the men raised to her, she thought that it was so they might have been raised to Riordan, and she felt an envy of Riordan. She felt an envy, too, of those young men he had so entranced that year after year one and another had set out to the west to find him and bring him back to leadership again. She felt an envy of Sean because he alone had been so drawn by the spell he had come at last into Riordan's very presence. She felt she would want nothing more than to be so entranced by something or by somebody.

Behind her Sean was appointing the Cabinet of the First Government: 'Riordan, of course, will be President and I will be Home Secretary and you will be Chancellor of the Exchequer and advise all of us.'

A man with a long wand came along lighting the lamps by the river. The reflection of the yellow lights lopped about on the water and tipped the wet cobbles.

She had been born near all the enterprise of Belfast and had lived much of her childhood in London, so Dublin, with its lost air and lost wealth, had often seemed pathetic to her. But now she knew there was no one to pity here. There was no indifference.

There was poverty more complete than any she had seen before but it had a dignity that deprived it of squalor. There were the louts and the wreckers and the fools who fired revolvers at anything and everyone, but through all their loutishness was the strain of passionate feeling raising them above the common loutishness of the world. They might suffer and die, but there was no pathos in them. In their death and suffering was nothing of the futility that corrupted so often and made pathetic the death and suffering of others.

Poverty here did not flinch the nerves. It was the dark creeping forbearance of indifference that gnawed into one. It was that indifference thrust in upon itself that caught one with the sickening guilt of pity.

Sean said: 'It would be good to be caught up on a wave of faith in something, in anything; to be caught up and carried right over to death without a moment's pause to lay one's hand upon one's heart. . . .'

Ah! Yes.

. . . Without the panic pause of apprehension, the back glance, the catch of the breath, that glimpse of oblivion revealing death nakedly so one knew it too hideous a price for life lived even at its fullest.

But she was of the North and of England where men

achieve and grow rich because there is always in their mind's depth, doubt like a weight to hold them back from the barren brightness of the skies.

The men from the jumping were all passed. She turned from the window. Arion was looking amongst a heap of clothes, books and papers lying in a corner, for a chess board. He had suggested they should play in an attempt to quieten Sean who was coughing violently. He found the board and, one by one, the pieces. But Sean would not give his thought to the game. He made stupid moves and laughed at them. His nerves were restless. Arion had lit a cigarette. Sitting there with the cigarette hanging from his lips and his eyes narrowed against the smoke, he had an unfamiliar, rather sinister look. He played quietly, ignoring Sean's fooling. He was not flattering him to-night, but that did not seem to make any difference to Sean. Rather it seemed to increase his excitement and confidence. He could never take Arion's disapproval seriously. He understood his beloved Arion.

Listen to me, Arion! I want to talk about myself. I can't play any more. No, no, no. . . . He scattered the pieces. Listen to me. He started to speak but was interrupted by a fit of convulsive coughing.

Arion watched him for a moment through his narrowed eyes. Then he glanced at his watch and stood up. In a cold, expressionless way he stood and watched Sean.

When Sean's cough relaxed and he looked up with his face red and his eyes streaming, Arion said: 'We must go. It is half-past nine. I don't want to be caught by the curfew.'

Sean pretended not to hear; he turned his head and looked down at his pillow, then lowered himself slowly down on to it. He said with weary impatience: 'This exhaustion is a nuisance. It makes me angry. It doesn't gain anything from me. I won't let it. It just makes me angry.' He spoke as though it were something outside himself and armed against him.

Arion stood without saying anything. Sean went on quickly: 'If only I were as strong as other men! If only I had the strength to do a hard day's work as other men can! Then there'd be nothing I could not do.'

Arion repeated: 'I am going now, Sean.' That time Sean had to hear and as he raised his eyes Elizabeth saw in them the deep-hidden panic fear of being left alone. Once alone he would sink into the despair that follows exaltation. He raised himself on his elbow so he was outside the circle of the lamplight and his face was in shadow. His flame was dimmed. It was as though a breath of carbon-dioxide had been wafted towards him so his flame dipped and faltered. The twist of his subtile, unhappy looking mouth gave away all the strain he was so careful to hide.

Suddenly she felt a revulsion against his difficulty and the complexity and perplexity that would make him uneasy company. She'd had enough of difficulty. Dear God, she did not want to be troubled any more.

Looking round the room, she hated it and its sordid bareness. She hated the darkness lying like a doom in all the corners. The dark here was like a black cloud of carbon-dioxide encroaching upon the light, creeping upon it to extinguish the flame of the spirit. She made a move to hasten Arion's going. Sean saw her and she felt his enmity. Something within him said with bitter enmity: 'I hate you,' and her mind replied: 'No more than I hate you.'

Her movement had exonerated Arion. Now she was to blame. She was forcing him away. Arion smiled a little, following every inflection of their thought with his mocking and formidable intellect.

Sean put out his hand to Arion. Stay, stay, Arion, and save me from despair. He lent towards him, trying to touch him, but Arion was just out of reach.

Arion would not stay. Detached and methodical he gathered up the chessmen and stood them in rows on the table. Then he said: 'No, I must go.' He opened the door.

Sean, propped on his elbow, his face flushed and damp-looking, watched him. There was apprehension and blame in his stare. But he would not blame Arion.

'Please, Arion, stay!'

Arion waved a hand to mitigate his going, and went. The door closed on Sean's pleading. Elizabeth followed Arion down the stairs. She had not spoken a word since they entered.

Out in the street she said: 'Why wouldn't you stay a little longer with Sean?'

Arion raised his eyebrows, feeling the question intrusive: 'He must learn self-sufficiency,' he said.

She said angrily: 'Don't you realize he is not suffering from a lack of self-sufficiency but from the undermining starvation that comes of attempting to be self-sufficient when he isn't! His nerves are on edge with hunger.'

He walked beside her coldly impassive. He walked

with his hands in his pockets, his shoulders drawn back, his head thrust a little forward. He was quite frigid and withdrawn in a fury of resentment of her intrusion. He knew their relationship possible because each respected the reservations of the other. Now he felt she was making it impossible She was trespassing. He could only withdraw into the impregnable core of his silence and shrug his shoulders.

She knew he resented her intrusion. She knew she was in danger of being completely excluded, yet she went on. She was caught in sudden wild anger with him that he should suppose himself privileged to act always unquestioned. She felt an anger that was half jealousy at his belief in his own security. No one was secure against him, but he was secure against everyone. It was as though he were insured against hurt. His satisfaction was complete. It was not self-satisfaction. Something had given him this complete satisfaction so he could look desirelessly at everything else.

He was held to her by a physical need, but by nothing else. He could go when he wished. In a moment, in an instant he could turn and go, but he did not wish. He was fastidious and attracted. The relationship was convenient, and possible because of her respect for his reservations. He repaid her, as he repaid no one else, with equal respect.

And she did not want it. She did not want the cold equality of their mutual respect. She wanted not only the passion of their physical union, but the deep and passionate hold of mental union. She was weary of her own solitude. She wanted to be saved from the solitude of her independence. And she wanted Arion, not Sean,

to save her. She had felt sudden revulsion from the
difficulty of Sean. She wanted to be admitted into
understanding with Arion, into the secret of his security.
At her revulsion from Sean she felt sudden, desperate
need to escape her instinct towards him. She wanted
to escape into Arion.

But there was no response in Arion. He walked
beside her, secure and withdrawn, in cold lipped
disapproval of her approach.

She burst out in anger: 'Why did you ever start this
affair?'

After a moment he answered quite lightly: 'To
gratify my curiosity.'

'And now is it gratified?'

'Yes — with regard to your sensual reaction to me.
But your self is still a mystery.'

'I will always remain a mystery,' she said, 'whilst
you refuse to see me as a human being.'

'Why should I refuse to see you as a human being?'

'Because you resent me. You resent my humanity.'

He thought for a moment, then he said: 'Perhaps
I do.'

'But why?' she asked.

'I suppose for the same reason that I resent religion
and politics and good causes. I am afraid of their
getting a hold on me. If I am brutal it is the brutality
of panic.' He was smiling again. He spoke as though
he were being frank and truthful, yet it was getting her
no farther than his evasion had done. She felt herself
up against his obstinacy. Because I have said I cannot,
I will not. She was powerless against his obstinacy and
knew he would tell her nothing.

'Why should you be afraid of anything getting a hold on you? I want something to get a hold on me — and nothing does.' She looked at him. His expression did not change. She added at last: 'But perhaps I am more elusive than you are. Perhaps nothing can get a hold on me.'

But she felt that something had got a hold on him. His was the freedom of belonging completely to some other thing. He was free from himself — so it seemed to her — and, his freedom being complete and perfect, he could not risk its disturbance by the claim of any other thing. So he rejected her and she was hurt. She was more hurt than she would have felt possible. She walked beside him bewildered and unhappy and subdued. Soon she wanted him to be hurt too, and said with spite:

'Something's always getting a hold on you. I expect you left England because of some woman and you'll leave Ireland because of me. Wherever you go your sensuality will get you mixed up with some woman or other, and then you'll have to run away from her.'

He said, undisturbed: 'You are right in a way. But you are more wrong than right.'

She insisted: 'Your sensuality will trip you up in the end. It's a fault in you.'

'Oh, yes,' he laughed. 'Another of the endless faults in oneself that one not only cannot overcome, but does not particularly want to.'

Against her will she asked painfully: 'And when you lie with me — it doesn't mean very much?'

He was silent for a moment, then answered in a gentle voice: 'It means a great deal at the time.'

His gentleness stung her. She felt she had betrayed

herself. She felt she had shown him her weakness so he need resent her no more.

They were at the house. On his landing she did not pause with him but flung herself upstairs to her room.

By the light of the street lamp she could see the housekeeper's cat curled up on her bed. Because she was fond of it, it was often in her room. She sat down on the bed beside it and stroked it quietly. The cat's coat was cool and silken like fine china, but beneath was warmth and a fierce, living tension. It awoke and stretched itself and began to purr. She felt its body vibrating and lifted it and let it lie half asleep in her arms. Then, with a quick movement, she caught it to her breast so it could not move. She held the small, living body with cruel strength and buried her face in the firm, lithe neck. The cat did not struggle but waited until she should relax her hold and it could get away. It lashed her thighs with its strong tail. In a moment her hold had become all cruelty. She gripped the straining body fiercely and the animal gave a sharp cry of pain. She released it at once and let it fall heavily to the ground. It gathered itself together and stalked away, then paused and started to lick itself with stabbing movements of its bright little tongue. After watching it a moment she went and knelt down beside it and with one finger stroked seductively the seal-soft fur behind its ears. It looked at her, then went on with its washing. Something in its detachment touched her profoundly. Tears of self-pity started into her eyes.

She jerked herself to her feet and, as though controlling herself with the same movement, the tears disappeared. She went and stood by the window. It was after ten o'clock. The street was deserted. She could hear someone moving in the room beneath her. In the room beneath that Arion would be at his desk writing.

She shivered a little. She put on her coat before leaving the house again. Once outside, she walked quickly and cautiously against the wall. At times she broke into a run and laughed to herself as she ran. The air was filled with a warm, rippling wind that exhilarated her curiously. The empty streets had a hard, metallic, naked look that was in some way exciting.

And she was going to go back to Sean. To do so was undignified, she knew — but she'd let no mere dignity stand between her and her will. Later if she were troubled by a memory of indignity she could easily transcend it with a mood.

She dodged into an alleyway from half a dozen Black and Tans patrolling the back streets. They tramped past and she sped on. She had to cross Grafton Street and that brought her out into the open. But she was in luck. She met no one until she came to the riverside. A policeman stood there staring down into the water. He had a dull, quiet look rather like a reflective horse that stands with its head over a gate. She edged softly along by the wall that he might not see or hear her.

Suddenly there came a ripping flash of rifle fire from the roof above her head. She caught her breath and stood paused to run, fearing he would turn and accuse her of firing. But instead he doubled up and sank down into an untidy heap on the road. Someone on the other side of the river blew a whistle. There was a sound of running from all directions. She opened

63

Sean's door and stood panting in the safety of the dark stairway.

When the door shut all sound seemed to cease, then there was a muffled, hustling noise from the street outside. She waited until everything was quiet again before tiptoeing up to the landing. There was no light under his door. He was lying in darkness. She opened the door and entered the room. Moving lightly she went and stood beside his bed. The room was so dark she could scarcely see his face on the pillow, but she could feel his eyes fixed on her. For a long time they looked at one another in silence; then, suddenly, he called out loudly in a strange voice:

'Who is that?'

She did not answer.

With a sudden movement that had in it the deliberation of fear he switched on the lamp. When he saw her he looked surprised and annoyed. Before he could speak again she said casually: 'I left my gloves.' She went to the chair and picked them up. But she did not go. She stood and watched him and he watched her uncertainly. At last he said:

'Why did you come in like that?'

'Like what?'

'Like death.'

She felt the imaginative fear in him and something hurt her throat. But she had to be wary of his enmity. She felt him like a wild creature that would run were she to move too readily towards it. So she paused, pretending she had no intention of coming at all. She said in her quiet, casual, reasonable voice: 'I thought you were asleep and did not want to wake you.'

They looked at one another again. She had her gloves but made no attempt to go, and he did not seem to expect her to go.

He looked older and greyish. The fever had left him. He looked very ill and sunken. He looked now as though his temperature had fallen below normal. He just lay there greyish and sunken into greyish, dirty, uncomfortable-looking pillows. The wonder of him was gone. He lay absorbed by his own misery and fears, uncaring of outer things; even uncaring of her intrusion.

Indeed, discharmed, no longer reflecting Arion, it did not seem an intrusion to him. In his house and in his mind anyone could come and go as they wished. He was not of Arion's generation. Anyone could say what they liked to him and he what he liked to anyone. Why hesitate before asking what you want to know? Let us out into the open and accuse our enemy on sight:

'Why don't you leave Arion alone?' he said.

'I can't.'

'He doesn't want you. He told me so himself.'

'I know. And I don't want him.'

'Then why don't you stop seeing him?'

'Why doesn't he stop seeing me?'

'I don't know. I suppose you hold him in some way.'

'And in some way he holds me.'

'Couldn't you go away?'

She made a little reasonable movement with her hand: 'This is my own country.'

She knew him convinced. She could sense at once his change of attitude. He had a volatile, almost too swift understanding that robbed him of the strength of prejudice. His intelligence startled her a little. She had not expected it. A certain blustering, febrile imagination — yes; but not that intelligence of understanding. She hesitated, less sure of herself:

'You understand that?' she said.

'I understand Arion's power.'

That annoyed her — the assumption that the power was all Arion's. She moved nearer to him and sat down on the edge of the bed.

'Why do you need Arion?' she said. 'Have you no power of your own?'

He looked at her reflectively for a moment, acknowledging her intelligence as a few minutes before she had acknowledged his. He answered simply: 'I am too much influenced by moods.'

She nodded, again acknowledging him. 'I know. I understand.'

It was true. She did understand. She knew he wanted to say: In some moods I feel myself irresistible, but in others it is as though I were foredoomed to failure and all my fighting useless. I must have Arion and his belief in me to reassure me. He bridges the abyss for me so I can cross to new confidence.

Although he had said so little of this she was surprised that he had said so much. She was surprised that he knew his own weakness. She had not thought of him before as self-aware, and now she realized his relationship with Arion could not be, as she had supposed, the elementary relationship of ingenuous inexperience confiding in maturity. It must be something more subtle and complicated than that.

She felt a new respect for Sean. He was not the

negligible dreamer Sean she had at first imagined him to be, nor altogether an impulsive and impressionable child. She was not going to take him from Arion by merely willing to do so. Not a bit of it. And she felt sudden jealousy of Sean's relationship with Arion and sudden urgency in her desire of him.

She said: 'What happened to distract your confidence? When did it fail?'

It was clever of her to ask that, but his expression did not change. He lay as before, frowning at the light. Slowly, without hesitation, he said: 'When I was a child I was quite wild and nobody could do anything with me. I used to go out and get lost in the Wicklow Hills and wander about for days without food. I seemed to live on a sort of mental elation so my body meant nothing. I used to think at times I could control my body completely. I wanted to control it so I would be free of its necessities.'

He paused and turned his head from the light, and she leant forward and switched it off. She knew it was easier to talk in the dark.

Quite quietly and suddenly he started to speak again: 'There was a fierce sort of power in me then. It was like a sea beating about inside me. Sometimes it was quite calm but often it was a violent turmoil so it seemed to surge up and choke me and I had to scream out and thump my fists against things. People thought I had a terrible temper.'

In the darkness the chill barrier of his enmity seemed relaxed. She knew now it would be possible to approach him without risking rebuff, but she did not move or speak.

He said: 'I used to wander over the hills in a sort of vision. It was as though I could rise out of my body and fill the whole sky. And then I felt there was nothing I could not do; there was nothing I could not achieve. I used to think then I was the one who would liberate Ireland and save her from the civilization of England. I would save her from the greed and ugly industrialism of the North and of England so she would become a sanctuary for the imagination. And I would do it of my own power. And then one day in the winter, after I had been walking for a long time in the rain, my body seemed to drag me back into itself and I found I was ill. The funny thing was I couldn't forget that I was ill. I could only be conscious that I was burning and shivering and feeling sick. The cold and the wind and the rain suddenly seemed brutal and unbearable and I started to run to get away from them. I kept thinking of the warmth of our house and my bed where I could lie down and sleep. It began to get dark. The hills looked desolate. There was no friendliness in them any more and I was lost. The rain splashed on my face. I ran and ran, sobbing and gasping for breath. Then, suddenly, I fell down. I just toppled over as though I'd done it deliberately, and I couldn't get up again. I crawled over the grass until I got to the road. . . . Next morning some people in a trap found me and took me to a hospital. I had pneumonia. I got better, but after that I could never quite lose hold of my body again. I was almost adolescent then and that made things worse. I had a pain in my chest and I coughed and I would get terribly tired. That was the worst of all — that tiredness; it would come down on me like a sickness.'

She nodded: 'I know it. It's like the weight that drags down the balloon.'

He agreed: 'Yes,' pleased by the simile, taking new interest in her, 'I could escape sometimes into a sort of delirium, but it wasn't the same. It wasn't a voluntary escape into sanity, but an involuntary escape into a sort of insanity. Because my body was weak now it was stronger than I was. All my will was taken up in the effort to make myself do things — eating and moving and just doing things. It took me all my time to live so I couldn't escape beyond living. The tiredness was always there like a whimpering child that worries you until you determine to ignore it. You know what I mean! You talk and laugh and pretend it isn't there, but the more you talk the more insistent it becomes so you cannot forget it. It's always there — the tiredness — like a snivelling brat always at your elbow. How I hate it and resent it.' He caught his breath quickly. 'Hate it, hate it, hate it! And you have to give in in the end. However much you fight against it in the end you fall back on your bed and lose consciousness gladly. It was after that illness I began to realize it was possible to fail. Once I realized it, I could never forget it. I never do forget it except when Arion is here. He infuses me with his own confidence, and with power that is like my own, and I feel infallible again. But when he goes I remember I can fail.'

After a moment she moved towards him and pressed her hand against his thin, cold fingers that lay dully on the coverlet. 'But you can't fail,' she said.

He said nothing. He lay grey and drear against the

grey pillows and did not speak. She gripped his hand and lifted it, but there was no response in his fingers. With a sudden movement she put her hands to his shoulders and tried to lift him, but he was too heavy and she could only shake him and say: 'You can't fail. Do you hear me? You can't fail?'

'Why do you say that?' he asked dully.

She could think of no reason to give him. What did she care whether he could fail or not fail! What did she care about the liberty of Ireland! All she could feel was a jealousy of his need of Arion and jealousy of his faith in Ireland. She wanted to put her hands round his neck and press her face into his breast. In her new respect for him she had felt the male pride in him and her desire had leapt to it. She was caught in a sudden convulsive tenderness for him that left her without pride so she thought only of a means of gaining him.

She and Arion met like combatants. They were thrown together, body to body, in a sensual transport that was like a lust of combat. And when it was over they separated coldly and lay apart like enemies. But as she touched Sean she was enchanted into this delicate tenderness and her body trembled. She wanted to bend to him and cover him with her body. In contact with him she wanted to close her eyes and lose herself in consciousness only of his body. She wanted to absorb him completely into herself as though he were an unborn child and she in possession of him, carrying him with her, a part of herself.

He lay unresponding and uncaring. He did not ask her again why she had said he could not fail. He did not believe her and did not care why she had said it. She had no power over his daemon.

He moved a little so she had to take her hands away. She could sit there if she wished — he did not care — but he did not want her to touch him. He lay without thinking very much. Dully and unhappily, he wanted Arion to return and comfort him, but he knew Arion had no intention of returning. He lay for a long time silent and, suddenly, she thought to tell him of herself:

'I come from the North.'

'I have never been to Ulster,' he said as though he were making conversation. 'What is it like?'

She knew he did not want to know. She knew he was irritated by her voice that was distracting him from the profoundly contemplative tranquillity of his despair. She set herself deliberately to irritate him. Better that he should be irritated into consciousness of her than that he should be absorbed by the absence of Arion.

She answered him: 'Rain, wind and cold. We lived at Carrickmoy. It's just where the coast turns round the corner into Belfast Lough.'

All the houses there faced the sea. It would have been funny to have lived in one that did not. It would have been like sitting with your back to the driver in a bus. In the winter the spray was flung over the roofs and flooded the back gardens. Her cousins used to roll their trousers up to their knees and bale the yard with buckets. The salt killed nearly all the plants. Only the aconite lived through the winter and in the spring its leaves would glitter with salt as thick as hoar frost.

She told him all this and other things about Carrickmoy. When she paused he did not say anything, so she
went on telling him her memories of things. They
were memories that had been with her so long it seemed
everyone must know them and she had not thought to
tell anyone of them before. They seemed part only of
herself and now she was bringing them out and wrap-
ping them about him as though they were herself; as
though she had woven them out of herself like a web
to spin about him.

He lay unprotestingly silent. When she saw he
made no attempt to resist her with interruption, she
went on quietly. She started to tell him about the
shore at Carrickmoy where she used to play during the
summer holidays with the other children. The shore
was the playground of all the Carrickmoy children.
When they went back to school they would go every
evening to climb the rocks by the light of the long sunset.

They were cruel-edged rocks, deep-crannied and
treacherous as glaciers. They were all thrust like combs
into the sand. They were so tilted and thin you felt if
you leant on them they would fall down flat, but they
were immovable. They were harsh and grey, as old as
the earth and as immovable. Even the sea could not
influence them. Here the coast's formation had not
altered an inch in a thousand years. The shore was
steadfast; the tide marks unvarying. Without avail the
sea was tender and insistent, or, storm-goaded, hurled
at the rocks blow upon blow like cannon fire. Always
it must fall back and admit that for all its effort it had
washed away no more than the footprints of the feet
that had been walking on the soft, clinging sand.

Through all the ages no more than footprints of ape and great elk; dodo and dinosaur; of king, saint and ship-wrecked Spaniard; of fugitives and rebels long dead and those still living Orangemen who, here from indrawn boats at midnight, unloaded arms to protect themselves against the South when it would seem no other would protect them. Daily it washed from them the footprints of the children who clambered, with the wild unawareness of danger that makes for safety, up to high tide mark to find above it the rocks, dry and rough, grass tufted and mottled with rosettes of yolk-yellow lichen.

But not a dust drain. The rocks were made of iron and stained the sands with rust.

Strange things were washed ashore here. Here the children found the bodies of the whip-tailed skate and of devil fish that were good to eat but when caught had to be beheaded at sea that their frightful appearance might not frighten away custom. Sometimes they found dead monsters that, living, ventured so seldom towards the land there was no common name for them. Amongst the stones they found coins worn thinner than paper and the marvellous, fine vertebrae bones of great cod, and sometimes lifebelts and wreckage bearing the names of ships long ago lost and forgotten. Once they found a sailor's tunic and once a plait of yellow hair.

She did not know if he were listening or not. It did not matter. She spoke in a deliberate monotone, trying to drug his upper consciousness with the waverless persistence of her remote, nerveless, little voice.

And once when she was climbing alone at that grim

moment of a winter's day when, the dark poised but not yet fallen, everything stands out blaely chill and clear in the last of the light, she came across a drowned man and woman roped together with a clothes line. Their hands, fallen apart, and their blank faces were a clear, strange, flower-like blue. They were strange, like sea-creatures, scarcely frightening as they lay there so quiet and apart, regardless of everything and of one another. They lay silent, all their passion frustrated. She stared at them until suddenly, in panic, she sped back over the rocks as though winged. But at home when everyone asked her what had frightened her she would not tell. Next morning they were gone. The sea had taken them away again.

She paused in the darkness, grown gradually remote from him and uncaring of him as she returned in memory to the lonely and rebellious child she had once been. Unexpectedly, he said: 'Go on.'

She said: 'There was a great pool of water ringed round by rocks and the sea wall. It was called the Chalybeate Hole. Some people said it was bottomless and others said: No, because nothing can be bottomless, but it was as deep as the deepest part of the sea. Years before a quarry had been there and one day in a terrible storm the sea had broken its way in and drowned three of the quarrymen. It had been abandoned then and the pit had gradually filled up until it became a sort of sea lake. It was always dark like indigo. Although there was seldom any movement on its surface people said that even the strongest swimmers were dragged down beneath the water whenever they tried to cross it.'

The children thought the ghosts of the three drowned men seized the swimmers and nothing would induce them into it. The sea was safer and they would jump feet first from the overhanging cliff down, down to strike the surface and sink nearly two fathoms before rising again.

Elizabeth could not swim well and dreaded striking the icy northern waters. More than that she dreaded the struggle when, sinking, she felt she would never be able to breathe again. When sea-weed touched her she became panic-stricken, possessed by horrors of octopuses and sharks, and would lash the water back to the safety of the shore. The children, spiteful, shrew-tongued, never really liking her, saw through her denials of fear and laughed at her. Once, when they all joined forces to deride her, she climbed up the sea wall and leapt down into the Chalybeate Hole. The others stood round agape and fearful eyed, never expecting to see her emerge alive. But she came to the surface and swam leisurely to the shore. As she waded in she pushed her hair back from her white face and whistled to show them all how little she cared. They never learnt that when she went to the cave to dress she vomited and sobbed in a transport of nervous terror.

'One day,' she said, 'I went to a deserted part of the shore and came across an old swimming pool boarded up and forgotten. Because it was very small and dangerous and unsanitary it had been closed up when the new one was built. Of course the waves had washed over the boarding and flooded it. When I found it a whole garden of coloured sea-weeds were growing from its sides. Marvellous colours — viridian, brown and flamingo pink — just like a garden. I never told anyone.'

He looked across at her, a vague shadow sitting curiously apart amongst the shadows of the room. She seemed to him outside the range of his sympathy. He could see the child she had been in complete under-standing of it, and yet with indifference. It was too like the child he had been. His sympathy was for himself and yet for no one like himself. In drowsy indifference to her, he let her talk on.

She was talking about a little town called Ardglass to which her uncle had taken her one evening at the long, slow setting of the summer sun. As she thought of it she saw as vividly as though it were imaginary the little, quiet village where nothing at all moved in the evening light. To her it had seemed not so much de-serted as never inhabited, a town that had grown of itself, for itself, like some undiscovered glade in a dense wood. Round the curved black rocks on the beach the untrodden sand lay flat and firm as metal and on it a tower was built. Yes, on the beach of all places! A tower of breaking and falling white stones, no taller than a tall man. The gulls congregated within it and swept through it. It did not seem strong and ancient like the other towers that were dotted over the Irish hills, but even her uncle, who knew so many things, did not know why it had been built.

A sturdy pier of flints curved like an arm into the sea. What curious traffic paused here? Her uncle told her how the pier became crowded with activity when the herring shoal was passing. Talking, he filled the village with girls who followed the mighty shoal down the

coast and with cotton bound fingers gutted and packed
the fish so quickly their hands moved faultlessly
with the speed and beauty of machinery. Then the
pavements became slippery and aglitter with fish-
scales; everywhere the sound of voices and the raw
grinding of the lorries navigating hardly the tedious
and crooked streets. For a while the village had its
place in time, then the shoal passed, the fisher boats
pursued it, the girls, the barrels, the lorries were gone
in a night, and it slipped back out of time to sleep again
in eternity.

Someone had said to Elizabeth: 'That's the Irish
Sea you're looking at.'

At Carrickmoy there was always the Antrim coast
to obscure the horizon, but here she could gaze over
the peacock darkening of the waters to where the mists,
lying layer upon layer, reflected the sun setting behind
her. Her uncle said: 'England is over there if you
could see it.' And she thought how she might set out
on such a strange evening as that, on such a strange,
calm sea and row right out of sight of Ireland and still
seem to have before her, nothing but the sea. The night
would come and go, then in the crystalline morning
light there would appear the pencil line that would
slowly broaden, darken and deepen and become England. It seemed to her that in England she would
cease to be a stranger to others and to herself.

Her father was in England. Her mother had come
for a holiday to stay with her people in Ireland and she
had stayed three years. Something was wrong somewhere between her mother and father. Everybody
knew and said nothing about it and she could not ask

questions. Then one day she was told they were going back to England — she and her mother and Richard, her brother. They were going in a week's time. Then it was to-morrow they were going. Her excitement was like the suffering of anxiety. And the interminable days that would not pass then, and now had been passed on years and years! At last it was to-day — that evening — they were going. . . . And then she realized their going. They were leaving Carrickmoy behind, perhaps for ever.

She went down to the shore and sat on the rocks. Towards evening someone called from the sea wall and looking back she saw one of her grandmother's servants beckoning her to return. The servant had told the children to call her and they, feeling strange events in the air, were hurrying towards her. She arose and went towards them, but as she neared them she felt she could not speak, she had to turn her head aside and hurry past. They, glimpsing her frigid mask, felt repudiated. They looked after her, then one of them said: 'She's going away to-night. She's going to England.' For a moment they were silent again, then one of them said with sudden vicious passion: 'Aye, and I'm glad.' 'So am I.' 'So am I,' said the others. They started to call after her: 'We're glad you're going. We're glad. We're glad.' She could not glance back over her shoulder because of the tears streaming down her face. For the first time she started to run that she might not hear their voices.

When they had said good-bye to everyone, her Uncle Vellert drove them in his car to Belfast. As they left Carrickmoy behind, Mrs. Dearborn said: 'I've a feeling I'll never come back here or see my mother again.'

She spoke in an acute, strange voice and Vellert, always full of foreboding, always failing and being hurt and disappointed by things and feeling sorry for himself, nodded gloomily.

It seemed to Elizabeth, too, that she would never see Carrickmoy again, and yet within two years her mother and father and Richard had been killed in the railway accident and she was returned to Carrickmoy to live with her grandmother. But she was a different person when she returned. For one thing she had lived through those two years during which her parents, hating one another and attempting to live together again for the sake of the children, had fought un-ceasingly and unceasingly spat at one another their deeply rooted hate. For two years she and Richard had lived in nervous apprehension against the background of upset. Every day when they returned from school they would tiptoe into the house and stand in the hall and listen for the sound of their parents' voices. If, as they usually did, they heard them raised in anger they would creep upstairs and hide themselves in their rooms away from it, out of sound of it because it was so un-bearable. Their parents were too absorbed in their own unhappiness to think very much about them. Gradually they learnt the trick of reservation. But that is not self-sufficiency. So, when she returned, she had learnt to ask for nothing and to expect nothing. But as they drove to Belfast she was still the vulnerable child and Richard, too, she remembered, had been different then from what he became before his death. She remem-bered how he used to irritate her by showing off.

Vellert said when they got on board the steamer: 'I'll
go and ask the captain to sound the siren when you
pass Carrickmoy Bay. We'll all be listening for it and
know you're thinking of us.' And Richard, very
charming, very much the little gentleman, said: 'Can
I come, too, Uncle Vellert?' Elizabeth made a face at
him and he put his tongue out at her and, self-consciously triumphant, strutted off holding his uncle's
hand. She would have followed them, but her mother
said: 'Come back. You don't want to go with
them.'

She stayed, obedient by force of habit, yet rebellious.
When her mother did not want her to do a thing she
told her she did not want to do it, and there was something peculiarly irritating about that. She stared after
Vellert and Richard. Of course Richard, the spoilt
cry-baby, must do what he liked, but it was Vellert she
blamed. He was her beloved uncle — her tragic,
romantic uncle at the thought of leaving whom she
had cried last night — and he should have asked her to
go with him.

She watched him go regardless of her. Tall and thin
in his wide-brimmed, black hat and flapping black
overcoat, his large feet looking splayed in their broad-
welted, hand-made shoes, she watched him and decided
she hated him.

As soon as her mother's back was turned she
wandered away by herself to the stern. Leaning over
the rail, she looked down into the gaping hold. She
could see the crane lifting bales and packing cases
from the quayside and lowering them to the waiting
men. Cattle were being driven aboard. The air was

full of their deep, apprehensive lowing. Somewhere below, tightly packed and wretched with fear, pigs, shipped hours before, shrieked perpetual protest. Dozens of voices flung themselves across the din and above all, slowly effortless, sounded the rising and falling creak of the crane. Long, shivering greyhounds, their tails curled beneath their bellies, were led tight-held across the gangway. They gazed shyly aside and clung to their keep rs. Then came the thoroughbred horses blindfolded and heavily wrapped, timid and submissive, suffering themselves to be led without question down below. But the black bull following them had to be dragged by the rope through the ring in his nose. One man lifting his stick struck it with all his might a blow athwart its flanks. The beast swung upon him with a fury of hatred and lowered its head as though to charge the man, but the man dodged aside laughingly, and struck it again, this time across the eyes. As though blinded and seeking light, it raised its head and gave a strange, long, piteous cry. All its pride fallen it went now as meekly as the horses. The men laughed across to one another and, as they gazed after the bull, a strange grimace broke over the faces of the soldiers in the steerage.

Elizabeth, fascinated, watched intently every movement below. She breathed in the smell of brine, rope, bacon and blood peculiar to ship and quayside. The dusk was growing; people moved about in the shadows as though they were in deep waters; the red light was dying over the mud flats; the whiteness of white things seemed to flash in and out. Suddenly the soldiers in the steerage, looking up, saw the small oval of her face with its serious and intent eyes. They called up to her, laughing and waving. She stared at them and blushed indignantly, then turned and ran away, everything spoilt for her.

'Where have you been?' asked her mother. 'Your uncle Vellert has gone. He couldn't find you to say good-bye.'

'I was only just down there,' she pointed to the stern and reflected, bitterly, that he could not have looked very far.

When they went down to their cabin, Richard said: 'I want to go up and hear the siren.'

Mrs. Dearborn said: 'No, it's too cold. If we don't go to bed we'll get seasick.' The engine was chugging as though it were in the next cabin.

Richard whined: 'I want to go up and hear the siren. If you won't let me go up I'll scream.' And he opened his mouth to scream and lifted his foot to kick the matchboarding of the door.

Just in time Mrs. Dearborn caught his shoulder, shook him, and bundled them both up the stairs to the main deck. It was quite dark now. Black masses of wharves and ships slid past them. Red and green lights floated on the waters. Although it was summer the wind blew ice-shrill from the east. They could see the lights of the Belfast road up which they had come a few hours before. Tiny trains, each window lit, their furnaces afire and trailing sparks, sped along the coast line. The ship went very, very slowly down the Lough. To port the Antrim coast receded dimly, to starboard the Down coast remained near and intimate.

Mrs. Dearborn, Elizabeth and Richard walked

round, stamping their feet and shivering with the cold. The soldiers watched them curiously. Again and again Mrs. Dearborn appealed to Richard to come below, but any hint of action caused him to open his mouth in a threat to howl. Elizabeth, silent and involved, walked beside them. Her mother said: 'There's no need for you to stay. You know how sick you get. Go down and get into your bunk.' But she neither answered nor went down. So the three of them walked round and round.

At last there appeared beyond the hump of Slane the haze of the Carrickmoy lights and, suddenly rounding the point, they faced the wide arc of the lamps of the Promenade. Each one gave a little gasp and they were glad they had stayed on deck. The boat went unheedingly on until it seemed they would at any moment be past.

Richard said: 'Oh! He's not going to sound it.' But even as he spoke there came from the darkness above, the siren's long, melancholy cry of farewell.

When Elizabeth stopped speaking she sat for a long time silent, waiting for Sean to say something. But he said nothing and, when she leant towards him, she saw he was asleep.

Arion sat at his desk and wrote letters. He wrote to his wife a long letter full of kindly inquiry in the remembered formula of a dead relationship. He scarcely mentioned himself. He hoped she was well and happy and he enclosed a cheque for eighty pounds, her monthly allowance. He wrote to his children. He wrote first to Peter who was at Eton, and then to Anne and Celia at their school in Kensington. Although he seldom saw them, they had not grown strange to him and when he met them he was not irritated by the affectations of their adolescence. He accepted them as they were and had no wish to change them. He had no wish to change anything.

His room was lofty and wide. It had been the drawing-room of the house in a more prosperous century and some of the old furniture purchased with the house had been left in it. The writing-desk was of satinwood inlaid with marquetry, fitted with all sorts of little drawers and cupboards and sliding panels. He thrust his letters and manuscripts and bills into them and left them all open. The caretaker, broom in hand, duster tucked under her arm, spent half her morning reading them and trying to piece together his history. He knew this and did not care. He felt as secure from discovery in this world of humanity as another man might feel in a world of dogs. What could they understand or, understanding, communicate?

He wrote to Peter about the burning of the Customs House and the great wall of flame that had lit the Dublin sky for three nights. It pleased him to write well and, knowing the boy sold his letters to a house-master who hoped they'd be of value some day, he wanted to give the man something for his money. He wrote to Anne and Celia about the drive across Ireland to Costello. They were impersonal, pleasant letters, asking about their hopes and successes but offering no advice and never mentioning himself. When he had finished he put them in envelopes and addressed them in his curious, very small handwriting. He put them all in a pile on top of the desk, then sat and looked at the last blank sheet of notepaper lying on the blotting pad in front of him. After a moment he wrote his address on top of it, then for a long time wrote nothing more. He sat with his cheek pushed up by his fist and dug the fine nib of his fountain-pen into the blotting pad. Suddenly, with difficulty, and painfully, he wrote:

'My dear, I do not want to write to you but . . .' He paused again.

My dear, my dear, I do not want to write to you. I will not write to you. I have said that I can live without you, and I can. Yes, even without you. I have turned my back on you and come to this desolate city to live amidst fighting, pillage and foolery, because I can live anywhere. Alone, I can live anywhere. I do not need you. I do not need anyone. I do not need anything.

He got up and went and looked through one of the two glass doors that led out to a tiny balcony above the street. The street looked greyish and void in the lamplight. There was no answer there. He crossed the room and went through the folding doors to the little room in which was his bed and wardrobe. It was dark. Only the open window glimmered. He leaned from it and looked down into the well of the yard and across at the backs of houses. Everything was dark. The windows were black, impenetrable pools of ink. Only the sky had life. It glowed a deep, rich Persian blue and was set with the motion of little stars. He looked up at the sky, waiting for his brain to clear and regain tranquillity. But it would not clear. His need struggled within him. He thought that perhaps if he went to Elizabeth he would know peace again for a while. But, remembering what they had said to one another that night, he would not go.

'My dear, I do not want to write to you . . .' And in four months he had not written to her; so she, not knowing what had become of him, had not been able to write to him. Of course he should have let her know his address in case there was something she wanted to tell him. Just in case. In three months so much can happen. She might be ill. She might be dead. His instinct told him she was not; yet, at the thought, he caught his breath in a spasm of intense, almost physical pain.

But I do not want to write to you. I do not want to hear from you. If you are dead I do not want to know. Isn't it from the tyranny of such knowledge that I must escape? From the pain, the unalleviable decadence of suffering; that decomposition which is need and need's frustration and wrecks dignity and flounders one in despair.

And you said, smiling: 'Is it because you are so afraid of losing things that you'll have nothing?'

Laughing, you said: 'A great dancer who loved greatly his dancing might in heaven dance for ever. Or another who loved chocolate eat as much as he wants. Why should we suppose heaven a perpetuity of something we do not want.'

But it is not only that. Explain a man to himself, dissect him until no dust-grain remains and he will answer slowly: 'Yes, that is true. But it is not only that.'

Arion returned into the sitting-room and walked aimlessly round the furniture. 'This', the caretaker had told him, 'is the best room in the house.' And he had been quite pleased to be in the best room. He could have stayed at an hotel, but at times he was surprisingly economical. He was careful with his money and generous only to those who had done him an injury, or were obviously out to take all and give nothing.

On the wall above the writing-desk hung a large Regency mirror. When he turned towards it he could see himself sauntering round the chairs, his shoulders thrust back, his head forward, his hands in his pockets. His face, pale and thoughtful with its large forehead and eyes and dwindling chin, pleased him with its attraction of intellect. He moved towards the mirror and his eyes, heavy lidded and drooping at the outer corners, watched him with a sombre stare that was almost morose.

It was strange that people spoke to him and took his hand and told him jokes; strange that women slept with him and held his body in their arms and kissed his mouth; strange that men came up to him in the street and borrowed matches or begged pennies, and women accosted him and children asked for cigarette cards; strange that he smoked and drank and ate food and digested it and passed the waste from his bowels; strange that he was treated like a human being and behaved like one when he was in fact this secret and uncommunicable self, apart from all living things. He leaned forward and touched his reflection in the mirror and felt the ice-hard, ice-cold glass beneath his fingers. He smiled. His expression did not change. It seldom changed. His permanent facial expression had not altered since he was a young man. He passed through life and suffered event, but it seemed to leave him unaffected. It was as though he moved in another dimension. Event had no substance for him; it left him uninfluenced.

He liked to feel the glass unyielding beneath his fingers.

Consider the great jungle of contacts trellised with leaves impenetrable, set about with flowers that are living flames, set about with monstrous flowers, bloody, ashen and agape for air. Consider the sultry air of the jungle dripping miasma, terribly living and ahush in the pause before leaping like the tarantula. Step and sink into the marsh ground alive with the writhings of snakes and at each step disturb toads and a hundred side-flying emerald lizards. In all the darkness strange eyes glint as they turn and seek. In all the darkness there is a wavering of forked tongues lashing their iron-hard heat. Consider the great trees, black and formless as waterspouts, swirling so swiftly they seem at rest, yet evade the sight.... Fly from the great trees that draw the spirit into their black vertigo. Trample down the insinuating tendrils and the fierce clinging serpents; leap from the darting tongues, slash aside foliage and flowers with the strength and un-thinking speed that annihilates fear until at last there is daylight a little through the leaves, the leaf curtains thin, there is space between the tree trunks and one can move without struggle. Now the fringe. In a moment, freedom. Pause, dizzied with effort, gasping exhaustion. At last one is out of it — the jungle.

Consider the great desert of freedom.

Arion looked into his own eyes, surprised they betrayed nothing. Large, rather gentle eyes, subtile and not happy. He jerked himself from their hold and returned to his sauntering round the room.

Consider the great desert of freedom. It stretches beyond the horizon into a brazen sky. It stretches beyond the sky into the space behind the stars. It stretches beyond space and encompasses eternity. And for oases? Only these cacti, spiked like hedgehogs, inviolable as oneself. Respect them. Respect them? Certainly — until I thirst and then, thirsting, break off the protecting thorns, break through the flesh and find, encased in crystal, purely and sweetly set, the water in their hearts. Drink of them and leave them dry so their flowers fade. Drink, leave them dry and open to the torrid air so their hearts wither. Maimed and withered cacti, despoiled beyond the power of healing! And you, my dear Arion, have you no regrets? Of course. Do not suppose, now I am satisfied, that my respect is lessened. Not at all. But mine is a long journey westwards beyond Lucifer and I must hurry on. Good afternoon.

Suddenly he crossed to the writing-desk and took up his pen again. 'My dear, I do not want to write to you, but, in case you should need me, this is my address.'

A fourth letter added to the pile. Now he could undress and go to bed and sleep.

TUESDAY

WHEN Sean awoke it was morning. He turned his head and looked from the window and saw above the line of roofs, a clear, blue sky. He sat up. The day was fine. The air, blowing cool through the open window, was full of brightness. After a week of rainy days this della Robbia blue and white morning was startling in its beauty. He felt an exhilaration of delight. He was better. He was quite well. He would get up and go into the country.

As he got out of bed he became aware of Elizabeth lying asleep across the foot. He felt no surprise or annoyance at her being there; he only hoped he would be able to dress and escape before she awakened. But she opened her eyes as he looked at her and sat up and ran her fingers through her hair. Then, suddenly, he was quite glad she had awakened. Now he had an audience for his gaiety.

'A marvellous day,' he said and started shaking out the clothes lying about the room and hanging them up on hooks on the wall. He moved in a light, half-dancing way, doing everything with a mocking sort of care, feeling all the time on the verge of laughter.

He felt her watching him and, glancing over his shoulder, met the sullen resentment of her eyes. He did not know what was the matter with her and, to ward off discomfort, he started speaking excitedly and laughing.

'When I was a child I used to have visions. Once I saw the Archangel Gabriel with his feet on the earth and his head in the sky and his wings encompassing the horizon. His wings were like blue pearls. Look, you can see them now behind the Four Courts — those vast and terrible wings!'

She turned her head away from him as though irritated and said: 'Where is the bathroom?'

He said: 'Next door.' She got up and left the room as though he had done her an injury.

That puzzled him, but he did not think much about it. He was thinking about himself and the fantastic brilliance of his mood. Now his need for Arion was dwindled almost from his mind. Its memory was quaint and incomprehensible, like an out of fashion garment. His confidence was of himself now, and he had forgotten how it could fail him. When he was depressed he neglected his meals and would not give a thought to looking after himself. But, now his power was recovered, there was no job too menial for him to tackle and execute with care. Now he would tidy the room, and make the bed, and wash the dishes, and speak with charm and understanding to the people on the quays whom he had passed in surly hate the day before.

When Elizabeth returned he took his clothes into the bathroom and bathed and shaved and dressed. Then he went and bought bread and milk and eggs and bacon and returned and cleaned the frying pan. Elizabeth sat on the bed and would not help. She seemed angry and he could not understand why. At last she said:

'Is Arion coming round this morning?'

'Arion? No. I don't think so. Why?' She shrugged her shoulders. He thought she had been making conversation, so continued it: 'I'm going to borrow his car and go into the hills.'

For a moment she was quiet, then she said with a quick uncertainty: 'Can I come, too?'

'Yes, if you like.' He was surprised. He simply could not make her out at all.

She knew he did not want her to come and yet he said: 'Yes, if you like.' And she thought of Arion who, even had he wished her to come, would have paused, considering the matter, before he said slowly: 'Yes, I think perhaps you might.'

She took the egg and bacon he had fried for her and sat eating in silence. For a while Sean had nothing to say, either. He was startled into silence by the realization that she was coming to spend the day with him in the hills. He felt the folly of his spontaneous: 'Yes, if you like.' It should have been doubtful and discouraging. But, after all, what did it matter? If she wanted to come — well, she could come. He need not let her worry him.

He was exhilarated by his self-sufficiency: 'I have regained it,' he thought. 'Self-sufficiency? No. It is self-conceit.'

'What is the finest thing in the world?' he asked aloud and answered himself at once, 'Self-conceit. It is the only thing that makes life bearable. The inward conviction that despite all proof to the contrary you really are the marvel you know yourself to be. When this conviction is shaken you go down into the depths

where death is a welcome and just end, and you can
only regain life by regaining, no matter how, the
conceit that makes life bearable.'

She sat with her eyes cast down on her plate. Perhaps she wasn't listening. He didn't care. He liked to
hear himself speak his thoughts aloud. He often
thought if he could overcome his nervousness in
public he would make a great orator. Now listen, my
dear Sean, to this:

'Conceit is the best thing of all. Do you suppose the
meek will inherit the earth? Not a bit of it. Who are
meek but the hypocrites who hope to profit by their
humility — the meek little English lower middle-
classes, the meek little shopkeeper English-busybodies
with a sneer for imagination and a snigger for beauty.
How I hate them — the meek little busybodies who
come here to inherit the Irish earth and open their
shoddy little shops and potter about the street thinking
themselves the salt of the earth, the solid backbone
holding everything together and keeping everything
going. "The Irish can't govern themselves," they say,
"so we come here to govern and take the profits and
keep the country poor." The English have always tried
to ruin Ireland. It's part of their policy. They're
afraid of us — the pistol pointed at the English heart —
so the little busybodies potter round to see nobody gets
strong enough to pull the trigger. But when the
trigger's pulled — when Riordan or someone like him
pulls it — where will they be?'

Elizabeth looked at him critically from under her
fair, straight lashes. He thought of what he had been
saying and realized that he knew only one English

shopkeeper prospering in Dublin — a little man whose mere existence irritated him unreasonably and so provoked the onslaught. It seemed to him that Elizabeth knew this and was thinking him a fool. He thought she was judging him from the vantage of her superior years that saw in him the adolescence she had just escaped. He hurried on, speaking despite her: 'Supposing one morning they woke up and found it was still dark, that the earth had suddenly come to a standstill whilst they slept, and there they were stuck in eternal night unless they could do something to set it moving again! What could they do? Poor little busybodies! What a fuss! What a hubbub! The poor little busybody English with their pounds and halfpounds, their coppers and their silver so methodically divided in the till, and their safety-pins instead of farthings for change, and their stocks and shares and the tyranny of their pennies and halfpennies. What could they do but grumble about the streets and think that God, whom they'd kept pretty severely in His place until then, was treating them badly.'

Dramatically he went and leant from the window and, looking down, saw the rows of old books in the shops below. The magazines lay unruffled by the wind. The Liffey was motionless. In the light it shone drab olive and waxen like some old artificial fruit, and, beneath the shadows of its many bridges, it was a glassy *terre verte*. All the buildings stood flat against the sky like architectural wash-drawings — neat, cleanly drawn and unreal with their pale shadows.

Through the blank eyes of the Four Courts the sky shone serenely.

'Like a ruin in Athens!' he said. 'Stupid little busy-bodies, lift up your noses and look at the sky! By what celestial mathematics is the globe set spinning and the great stars securely set in their places that they fall not down upon your wooden heads? Why worry? Enough if you take off your hats as you go into church and see that your wives keep their's on, and give sixpence to the organ fund and a shilling towards the new choir surplices and look sidelong at Roman Catholics and remember God has got his eyes on you because he has nothing better to do.'

Elizabeth looked at Sean leaning from the window with one arm extended. Really in this mood he was rather blatant! How long would it last? Lately she had cultivated a taste for Arion's restraint, but the attraction towards Sean remained. She merely withheld her distaste for his mood, waiting until it was passed and he become tractable again.

He went to get the garage key from Arion. As he went he began to think of Arion and remembered how, the night before, Arion had left him when he called to him, needing him. He felt an inner, acid bitterness of resentment that was passionate and irrational. He began to wonder what he could do or say to show Arion how little he cared about him. He walked into the room and demanded the key as though the car were his, and then began to talk about events reported in the morning papers he had bought on his way. He walked about the room talking with a light half-contemptuous bantering confidence through which showed nakedly the raw edge of his resentment.

Arion, shaved and bathed and in his black dressing-

95

gown, sat eating his breakfast at a table by the open window. He had met this mood before in Sean and, understanding it, disregarded it.

'The key is on my dressing-table with the others,' he said. 'It is the Yale. You will need some petrol. Get what you want and have it put down to my account.'

'I can pay for it,' said Sean, insisting his annoyance.

Arion smiled: 'Just as you like. What were you saying is in your paper?'

Arion's grace was difficult to resist. It undermined Sean's anger until he began to feel himself drawn again into the circle of Arion's will. He wished he were not going alone to the hills; he wished he could stay here with Arion or take him with him.

'Will you come with me?' he asked.

Arion shook his head: 'I am going to write to-day,' and Sean knew him unpersuadable.

'But you will come to the meeting?'

'Yes, I will come.'

'I'll be back before dinner. I'll come and call for you about nine. You'll be ready then?'

'Yes.'

'Arion, you will come?'

'Of course.'

He went to the garage. Elizabeth was waiting for him there. He found he hadn't sufficient money to pay for the petrol so it went down to Arion's account. Before noon they were making their way out of Dublin.

Sean had nothing to say now. He could not regain the rapturous relief of his early morning mood. His visit to Arion had deprived him of something. He was scarcely conscious of Elizabeth sitting beside him. He felt troubled as though he had left something behind.

At Rathfarnham the car was stopped by R.I.C. men. Sean sat staring before him with his hands on the wheel while the car was searched for arms. He seemed, himself, now dulled by the humility he despised. At last they were waved on and came to the hills.

The sky had begun to cloud over. They passed from the main road to a lane and bumped over soft ruts until Sean ran the car on to a level grass patch. He jumped out, then he locked it and started walking up the slope. He walked as though Elizabeth were not with him but, suddenly, at the top, he turned and looked back for her. She had not attempted to follow him. She was strolling leisurely up the same slope in another direction.

He was annoyed with her for having come, and now was further annoyed because she was not following. He felt vaguely responsible for her as though he were her host. He wanted to be alone to brood over his disturbed mind. He wanted to comfort himself by walking over the hills alone in dramatic detachment. But, detach himself as he might from her, he felt her trailing vaguely after him and his thought was disturbed.

'Shall we walk to Sally Gap?' he asked with a peevish attempt to seem friendly.

'Yes, I should like to,' she agreed quietly, deliberately ignoring the difficulty of his mood. That was Arion's trick, but she could not have for him Arion's charm. No, she had nothing for him. He had talked to her last night about himself, but he had talked in the same way to O'Rorke and Finnigan. He had no great reserve. He talked to people about himself to win them to his cause and gain their reassurances against the ever-poised hostilities of the pit.

See, I am Sean Murtough, and this and this and this is myself! You believe in me, don't you? You are sure I will win? Say 'Yes'; reassure me!

Yet, when they repaid him with reassurance, he could never really believe it was genuine.

When he had talked of himself to Elizabeth she, in return, had done no more than talk about herself. And he did not want to hear about her. He wanted her to give him her vision of him, another facet of himself to add to the great self-vision he collected jealously so that in the end he might see, clearly-solved, the mystery of himself. But she — she was only interested in herself. She was nothing more than an egoist. He had felt her desire of him and felt she wanted to absorb him into herself. She wanted to make him no more than part of herself.

Then she had slept on his bed all night! Well! That gave her no hold on him. And, anyway, didn't she realize the impossibility of getting a hold on him? Couldn't she see that he was given wholly to Arion and to Ireland?

The rain had begun to fall with a fine lace-like quiet. Whins blossomed everywhere. They were so startlingly bright in the rain the hillsides seemed patched with sunlight. As they went down the hollow towards the village the bare lane changed and larch trees, heavy with water, swayed against the delicate grey of the sky. From the branches hung the chenille of the young green. The black, powdery earth beneath them was mixed with cones and pierced by the down-soft, uncurling heads

of the young ferns. It had been a cold, wet spring and
things growing on the unsheltered hills were opening
late. The delicate, decorative spring quality of leaves
and plants was not yet lost in summer coarseness.
Elizabeth, prying into the banks, found a solitary,
remaining primrose. Sean watched her as she bent
over it and, with a finger tip, touched the silvery hairs
on the long pink stalk. She touched it with a sort of
absorbed tenderness. Her profile stood out against the
grass green with a cameo calm, motionless and set in
her absorption. Her hair, pale, wraith-fine and tangled
with wet, slipped forward across her face. She pushed
it behind her ear and raised herself and stood droop-
ingly, looking down at the flower.

He thought: 'She is one of those people who must
love someone or something. That's what's the matter
with her. She's like those awful women who must flow
out all over things — like treacle. She can't be sufficient
to herself. She's got nothing to hold on to in herself,
nothing but this gluey tenderness trickling out over
things so, once caught, they're done for.'

He had a distrust of women he knew to be absurd
and yet could not overcome. He knew the cause of his
distrust, yet it remained. He was sometimes attracted
to women and had slept with two or three, but without
pleasure because of his distrust that kept him always
alert to fly from them before they bound him irrevocably. Friendship was safer and more satisfying. A
woman in return for himself could give him only
herself which he did not want. But Arion, given Sean,
returned a magnified Sean, an aureoled, amazing and
prevailing Sean. One could ask no more.

99

She said: 'It's the largest primrose I've ever seen.'

He said: 'I never look at them. They're anaemic flowers — very overrated.'

He walked on. The air here had the damp warmth of a hothouse and was affecting his chest. He was beginning to feel tired and breathless. Under his collar-bone the ache was returning. So he wasn't better yet!

And he knew he wasn't better. His grandfather had died of consumption and, although his parents had been healthy enough, two of his three brothers had died of the same disease. But he would not admit even to fear of it. He would not admit it to his thought, holding it back with his will as though by so doing he was warding off its physical attack. But, with his lower consciousness, he brooded on it and faced it and came to terms with it. The terms were these — if he succeeded, then he would escape it and be well; if not — then death would be something to fall back on. Until he was declared success or failure, it might not touch him.

He took a deep breath to accentuate the pain and felt it with anger, wondering if it could be getting an unfair hold on him! He wanted to deny it with a fury of anger, but the pain remained. He looked around him at the blae, dim rises of the hills drained through the delicate jasper-grey purity of the air until they seemed no more than washes of colour superimposed in odd shapes one upon the other. Breathing deeply the smell of earth and moist young leaves, he was hurt with a sombre jealousy as he thought of death and of others walking in the spring here when he was dead. For he felt the hills had for him meaning and beauty they could have for no one else and they were, therefore, his.

Suddenly, surprisingly, the light changed. The sage gloss of the grass leapt into green flame eclipsing the inner-burning brilliance of the whins. The distances darkened into blue. Elizabeth stopped involuntarily and laughed with pleasure. Sean turned on her his frowning, despondent eyes in irritation. He wished he might cast over her the shadow of his bitter anticipation of death. If he were indeed dying, then he would pain her with his near death. But he wasn't dying — so he'd say nothing, for, by speaking aloud, there was no knowing what fiend's curse he might bring on his head.

By noon they'd walked two sides of a triangle and were at Enniskerry. To return to the car they had only to walk the third side, so they seemed to have plenty of time. They sauntered into the village to find an inn. The grey of the sky had been rolled back to reveal the under blue, and up from the east came great white clouds seeming chiselled in marble.

The return of the sun played his mood over with a febrile laughter. He became perversely mocking of everything about him.

They found a little inn and sat down to eat. When they were served and had started eating, a group of American tourists whom even the trouble could not keep away, entered and ordered luncheon loudly. Sean watched them with cynically critical eyes and set to inventing malicious fates for each of them. He had a surprising wit and Elizabeth laughed with him in spite of herself.

'Let me draw them,' she said and he found her a

pencil and a piece of paper and she drew spiteful caricatures of the unfortunate Americans in the throes of the fates Sean had invented for them. Amused by her drawings, he invented wilder and more improbable situations in which to place his victims. She drew rapidly over menus and envelopes — grotesques and caricatures — until they had laughed themselves into a sad and exhausted emptiness.

Without speaking, with a sort of weary yet effortless movement they climbed to the top of a near hill and threw themselves down on the grass. The grass was short and hard and still damp. They could feel its cold penetrating their bodies whilst the sun burnt pleasantly into their hands and faces. They lay a few yards apart. During their walk and whilst they had laughed at the inn, a strange, almost perverse sympathy had grown up between them so they could be silent now like old friends. Sean spoke first. He was lying on his belly, his head propped on his hand.

He said: 'When my father was a young man he once met Parnell walking alone over this grass.' He laid his palm flat upon it as though he were fitting his hand into the footprint of a man. 'The grass is still here,' he said.

'Not the same grass.' She disliked the morbid insistence upon death that had prevailed through all his laughter during luncheon. She felt it deliberate. She felt it a sword which he swung round and round swiftly before him to make an invisible barrier through which she might not pass.

'They are the same hills,' he said. He roused a blunt antagonism in her.

'Are you afraid of dying?' she asked.

He turned his head away and looked down into the hollow below where the traffic turned sharply on to the Dublin road. She saw his face blanched by sickness and gauntly hard-limned. His mouth, that in repose had a natural smile, was caught rigid in a tetanus grin of hate.

He felt her watching him and felt her antagonism change to compassion. When they concerned him, he felt the thoughts and moods of others like a variation of the atmosphere about him. Her antagonism steeled him, but he could not bear compassion. His voice was frigid and mocking repudiation: 'On the contrary, I look forward to it. This life is an insult to one's intelligence.'

He smiled mockingly at her, then turned his head aside and, after a long pause in which she said nothing, he started to speak quickly and quietly: 'One night in the spring I went out to post some letters and a woman who was walking along the pavement in front of me started shouting at the top of her voice about these Christians who had turned her into a harlot. I went into the post office — nice and warm after the cold street, and quiet and primly conventional. The girl behind the desk said: "Yes?" (She was much too proud to say "please".) I said: "Two twopenny stamps, please." She gave me them and I licked them and stuck them on the letters. When I returned to the street again the woman was out of sight. I thought: "Thank Heaven! Saved from having to do anything for her!" '

With a cynical gesture he rolled over on to his back and stared up at the sky. 'But, after all, what could I do for her?' he asked in a subdued voice. 'It's an impertinence to shove us head first into this mean, miserable, little cinder of a world; to pick us up out of oblivion and rub our noses in injustice, cruelty, sordid poverty, hate, malice and suffering we are powerless either to avert or alleviate. For all I know I was not unhappy before I was born.'

'Haven't you been happy since?'

'I can't remember.' He caught his breath and went on in a slow, self-conscious voice: 'I had three brothers. Two of them died of consumption.'

'And the other one?'

'David? He was quite strong and very good-looking. Everybody liked him. He was executed after Easter Week Rising.'

Oh! Yes. She remembered. She had heard of David Murtough. She should have had the sense not to ask about him. But Sean was not thinking of David — the fair Hermes, armed with strength; rightful victor yet earliest fallen — he was thinking of himself.

He said: 'It is an insult — this life! There are so many possibilities for good in one and so little use for them. At every turn the insults, misunderstanding and fickleness of others repudiate your generosity until at last in self-defence you, too, must insult, misunderstand and play false.'

She wanted to respond to him then, but she could not. She could only say in a half ironical tone: 'And what about Arion?'

'He's different.' Sean paused a moment before adding with a sort of glow on his face in a whisper: 'One would gladly do anything for him.' Suddenly he said with a roused, flushed interest: 'Have you read that story of his where the woman is sitting alone in the house waiting for her lover to come? She does not know that he has gone off with someone else and will not come again. As the hours pass she begins to feel that awful dread of suspicion. It numbs her. You can feel it. It is like the most terrible suffering. Then, suddenly, the wind rises and raps the branch of a tree against the door. Although it has done that often enough before she has not heard it; but now she hears everything. She starts up with her pulse racing, trembling with relief and excitement and calls out "Come in." She stands staring at the door, but no one enters. After a few moments the wind raps again. Again, almost sobbing, she cries "Come in. Come in. Come in." But there is no one outside. . . . '

She nodded. Yes, she remembered it. Surely it had been written for her, not for Sean.

'And,' he went on, still excited, 'do you remember *Prelude and Fugue*?'

No, she had not read that.

'In it he says somewhere that there is only one impregnable stronghold, and that is indifference.' It had been a curious book, half novel, half treatise, in which a young novelist, himself lazy, drunken and self-indulgent, had conceived a character living off the force of its own indifference. In the next generation the conception was copied by Nature when she wanted to make an individual. And the individual was copied by man when he wanted to make a type. Later the type became a prevailing type, gaining ground, until, in the end, it overcame Nature herself and destroyed everything. The book had not been easy reading. Sean could not remember much of it. He could remember most distinctly the sense of smiling logic and detachment pervading it, that he knew was the author's only self-revelation.

When he had met Arion he had not stopped to think if he were meeting a stranger. He had said to him: 'For all I know I was not unhappy before I was born — but I haven't been happy since. I know I'll die of consumption like my brothers. I didn't want life and now that it's been forced upon me I won't be trapped into wanting it. I've got no patience with the fools who swallow the insult and grovel for more. I mean to achieve the indifference of the individual in your *Prelude and Fugue.*'

And Arion had smiled, saying: 'But you must not take that book too seriously. After all, what would you gain by achieving indifference which would be only your own annihilation and the annihilation of the race? Nature would merely start all over again with another species as hungry for life as humanity was once. I feel it is not in you to turn your back on life and face annihilation.'

Then Sean had told him how as a child he had walked on the hills drunken with the consciousness of his own will. Arion had said: 'I know. I know.' He had captured Sean and filled him with the desire to act and sent him forth to find Riordan. He had drawn him back from his first advance into indifference. He had returned him to life and anticipation.

And he had found Riordan.

He sat up, suddenly laughing and pleased with

himself. That had been no easy job. Now all he had
to do was bring Riordan to Dublin.

He raised himself on to his knees so he knelt beside
her, towering over her and laughing, carried up suddenly to confidence by remembering he had succeeded
once. He said rhetorically:

'The mind, once released from life, will have all
space for its perception. Here it exists in a penumbra
that is only the outskirt of a distant light. And what will
death be but a stepping from shadow into light — a
step that would take a million years of mortal walking,
yet, at death, takes one in an instant beyond Cassiopia
and Orion's belt, beyond the dog and the bear and the
seven stars of the Pleiades . . .'

She lay in his shadow without moving and interrupted him with a frozen and precise brutality: 'No
one but a fool thinks death will take him farther than
his grave — and it's dark enough there.'

He knelt still and silent, staring at her with a
passionate hate. For some minutes they looked at one
another, their faces in shadow. Then he stooped over
her as though she were drawing him down with her
will. With the curiously satisfying and yet uncanny
sense of a thing inevitable and foreseen, she put her
arm round his shoulder as he lifted her and kissed her
mouth. With a shock of desire, he felt her lips part
beneath his and, at once, he moved away from her. He
let her fall back again to the grass and looked at her
with anger. He felt she had gained a victory over him
and was white with fury against himself as he knelt
there, staring at her.

He saw her close her eyes against his anger. She

looked older with her eyes closed. Suddenly he saw
that here was no adventuress who had overcome his
beloved Arion and now was trying to overcome him.
She had a forlorn look, lost and unsatisfied, and when
she opened her eyes they were full of tears.

Despite himself he lent towards her and said: 'Why
do you look as though you are hurt?'

She answered bitterly: 'Perhaps I am hurt.'

She tried to rise but his hands held her down and
she did not struggle. Now his movements were
instinctive; he was lapsed from thought and self-
consciousness into a deep instinctive sympathy with her.
Restraining her with his arm across her waist, he lay
down beside her, curiously and gently abandoned like
a tired child rather than a lover. They lay in a sensual
transport of content that scarcely touched consciousness. The sunlight deepened. The grass warmed and
dried and moved in their ears with a delicate, almost
inaudible rustle. Traffic purred along the road below.

She felt his hold on her slacken. After some time
she sat up with blurred eyes. They had been lying still
for an hour or more and he was almost asleep. Her
movement awakened him. He lay watching her as she
clasped her hands round her ankles and rested her chin
on her knees. She had a drowsy, voluptuous look like a
cat roused from sleep. She yawned with a contented
vagueness.

With a sudden, rapid movement he gripped her arm
above the elbow and pulled her down again. With a
wild, almost savage desire, he covered her with his
body and pinned down her arms beneath his hands. He
felt her respond to his physical contact and with sudden

violence he bit into her lips until, in pain, she wrenched
her right arm free and tried to thrust him from her.
Determinedly he broke down her arm's restraint and
crushed her hand between his breast and her's. They
struggled in a furious embrace until their excitement
subsided. Then they lay for a long time breathless and
exhausted, listening to the beating of their own hearts.

Suddenly Sean jumped up: 'It's getting late. I have
to call for Arion at nine.'

She rose meekly, saying nothing. She had a wounded
look, and that pleased him. That he could wound
her filled him with a sense of malicious power. He
caught her hand: 'Come on. Let's run.'

He pulled her down the shaded slope. The sun was
almost set. They sped over blue grass in a blue light.
The whins were lightless and around them diffused
shadows hung like a mist. The evening smell freshened
the air. In the grass the lanky, ill-fed buttercups were
tightly shut and the grey scabious indistinguishable
from their leaves. The twilight was falling quickly. Be
fore them things hovered indefinitely, liquid, quite dark
beneath a bright, clear sky. A bat swept round them.

Sean pulled her to where flints had once been
quarried and a cliff side fell sheer down to the road.
He swung her round and brought her to a standstill on
the very edge. The pit, filled with brambles and giant
nettles, gaped blackly beneath them. On the sides a
weedy flower grew in clots, red in the daylight but
darkly purple now like arterial blood.

He said: 'Suppose I were to jump over and break my
neck and lie in a heap amongst the nettles! What
would it matter then that I left the Catholic Church,

couldn't eat eggs, had been sick once in public, knew *Prometheus* by heart, had seen the Archangel Gabriel and found Riordan when no one else could find him!'

The ground crumbled away beneath her toes. She stepped back nervously. Something in the place touched her with terror and a sort of hysteria. She put her hand on Sean's arm and he moved from her like a wild creature that will not be touched, but might in an instant dart out a sting. He laughed maliciously so, in that uncertain light, the lines of his face seemed to twitch upwards like a faun's. He had an odd face, she thought.

He said: 'Did Arion tell you that I am dying?'

'We are all dying.'

He looked very pale and intangible; curiously enchanted and remote from her. And she had thought that she had captured him.

'Yes. You may die to-morrow,' he said, 'and you may live another fifty years. But I will not live another six months.'

He saw the rebuke in her eyes and was delighted with himself. He was intoxicated with the moment. He, Sean, had caught the moment ineluctably in his hand and was turning it like a crystal in the twilight to catch whichever colour he pleased.

You suppose that you have caught me! You suppose that you have netted the unicorn! But I am the dying Sean, the tragic Sean, who is beyond the touch of any mortal woman.

She looked aghast: 'It's not true,' she said, realizing it was true even if he did not believe it himself.

In a chaotic whirlwind of delight he caught her

wrist again and ran with her round the edge of the pit to the road. She stumbled after him, numbed within the delicate, soft core of her heart. She was thinking of herself. She was thinking that there was no one in the world for her, that she was doomed to solitude. Yes, she was doomed. Her eyes filled with tears. She had an unbearable horror of solitude and an all-pervading need of companionship and affection that had never been satisfied. She thought of her lonely and unhappy adolescence when she had lived with her puritan, unloving grandmother. She thought of the years she had lived alone in Dublin. It seemed to her she could make not permanent friendship, arouse no permanent love. Only a curiosity, an excitement which, at the very instant of her eager response, failed and left her naked. And she might live fifty more years. . . .

She began to sob.

He took no notice of her. He was thinking of himself. That the germ was in him from his birth.

'I am doomed,' he said.

She said: 'So am I.' She pressed her free hand against her eyes. 'I am doomed to loneliness.'

He turned and looked at her and she abandoned herself to a fit of sobbing. He turned from her; then, against his will, looked back and stood watching her. Her sobbing troubled him. In some way she had indeed bound a thread about him with which she could pull him to her. There was about her an aura of physical magnetism that plucked at him as it plucked at Arion. He felt desire of her as she stood there crouched and sobbing. He was caught in a tenderness of pathos and desire. He took her hand from her eyes and looked at her. She hung her head. He put his arm round her waist and she pressed her face against his throat, comforted and sobbing weakly. She felt sick and dizzy with crying and leant against him. After a while she said in a small voice: 'You have to meet Arion.'

Oh! Yes. They moved on slowly, their arms about one another. It was quite dark now. The darkness had a dazzling quality. It was clotted in the valley where they walked to an onyx depth that moved and quivered with an inner black fire. It lay before them like a black wall against which they put out their hands to touch only empty air.

Sean said he knew a short cut and they walked up on to the grass. There they stumbled over rabbit holes and started to laugh again. They came to a standstill beside the fenced flower garden of a week-end bungalow. The white flowers of the tobacco plant glimmered and filled the air with perfume. Sean struck a match to find a way round and, dimly and curiously coloured, there appeared yellow rock roses, purple orchids and large blue clovers. A moth with furry body and tiny, delicately quivering legs, came fluttering to the light. Sean dropped the match, but before he did so Elizabeth had seen the shadows hollowing his cheeks and his eyes; and he had seen her face haloed with its tossed, pale hair watching him intently. He put his arm round her again and they felt their way forward. She held to him in a sudden tensity of grief. She pressed her body against him, stricken beyond telling.

'It isn't true?' she whispered.

'What isn't true?'

'That you are dying?'

Abruptly he loosened his arm from her body and she felt him draw away from her. His body, his mind, his whole consciousness drew away from her and left her alone there in the darkness.

She put out her hand to find him, but he evaded her.

She shuddered and called out: 'Sean.' But he wouldn't answer. She could hear him walking about a yard from her, withdrawn from her. A shadow moved at her feet. She cried out in panic: 'Sean, where are you?'

His voice, cold and discouraging, came from quite near: 'What do you want?'

She didn't answer, but followed him in silence until they found the car.

Sean drove swiftly, accelerating until the telegraph poles, lit for an instant by the headlights, flashed past one after another like the leaves of a book. Elizabeth looked up and saw the star pattern above their heads unmoving for all their swift flight beneath it. It was curious to look up from the hurrying road to that static pattern above. She wondered where they were going. She knew Sean would not return to Dublin that night. He dared not risk challenge and incur suspicion whilst his project hung so, midway between success and failure. At last she asked: 'Where are we going?'

He said: 'To an inn not far from here.' His information was polite and vague, given to a stranger.

He swung round from one lane into another and then into another. She marvelled how he found his way in this dark night without a pause to reflect it. He must know the hills by heart.

He was worried about Arion. He should have gone for him. Supposing that now he was not arrived! But he would be there. He would be waiting for Sean and worried, too. He would be saying to the others: 'I wonder what has happened to Sean. He was to have called for me about nine and here it is eleven or more, and no sign of him!' Sean strove to force the car forward with his will. His will was in his foot that pressed the accelerator. They turned corners madly and came to an abrupt standstill outside a small inn. It was still open and brightly lit. Licensing laws were not taken too seriously outside Dublin. Sean jumped from the car and strode through a door marked 'Public Bar'. When he did not return, Elizabeth stood on the car seat so she could see above the frosted glass into the tap-room. A man stood behind the bar polishing glasses. At a table at the far end of the room four men sat and looked up at Sean who was talking to them. His hair had been blown by the wind in the car. He had a distracted look and glared away from them as he talked. After a few minutes they seemed to persuade him to sit down. He sat down.

It was cold now. Elizabeth shivered and was curious and bored. She went into the next door marked 'Bar Parlour' and, taking a seat on the horse-hair sofa, waited for someone to become conscious of her.

A glass door led from the parlour to the bar. Elizabeth took a cigarette from her handbag, lit it and sat and watched the little gathering of men in the next room. Sean appeared to remember her. The man beside him rose and came to look for her. He glanced into the parlour, saw her and entered, smiling nervously.

He was a tall man with a short nose, short chin and long upper lip. She knew him.

He said: 'You are Miss Dearborn, aren't you?' He spoke with a slight American accent.

She nodded: 'Yes.'

He said: 'I have seen you in the car with Arion.'

'We live in the same house, so he sometimes gives me a lift.'

She remembered his passing them and smiling at Arion and looking at her; and Arion had said: 'That's O'Rorke. A good Catholic. Absolutely no truck with modern literary birth control. He produces a novel a year with the regularity of the Victorian mother.'

She sensed his dislike of Arion and that brought them to a standstill. She said at last: 'Do you know Arion well?'

He smiled, showing his two large, white front teeth: 'Does anyone?' he asked.

She smiled, too, rather liking him. 'What is your opinion of him?' she asked.

He closed the door before replying: 'He's deep, but I think you'll find him half explained by his eagerness to make a good impression.'

She was surprised and said: 'Do you think he cares what impression he makes?'

'Yes. I think it's the thing he cares about most of all.'

No. She didn't agree. No, she was sure that was not right, and yet . . .

Sean put his head round the door. 'What are you talking about?' he asked, worried, irritable, not wanting to know. 'I wonder why Arion has not come yet!' He crossed to the window and peered out: 'It's my fault. I've got the car. He wouldn't realize I wasn't coming until nearly ten and then it would be too late to get a tram or a taxi.'

'We can hold the meeting without him,' said O'Rorke restrainedly.

'I know. But it's my fault he hasn't come.' Sean spoke as though he felt the others were accusing Arion for his absence.

'Let us go back into the bar,' said Sean, and O'Rorke said: 'But what about Miss Dearborn.'

'Probably the landlord will let her have a room,' said Sean. 'She can sleep here.'

But she didn't want to go to bed. She wanted to attend the meeting. O'Rorke was diffident: 'It's a private meeting,' he said.

'She can come if she likes,' said Sean, still peering from the window. 'She already knows more than you do, for she was with Arion when he met me at Costello.'

O'Rorke shrugged his shoulders and went back to the others. She had not agreed with his valuation of Arion and so he had at once been on the defensive, at once distrustful of her. He said something to the others and they all turned and looked at her as she followed Sean into the room. They were all Dublin men that she knew by sight, though she had not known, and nobody knew, that they were associated with Sean.

Sharp, with his coffin-shaped face and black suit, was a solicitor. Daly was a master at the Art School. He had been there when she was a student. She smiled at him.

He had once been fond of her. He had painted her

portrait and she had sat for him for the figure once or twice. He looked at her and burst out laughing: 'But it's Miss Dearborn,' he said and turned to O'Rorke, 'My dear O'Rorke, you are absurd to harbour suspicions about her.'

Sharp, half won, bowed to her stiffly, but O'Rorke sulked on.

'Sit down, sit down,' said Daly, making room for her and catching at her hand with an amorous gesture. She eluded him, smiling, and sat down beside Sean. Daly made a face at her. The ease of their old familiarity was still between them. She began to feel quite amused and happy sitting there opposite Daly, still her admirer, and beside Sean. Then she became aware of the fourth man, Finnigan. He troubled her.

He was staring over her head as though impatient of the pause in proceedings her entry had caused. He was a little old man who was in continual physical pain. The strain of suffering was in his staring eyes that embarrassed and hurt people. Why didn't he die and leave others in peace instead of living on like this to embarrass and hurt them with his frightful, half-blind eyes? What had he to anticipate, but death? The others hated his presence at the meetings. He seemed to have no faith in their projects, yet he attended with stolid regularity. He attended as though to spite them. He had the money with which to finance them. As Arion did not offer to supply them with any and none of the others had any, his money was indi pensable. They had to bear with him. He seldom spoke, and when he did it was to declare his faith in the indomitable force of the British Empire.

'Then why are you supporting us?' the Irishmen would ask.

'Because I hate the English,' said Finnigan. 'But I've no hope at all of overcoming them. No hope at all.'

He seemed like an evil genius insisting them to failure. Often he would sit and chuckle cynically at all they said. Yet he was tormented continually by some internal growth and even whilst he chuckled would grind his hands one on the other on the top of his silver-headed stick until it would seem he must wear the metal through.

They were all older men than Sean. Sean, troubled by Arion's absence, feeling unsupported, suddenly saw them as strangers and his seniors. But he had the upper hand nevertheless. He had promised them he would find Riordan and he was the only one who knew where he could be found again. So he hid his discomfort by being petulantly authoritative amongst them like a spoilt prince amongst his tutors. They would have liked to box his ears and dared not. They looked at him as he sat with his hands pressed to his temples, his fingers drawing up his eyes so he had an Oriental look.

'You were going to tell us the arrangements you made with him,' said Sharp patiently.

Sean did not answer for some moments. Elizabeth sat close to him, uniting herself with his independence, amused by the enforced patience of the others. She disliked O'Rorke now and Daly had disappointed her a long time ago. She tumbled the other two in with the rest. She didn't like any of them; but she loved Sean.

Sean said: 'I will leave here on Saturday and bring him back with me on Sunday.'

'And where is he now?' asked Sharp.

'I am sorry, but Arion thought I shouldn't tell anyone.'

'I suppose you told Arion,' said O'Rorke.

'No. Nobody.' Sean turned and looked at the clock. It was midnight. He said: 'Arion won't come now.' There had been a restlessness in his bowels and a shuddering of nerves in his chest, but now he was sure Arion would not come he felt suddenly resigned and more kindly disposed towards the others. There was a sort of relief in his disappointment. He said: 'We should make plans to present to Riordan when he comes. We don't want him to think we've just been sitting here waiting for him to come and do everything.'

The man came from behind the bar and placed a bottle of whisky, a siphon of soda-water and glasses on the table. Elizabeth remembered Arion's telling her that he had introduced the rule that they should not drink until after midnight, in an attempt to end the rows that had broken up most of the earlier meetings. Daly filled the glasses.

The man started putting out the lights. He pulled the rings that hung on chains from the gas brackets. The yellow-greenish lights went out one by one and soon the bar was in semi-darkness.

Elizabeth refused a drink. Whisky made her sick. But Sean took his glass eagerly. The others who had been irritable and alert before, waiting for the respite of midnight, now sank back more comfortably in their seats. The man went off to his bed and left them with the place to themselves. As he went he put out the light in the parlour. Now the only light was a ray from a lamp outside that fell across the floor-boards and up the counter and touched with bright spots the dark glass of the bottles and the row of upright metal handles.

Elizabeth and Sean sat on a high-backed seat against the wall. She lent close to him, snuggling close to his body in the darkness. He emptied his glass at a gulp and pushed it over to be refilled.

'Yes, we must make plans.'

The others, warmed and allayed, moved closer to the table and lent forward in new friendship. Only Finnigan sat as before. His hands, with veins like blue cords laid across their backs, ground his stick top. His glass was untouched before him.

Sean sipped his glass, then lifted it: 'To the coming of Riordan who will clear the English out of Ireland.'

Finnigan did not lift his glass till the others had replaced theirs, then, with a creaking movement, he put it to his lips, sipped it and said sombrely, apropos of nothing in particular: 'The English have their rights.'

'Their rights are our wrongs,' said Sean aggressively.

'We have rights, too,' said Daly. 'We are a people and we should be a nation.'

'Yes, we have rights,' interrupted Sean: 'but it is not for our rights that we are fighting. We Irish are a nation of aristocrats. We do not claim rights but responsibilities. We are fighting for the responsibility of ourselves.'

'Anyone would think you begrudged us the money,' said O'Rorke to Finnigan. 'And if you do begrudge it us, well! We'll not be the ones to ask it of you.'

Daly patted O'Rorke's arm to quiet him: 'I'm sure

Finnigan begrudges us nothing that will buy the liberty of Ireland,' he said.

Finnigan smiled sourly into the bottom of his tumbler: 'It's a fine penny it's costing me — the liberty of Ireland,' he said.

'And you're a fine Irishman to be counting the cost,' said O'Rorke.

'I'm sure Finnigan's not counting the cost at all,' said Daly pacifically; 'and I'm sure Riordan will be the first to see that none of us is a penny the loser when he becomes President of the Republic. It's Finnigan himself will be Chancellor of the Exchequer and making a fine thing out of it, won't you, Finnigan?'

The little, bitter-humoured, old man said nothing. In shadow, his age indiscernible, his well-cut clothes and careful linen gave him something of the air of a Victorian dandy as he sat stiffly, his hands on his cane top.

'Isn't it a well-known fact,' said Daly, 'that every Chancellor of the Exchequer dies a wealthy man?' But there was no response in Finnigan. Daly, plump, pale, flaunting his good-humour that he wanted believed irresistible, turned his back on him and changed the subject: 'I wonder what great book Riordan has been writing all these years?'

'Something that will astonish the world,' said Sean.

'Did he tell you that?' asked Sharp in his calm, precise voice, turning his glass with his long, white fingers and raising his brows.

'He did not, for we had other things to talk about. But is it likely he'd be wasting his time and talent when he's got nothing else to do but use them? I've heard it said he could have been a finer poet than Yeats or Russell, but he chose instead to put everything into his passion for Ireland.'

Elizabeth lent close to Sean in a half-sleeping, sensual consciousness of his body. She pressed her nerves against him in pleasure, with a deep sense of peaceful security, feeling herself accepted by him, possessed by him and no longer worried to think for herself. When he put his hand on his knee she caught it and he let her hold it, not really aware of her as he drank and grew excited and talked.

'I've always heard that literary men are useless as leaders,' said Finnigan out of the darkness. 'They're too conscious of danger.'

'Why!' said O'Rorke, 'in the Easter Week Rising Riordan fought as though his life meant nothing to him. That's why the English are afraid of him. Riordan's no coward.'

'Finnigan didn't say he was a coward,' said Daly. 'He only said literary men don't make great leaders. He's right enough when you come to think of it, but I don't think Riordan would ever have been a writer at all. It's a leader he was, right from the start.'

'Not a writer!' said O'Rorke, half rising. 'Did you ever hear the like of that! Why, what about his great preface to his translation of Lenau?'

'I don't know why he wanted to translate Lenau at all,' said Sharp. 'Why waste time on an inconsiderable writer like that?'

'Well, to tell you the truth,' said Daly confidentially, 'he was attracted by Lenau's *Don Juan*. You know Riordan was a bit of a Don Juan himself on the quiet.'

'That's a lie,' said Sean passionately, banging the table with his glass.

'Och, sure,' said Daly. 'It's true enough. But what else would you be expecting from a fine, handsome man like he was, with a great voice and full of fire!'

'There's not a word of truth in it,' shouted Sean. 'He's a handsome man I know, because I've seen him, but he's the sort of man that wouldn't give a woman a glance over his shoulder even if she were smiling after him. Do you think I can't judge a man?'

'No man can judge another man in that respect,' said O'Rorke. 'Now, who would think that Arion had a weakness for women?'

With a furious movement Sean lifted his glass and threw it at O'Rorke. It sailed over his shoulder without touching him, but the whisky in it splashed his neck and shoulders. As O'Rorke was about to reply with his, Elizabeth awakened, sat up sleepily, and Daly caught his arm. There was a sudden, embarrassed silence. Elizabeth yawned and settled down again. She had not had much sleep the night before.

O'Rorke was wiping his clothes with a handkerchief: 'If that girl weren't here,' he said, 'I'd kick you round this room, Sean Murtough.'

'Do it, then,' said Sean.

'Not with Miss Dearborn here.'

'I'm sure she wouldn't mind at all,' said Sean. 'For it's such a sight you'd be trying to kick me round the room she'd have the greatest laugh she's had in years.'

'. . . and if she weren't here,' went on O'Rorke as though Sean had not spoken, 'I would tell you a few things about your friend Arion that would surprise you.'

'Indeed!' Sean became suddenly frigid and sober with anger. He sat upright in silence for some moments before he said quietly: 'If you said anything against Arion to me I don't think I would hesitate to murder you.'

'Is this, or is this not, a meeting to discuss plans?' asked Sharp coldly.

Sean flung round on him: 'Time enough to discuss plans when Riordan comes.' He relaxed back into drunken indifference. 'Give me another glass. I want a drink.' Daly got him a glass.

'You said you wanted to discuss plans,' persisted Sharp.

Sean filled his glass, spilling the whisky over the table. He touched his head: 'The plans are here,' he said. 'They are my own, and I, alone, will present them to Riordan. I found Riordan when no one else could find him. I cannot fail. There is power in me. When I was a child I was quite wild and nobody could do anything with me. I used to go out and get lost in the Wicklow Hills . . .'

Elizabeth yawned and pressed her face into his shoulder. He did not notice her. She slipped down in the darkness until she was lying along the seat behind him. She was fast asleep.

Arion sat at his desk writing. He had been writing all day. Secure and tranquil in a mood of ease of thought and vision, he had not wasted a moment in eating or resting.

Usually he wrote with difficulty, in a sort of anguished struggle against the intrusive and alien world of his senses. But that morning he had awakened in peace and, after Sean's visit, had set to work and worked undisturbed till dusk.

It was nearly ten o'clock before he realized his eyes ached, that it was getting dark and he had been straining to see. He went to the window and looked at his watch. He should have been out of Dublin half an hour before and at Sean's meeting by now. He found his hat and hurried down to the street.

He hailed a taxi that was beginning to make homewards and persuaded the driver to rush him out of Dublin to the comparative safety of the suburbs. The man, fearing to be caught out after curfew and lose his licence, would go no farther than Ballyboden. Beyond that Arion must walk.

He was not displeased. The sky, that in the city was made drab by the street lights, shone here a pure peacock green. Trees, on either side of the dark road, rose in a mist of darkness, their branches studded with the few evening stars. The air smelt of leaves. He walked on in the calm continuation of his mood. He was satisfied with himself. He had done a good day's work. Undistracted now, physically or mentally, he saw, with detached curiosity, the inner mystery of things and might pronounce on them his dispassionate valuation. His sensual self was non-existent. Hopeless, fearless, futureless, he was supremely happy.

Now he would wish himself alone in the Gobi desert. Now he would wish himself a stranger without acquaintances in the heart of some great city where everyone spoke a language he did not understand and no one understood his language. Could he achieve a perpetuity of this mood and live where life could not intrude and wreck his self-sufficiency, then he would write for ever undisturbed and, writing, discover completion.

Years ago his wife, when she was growing to hate him, had said to him: 'Your mind is outside life and, therefore, you are non-existent. You have no place in humanity. You are inhuman. You are monstrous — and non-existent.'

He had replied: 'My mind may seem monstrous now, but it will recur. To-day life may find it convenient to regard me as non-existent, but what will become of life when all minds are of the pattern it finds convenient to regard as non-existent?'

She had said: 'You have a sort of megalomania. You'll end up in a padded cell believing yourself Napoleon.'

She had really grown to hate him sincerely, brooding over her hatred and inventing injuries to secure it in her mind until it became a fixed passion. One day he had felt it tedious and had walked out of their house in Hampstead and never returned again. He had not hidden from her. He had merely gone to live by himself in rooms a few streets away. Their friends, who were expecting her to leave him, were surprised.

That had been ten years ago and he had not seen her since. He could scarcely remember now what she looked like. She had been a rather lovely woman. A great many men had wanted her and he had not, really, ever. It had all been against his will; all beyond his control. He had been helpless against the force of it. When he had left her his physical need of her had been torture. His body felt hurt and slighted in solitude. His nights had been agonizing. Yet he had not even thought of returning to her. That relationship was overcome.

Houses began to appear. He was approaching a village. He remembered that when they had last driven to a meeting, it was here that Sean had turned off from the main road into the lanes that led to the less frequented hills. As he came to the streets he noticed women come to their doors and, after looking from left to right, creep secretly out and down a turning. It was the turning he should take. He came to it and followed them silently.

The women all had black shawls over their heads. Their hands, gripping the shawls beneath their chins, glinted whitely. Occasionally a head turned and, for a moment, there hung in the night air the pallid oval of a face. Amongst the women a few men walked. All went towards an old chapel that rose from the shadows at its base to pierce sharply the rich sky. Each one, coming to the open doorway, entered and was lost in shadow. Arion followed. He tiptoed like the others through the porch into the church that was lit only by the votive lamps and a glimmer from the windows. The woman before him paused at the holy water stoup, then sank to the floor and knelt there a moment like a pool of shadow before gathering herself up to drift dimly and silently to where a curtain hung before the faintly lit steps to the crypt.

The steps were greyish stone. They glistened with damp. At every half-dozen yards a small blue bud of flame burned in a wire cage. The crypt was crowded so people were standing on the lower steps. Arion stopped on the step above them and, looking over their heads, saw, on the far wall of the crypt, a figure of Christ crucified, larger than life and daubed with red paint at the hands and feet and side. On the floor beneath the figure there lay, on a roughly improvised bier, the body of a young man. He had a pale, snub face and red hair.

Most of the kneelers faced the body but some were turned towards a counter attraction, a brand new figure of St. Teresa brilliantly lit by the naked electric light bulb hanging over her head. The straw in which she had been packed was scattered over the floor. She was not yet on her pedestal and stood with the congregation smirking in her pristine crudity and looking, amongst those dim women, rather like a gay lady that had come in by mistake and now was brazening out her embarrassment. The women crept round the hem of her skirt. One knelt upright on a chair before her with arms stiffly extended, motionless, with the bright, blank stare of someone drugged.

The artificial light hardened everything, yet, despite it, there was a darkness in the air. The people, crouching like frogs on the floor, were to Arion, inhuman and beyond sympathy. Only the body of the young Fenian seemed to him a living and human thing. He felt a sudden deep revulsion from the place and the figures that had for him the dreary hysteria of figures in Madame Tussaud's. He turned and made his way between the women standing on the steps behind him until he was out of sight on the top step. Then he took a notebook from an inner pocket and wrote:

A. If God exists he keeps himself well hidden.
B. Perhaps that is as well for him.

He returned to the road that soon dwindled to a lane.

Suddenly he thought: 'What made me go down there?' His mood was troubled. He felt, with the dread that came of self-knowledge, the first hint of a reaction from tranquillity. He had touched the peak; the descent was now beginning. He started hurrying to get away from the last of the cottages. He felt as though he were being slowly stripped of all the confidence that had muffled the poignancy of his senses and given him peace. He could do nothing to retain it now. The nakedness must be borne, but alone. It was like a recurrent symptom of a chronic disease from which no one must know he suffered. Whilst it inflicted him he must hide; he must suffer it out in the safety of complete solitude until it was passed and he might return again to view as the envied, the complete, the only uninflicted one.

He could not bear that anyone might suspect his sickness. He fled to solitude, the homœopathic cure for his disease that was an unendurable consciousness of his own solitude.

The hills seemed to grow out of nothingness and take their places around him. His contentment was evaporating like a mist through which was appearing, stark and undeniable, the independent existence of things. Here was the world outside himself, beyond his absorption or his control. He surveyed it with a sort of terror. He shrank within the tiny compass of his own body and surveyed the great stretches of the surrounding hills.

A silvery bloom of light hung over them. The moon was still hidden. The sky was tremulous with great and brilliant stars that seemed to be hanging on threads not more than a few yards above the earth. The sky appalled him. He stared up at it, resentful in his insecurity, and hated it.

After all, where was the force of those white spots spattered without design over a dark ground? Suppose it black spots on white and what resulted? The meaninglessness of an old blotting pad. One was tricked by a mode of presentation — no more.

Yet, even after its discovery, the trick worked. In the helpless downrush of his reaction, his intelligent and analytical awareness availed him nothing, but only added to his indignity. Now he was being carried away painfully by the maniac distress of the uncontrolled creative imagination. He caught at himself with a wild strength of anger knowing, even as he did so, that effort was futile now and would only exhaust him the more.

This was the remaining weakness assailing him, not often, but with the force and terror of an attack of angina pectoris. It was curable. His will insisted that it was curable, and it was curable. In five years — and if not in five, in ten — he would have evolved out of himself the power to resist attack. He would be cured of himself.

Meanwhile, he was attacked. The nervous exhaustion of the disease swept in upon him. He walked quickly and with a distracted fury.

Consider now the sublime lunatic striding his cell as

the sun strikes through him with the warmth of confidence! Am I not Napoleon? See, I walk so, think so, am so! No doubting it. I'll not allow myself to doubt it. . . . But at night, when the familiar, quilted walls have disappeared into the darkness and space has become boundless; at night when the mind treads insistent the black desolation of the universe beyond the stars — doubt can come then, and the terror of doubt. Waking at three o'clock in the morning a terrible, black chink of truth decries the brilliance of illusion. . . .

No, no, no. Scream it away. Let loose panic like a million yelping hounds to scream away truth; thump the padded walls and so regain the consoling certainty of imprisonment.

He came to a standstill, trembling with fury at his own imagery. It was beyond his control. His instinct was to rush to companionship away from it. There was the danger.

The moon was creeping up behind the hills. A whiteness rimmed the delicate line of the nearest hill and was diffused over the eastern sky. The faint iridescence lightened the air, moulding and hardening the plum-blue curves of the grass. Arion paused in the lane. The ground beneath his feet was pale and broken with ruts. Here the lane bent out of sight and fell slowly down to the inn.

He stood motionless, remote and small, lost in the folds of the hills. A ghost breeze bent the grasses. He shivered. For an instant his will prevailed and he regarded the earth as though it were the creation of his own mind. He stood above and detached from it — his creation. With the comprehension of a chemist, he stood remote from contacts in an exact, unemotional and unmystical appreciation of the pure hill-line against the whitening sky. In the instant it became no more than mirage. With a movement of his eyes he might disperse it all and be returned to the unvarying desert.

An instant gained, then the desolation of his solitude swept in again upon him. He ran forward until the light of the inn appeared over the hill edge. In another moment he might have run down to them in panic — the lost and unavailing Arion — but he held himself back in time. He stood on the hill brow staring down at the inn as though from the wilderness of space down at an inhabited planet.

He watched the movements of the tiny figures seated round the table in the bar. As he watched the lights were put out and, in the growing moonlight, he could see the inn like the grey and empty shell of a dead tortoise. A sense of uninhabited desolation came from it towards him.

Suddenly he could not bear the thought of Sean, O'Rorke, Daly, Sharp and Finnigan. The thought of their squabbling was beyond endurance, and beyond endurance the thought of this ridiculous conspiracy in which he had let himself become involved. It was all becoming distasteful to him. He thought of Sean in weariness of him, in weariness of them all. Amongst them he would only find his solitude concentrated more darkly within himself. Yes, he knew it. This was not a sense of loneliness from which escape might be made into companionship. It was not mere loneliness at all, but a profound consciousness of his isolation. His isolation was of himself, and inescapable. The need was to complete it. Completion would bring self-sufficiency and that was the cure for this assailing sickness. Completion was the only cure for these attacks when consciousness of incompletion made his isolation unendurable.

Meanwhile his need for contact was an anguish. He thought in bitter accusation: 'Why don't you write to me? You must have my address by now,' knowing all the time that she had not yet had time to receive it, much less to write. 'Why don't you phone or wire? Why don't you rush to me when I want you so desperately?' It was in this mood that his need for her was the destructive weakness. It was in realization of that that he had left London intending never to let her know his whereabouts again.

He turned his back on the inn and climbed up the slope on his right hand and walked away into the hills. The light was growing. He felt it playing like a persistent lightning over his nerves. At last he had to run down into shadow to escape it, but the intense pressure of the darkness was no more endurable. In this mood nothing was endurable. Nothing, nothing. . . .

He hurried as though he were being pursued, yet he almost wished he really were being pursued. He wished he might turn and find some human creature behind him and knew, even as he wished it, that were he to do so, he would frighten the creature in his disgust and hatred of its stupidity, its intrusion, its very existence.

God, how he wished that she were here and he might bury his head in her lap and lose consciousness!

Yet there was no knowing how even she might react to this mood in him. He had never let anyone see

133

when it had beset him. Never, at any time. Even when he was a child and it had been beyond his understanding, he had hidden with it.

Yes, he must hide. Even from her.

Do not come near me! He hurried as though from her, as though she were just behind him. Do not come near me!

Don't you understand that this is not me. Will-less, my words all gone, my imagination escaped from control, existing of the tremulous nervousness of my flayed senses, flinching at the very movement of the air about me — this is not me.

Don't come near me. You cannot follow me now.

And yet you said once: 'Do not think I do not know. Do not think there is anything I do not know.' And I did not ask you what you meant. I could not ask you and discover that you knew. This is not a thing to be spoken of, to be given the existence of speech. It is not a thing that can be denied or affirmed.

But how could you know? It isn't possible. Have you followed me through this impenetrable darkness? How could you even enter it and live, when it has killed so much of me? It isn't possible.

Were I to turn and find you beside me now, I would be lost. I would be abandoned to you. There would be nothing of me you would not know, nothing you might not possess. I would never recover myself from you.

So, you must keep away from me. Do not write. Do not come and see me.

I will go down by myself and recover of myself. Leave me to exist only of myself.

He walked until daybreak.

WEDNESDAY

ELIZABETH awakened to a glitter of light. The white, naked sun was streaming in through the windows over the tables, the sanded floor and the array of the bar. The glasses and silver dazzled. She closed her eyes and opened them to fuller wakefulness. She was lying alone on the seat. Sean had moved to a chair. She sat up and looked around her. The man was behind the bar again. As she looked at him he put down the glass he was polishing, leaving the cloth in it, and pulled a leaf off the calendar. The new, red figures said that this was Wednesday, the sixth of June.

She had met Sean for the first time three days before. She looked at him. He was sitting opposite her, upright and awake. She said: 'How long have you been awake?'

He said: 'I haven't been to sleep.' His face was white and sharp with an intelligent and acid keenness. His eyes stared and were dark-ringed from lack of sleep. He looked at her with penetrative intelligence. The fire was dead in him; he was coldly and unrespondingly sober. He sat with his head between his hands in a sort of timeless trance of sober and acute perception. At once she felt the chasm between them. She felt his will. She knew then that he had a will apart from Arion. Beneath the undulating surface of his moods there was an individual will. With a sort of hopeless weariness she felt it there and apart from her. She felt a sort of weariness of striving against the wills of those who stood apart from her and left her unsupported. She felt a hatred and weariness of the ineluctable solitude of the mind.

She looked round for the others. Finnigan was gone. His chauffeur had called for him hours before. O'Rorke, Daly and Sharp slept drunkenly in their chairs.

'Were you waiting for me to wake up?' she asked.

'No,' he said vaguely. 'No.'

'Had you forgotten me?'

He did not answer and she knew he had forgotten her and everything else. She said: 'It's nearly midday. When are we going back to Dublin?'

He said: 'I must wait for Daly and O'Rorke. They came by taxi last night.'

She said: 'Why don't you wake them?'

'Let them sleep it off,' he said. 'There is no hurry.'

'Aren't you going to see Arion to-day?'

'No. I don't want to see him.' His voice sounded to her small and toneless as though he were speaking on the telephone from a great distance.

She felt him apart and unequivocal. She had gone asleep beside her beloved Sean and had awakened to find herself faced by this stranger. She sat for some minutes on the seat pressing the palms of her hands into her eyes. She felt tired; rather faint and sick, empty as though gutted. She was quite empty and dull with disappointment. She had set herself to take Sean, sure of her superior strength, careless of him in her deep consciousness of her unattainable, loved Arion.

Now, when she thought of Arion, he seemed dwindled beyond her caring and her desire was all for Sean.

The air was heavy with the smell of beer and spirits. She said: 'I have a headache. I'll wait for you outside.'

She went out into the clear, clean morning. She gave half a thought to the idea of returning to Dublin by herself without telling Sean that she was gone. But she did not know how far she was from the buses; and she did not suppose her going would worry him much, so there was not much point in it.

The grass slopes fell back with a tender and modest air as though newly created. The sky was very pale. There was a soft sweetness in the air. She walked up to the hillside and sat where Arion had sat the night before. She looked over the delicate undulations of the hills. Men from the village were coming down the path behind her to the inn. They passed close to her yet their footsteps sounded muffled, almost out of hearing. They glanced aside at her curiously, but she did not notice them. Others came in twos and threes, talking until they caught sight of her, then approached and passed her in pregnant silence. She was not conscious of them. After a while they returned and passed her again, their heads unmoving but their eyes sliding to their corners to see her face set pale and rather coldly impersonal, and her thick white neck, and the first shadow of the valley between her breasts showing above the edge of her blouse. She aroused in every man a sexual curiosity, but nothing more.

The barman came out and asked her if she would have something to eat. He brought her a plate of cold beef and pickles and a dish of yellow gooseberries on a tray. She thought she was not hungry, but, when she started to eat, she ate everything. He came and took away the empty plates and said one of the gentlemen in the bar was paying. She did not think it could be Sean; she thought it must be Daly for whom she was still attractive.

The sunlight had taken on a deeper, harder brilliance when the four men emerged. She combed her hair and powdered her face before she went down to them. To her eyes, strained with looking at nothing, the men seemed to move in an indecision of darkness. O'Rorke and Daly were grumbling with a laughing stupidity as they got into the back seat of the car. Sharp, meagre and worried looking, sat in the front.

Sean was doing something to the engine. Looking at him, Elizabeth was touched by a sense of coming calamity that descended on her suddenly and without cause. She felt a shadow behind her and turned to see it, but it slipped from sight quicker than she could turn. She looked at the three men in the car. O'Rorke and Daly were commiserating with each other humorously and wishing themselves drunk again; and Sharp sat in his pinched self-consciousness wondering why he ever had anything to do with it all. Odd creatures! To be within the mind of one of them would be to be within an unrecognizable world. Amazing that Sean, bent there over the engine, with his gaunt face and pale, fine, forward-falling hair, was of their species. She felt kin to him, but he denied her.

She was squeezed in the car between Sharp and Sean. Sharp held his elbow stiffly from her. Sean touched her legs when he changed gear, but he gave no thought to her.

She was waiting for the others to go. She was waiting to be left alone with him. But when the three were dropped in Harcourt Street, there was no change, and she felt powerless to make a change. She was uncertain of him and of herself.

He said: 'I have to go and get my allowance from my father.'

She said: 'I know your father. I'll come with you.' She paused before adding weakly: 'I'd like to see him again.'

He said nothing. He drove to Merrion Square. She did not want to go and yet she could not leave him. She felt a curious dread at the thought of seeing Murtough again. She felt a folly in her going, but she had to be with Sean. As she followed him up the steps to the door, she said too loudly and with a stupid half-laugh, 'Why don't you live here?'

He never hesitated to tell anyone about himself. He said: 'My people were too close to me. They could infuriate me as nobody else could. They could make me lose my self-control. I wasted so much time in just being angry with them that I seemed to do nothing else. I had to get away from them and live alone in tranquillity.'

A servant admitted them. They went up the stairs to Murtough's door. When Sean opened it his father was sitting smiling at them as though he knew they were outside and about to enter. Smiling, almost on the point of nodding, as though to say: 'I knew you were coming. I knew you were together. There is nothing I do not know.'

Sean, standing in the doorway, looked as though he

were facing an enemy. He said: 'To-day is the sixth of June and you haven't sent me my cheque yet.'

'I thought I would like to see you,' said Murtough pleasantly, 'and your cheque is the only thing that will bring you here. Won't you sit down? And Miss Dearborn. My dear child, it is delightful to see you again.' Elizabeth moved forward to shake hands with him, but Sean remained in the doorway.

'I haven't time to stay,' he said. 'I need the money. Will you write it now . . .' He paused, then added an ungracious, '. . . please?'

Murtough laughed, holding Elizabeth's hand. 'My dear John, do come in. Why are you so sullen? You seem to turn every visit into a visitation.'

He was obviously determined to protract the visit and Sean, with cold and silent patience, withdrawn, determined to yield nothing, entered, closed the door and sat on the nearest chair. He closed his lips tightly and sat as though he were in a waiting-room.

Once he was seated Murtough appeared to forget about him. He pulled Elizabeth down to the chair beside him and started speaking to her as though they were alone. It was this she had dreaded. She sat uncomfortably, wishing herself safely away, yet held by curiosity, wondering what he really would say.

'What have you been doing with my son John?' he asked.

Elizabeth answered with the restlessness of discomfort, turning to include Sean, willing him to enter the conversation and release it from intimacy: 'We went to the Wicklow Hills yesterday,' she said. Sean was looking across the top of the pianoforte towards the open window. He sat detached from them, leaving her helplessly alone with Murtough.

'And then you went to the meeting at the inn?' said Murtough.

She looked at him, not knowing what to say, not knowing how much he knew or ought to know.

'Arion lunched with me this morning,' he said. 'Something detained him in Dublin last night.' Sean appeared to hear nothing. 'He said John had not returned from the hills and you seemed to have disappeared. I believe he was a little worried about you.'

'No, I don't think he would be.'

'No?' Murtough smiled his unceasing amusement. 'And who was present beside John and yourself?'

She looked at Sean. He gave no help and so she answered: 'O'Rorke, Daly, Sharp and Finnigan.'

'Oh! They are the conspirators!' He raised his eyebrows. 'Well! Well! Well! Daly — the rather plump young man who teaches at the Art School, and Finnigan! He is financing the plot, isn't he? Poor Finnigan! He regards me as an arch-enemy. . . . Something that happened years ago. A rather sordid story I won't repeat to you, my dear. He is financing Sean in the belief that if he gets enough rope he will hang himself.' Murtough spoke with a sublime lightness as though the whole thing were a tremendous joke: 'I often suspect it was he that betrayed my eldest son, David, to the English.'

Elizabeth looked up at him quickly, shocked, and shocked by the levity of his tone; but even his eyes were full of mocking laughter. The man was incomprehensible. She swung round to Sean. Sean stared unmoved out at the clouding sky.

'Then he may betray Sean,' she said in a worried, stupid voice, not knowing what to say.

'Sean doesn't think so,' replied Murtough. 'In fact he has implicit faith in him, so . . .' He shrugged his shoulders and changed the subject. 'And O'Rorke! Isn't that the man who wrote to the *Irish Review* condemning Arion as unintelligible? Arion, who prides himself on his exquisite simplicity! I wonder if he understands him any better now they are united in a common cause?'

She did not answer. She did not want to talk about Arion. But Murtough was insistent.

'And you?' he said. 'Have you penetrated the mystery of Arion?'

She was acutely conscious of Sean's presence: 'I haven't tried,' she said. 'I respect his mystery and he respects mine.'

'Then he is a stranger to you?'

'Yes. He is as much a stranger now as he was the first time I met him,' she turned on Murtough. 'We do not trespass upon one another,' she said.

For a few minutes Murtough looked at her in silence, half smiling, half repudiated. 'You are a strange child,' he said. 'In your way you are as unapproachable and unplaceable as Arion. You are like one of the courtesans of the ancient world who lived an independent life regarded as an equal by the men with whom they associated, not for profit, but from choice and for their own gratification. You must find a Grecian island and retire there with the few, sane intellectuals left to Ireland and escape this hell and scrimmage.'

It seemed to her as though he were putting a curse on her. She said: 'How do you know I want to escape it?'

'Surely everyone wants to escape it,' he said. 'Even Arion is weary of it.'

Sean turned now, abruptly: 'Did he tell you that?'

'No. I did not need to be told.'

Sean merely looked away from him again with a chill and silent contempt. His mood had scarcely varied since the morning. He was still silent in sober detachment like a sheer wall giving no foothold.

Because of Sean's patent enmity towards him and because he would not release her hand, but peered into her face and questioned her when she hated his questioning, she was beginning to feel an actual revulsion from him. She wished Sean would insist on going, but he seemed to have forgotten that he ever wanted to go and now to be resigned to sitting there for hours, if need be, in a coma of indifference.

She picked up a book that was lying face upwards on a stool beside her and looked at the unusual face drawn on the dust jacket. She read: *A Life of Baudelaire*.

'So you can still find something to read?' she said.

'Occasionally. But it is a discouraging search and one I can never hope to abandon. I must read. After Conolly has wheeled me each day three times round Stephen's Green there is nothing left for me to do but read now that I can no longer play the pianoforte. But at your age surely you are not complaining that you have read all the books?'

'I seldom read anything now,' she said. 'I read every book worth reading when I was too young to appreciate them and now I seem to have neither the time nor the patience to re-read any of them. For years, when I was a child, I had no companions but books and they made me discontented with circumstances, worldly wise, amoral and destroyed my faith.'

'No University could have done more,' said Murtough. 'You have had an excellent education.'

Suddenly Sean started to cough. After a moment he held his breath. Furious with himself, his face flushed and anguished and angry and his eyes swimming, he held his breath in a determined effort to stop coughing and he could not stop. He choked and coughed again.

At times his coughing had a brutal quality. It seized him with a dominating violence of brutality against which he fought for breath, for life itself. He fought to the black and frightful pinnacle of desperation. Then, of a moment, he would be able to make a terrible effort and free himself. It was achievement. A miracle. He could breathe again.

Exhausted by the effort, he sank back in his chair. His breathing became so faint Elizabeth rose instinctively to go to him. But Murtough, with his hand on her wrist, held her back. She looked at him. He was not looking at Sean. He had picked up the Baudelaire book again and he started talking about it, quickly, half-laughingly, as though tactfully covering up some lapse from gentility.

'It was written by a man whom I knew in Paris. He seemed a healthy, lustful creature, very casual in

his sexual relationships, going to a brothel to have a
woman as he might go to a café to have a drink. Yet
in this book that he has sent me, I find him writing
not only with insight, but with sympathy, of Baudelaire
who in his private note-book compared a lover's
embrace to a torture or a surgical operation.'

Elizabeth, seeing that Sean was now well enough,
sat down again and Murtough, releasing her arm,
opened the book and translated as he read: ' "With
what knowledge of an inner shadow does Baudelaire,
the conscious sinner, the voluptuary with his eyes
turned to Heaven, describe the embrace as a Black
Mass. Like all of us he suffers from violating the law
that must be violated if we are to remember its
existence." Elsewhere he says that the human face in
the grip of passion expresses nothing but a mad
ferocity and that the real pleasure lies in the certainty
of doing evil. Would you care to borrow it?'

'I can't read French well enough to understand it
all,' she said, resentful of his probing into her secret
darknesses and beginning to hate him for Sean's sake.

Sean, recovered and watching them, said unexpectedly: 'Our generation has no patience with
Baudelaire and his consciousness of sin. He is like a
man who, having been flung against his will into the
water, prays forgiveness from his assailant for having
got wet.'

'You would not ask forgiveness?' said his father.

'I would not let myself be flung in,' he spoke
aggressively, conscious of their relationship.

'You are stronger than the assailant?'

Sean flushed a little: 'I will be stronger,' he said, and

Elizabeth, meeting his eyes, saw in them only a self-conscious vacancy and she was hurt. She turned away, refusing to recognize the fundamental difference that must separate them in the end. She did not want to recognize it. She wanted to suffer out his misunderstanding until every hope was dispelled.

'Sean suffers from the inadequacy of living,' said Murtough.

'I think we all do,' she answered quietly.

'Only the young,' he said. Then, as she smiled her bitter unbelief, he said: 'As you get older you gain a satisfaction from your body that in youth cannot be understood. When you are young it is scarcely a part of you. It is scarcely more than an instrument you use for your needs. But when it has grown old with you and you are no more ridden by the needs that force you to use it with violence and hate, then you begin to regard it with the affection you might feel for an old comrade. You tend it carefully; you see every wrinkle and line upon it as scars of a battle you have fought together. You cease to resent it as an impediment. You are careful for it. It is growing old. It has suffered. If, by its weakness, it has forced suffering upon you, you, by your misuse, have forced suffering upon it. There comes a fusion of yourself with your body. You and your body become part of one another in a way impossible in youth. When you are young you marry with other bodies. When you are old you marry with your own and it becomes your constant companion. When you are young you are careful for the body of your beloved, but when you are old you are careful for your own. You guard it against extremes of heat and cold; you listen for every slight irregularity of its heart-beat. There is a pleasure of satisfaction in every twinge of pain it inflicts upon you just as though it had been inflicted upon you by a mistress or a lover. I lift my arm and at once, easily, swiftly, unfailingly, pain glances up to my shoulder and I feel a pleasant satisfaction. And so I can sit here, day after day, seeking no other companionship but that of my own body that is my comrade, my mistress and my self. The young pity the old and fear for themselves, saying that old age is lonely; but your pity is misplaced.'

'I think we pity the old,' said Elizabeth, 'because we pity ourselves. We are lonely and suppose that, growing old, we gain nothing but only lose the advantage of being young.'

'Then be reassured,' said Murtough. 'Youth at its best is a green and acid lime. Life sweetens as it ripens.'

Sean rose from his chair with a twisted smile. 'Thank you for reassuring us,' he said. 'We shall no longer be afraid of growing old.' He stood and looked at his father. There was between them a mocking understanding. 'Now perhaps you will let me have my allowance!'

'But you must stay to dinner.' No, Sean would not stay. 'You, Miss Dearborn, surely you will stay?'

Oh, no. Elizabeth rose quickly and moved out of his reach. She was apprehensive that Sean might go and leave her alone with him. She could scarcely stifle her revulsion from him. She felt captive there, crouched ready to fly when the door opened. She knew he was disappointed in her, that he had credited her with a maturity she had not yet achieved. She did not care.

He had supposed her to be mistress and shaper of events, and she was not. No, she drifted weakly like the rest of them. She had not taken Sean and she was not holding him for fun whilst the whim lasted. She was ashamed that she had so fallen short, and yet she really did not care. All she wanted was to be alone with him now.

She watched Murtough take out his cheque book and fountain pen and write the cheque.

'There you are.'

How she must have disappointed him! But she did not care. She was abrupt and merciless in her not caring. At last they were going. There was something cynical in Murtough's smiles and farewells. She did not care. At last they were out of the room. . . .

But Sean was no different and no nearer. He went down the stairs two steps ahead of her.

There was a sudden rush against the windows and when they opened the front door they saw the rain falling in glass rods that splintered on the pavement.

'It's too heavy to last long,' he said. 'We had better wait.'

He went upstairs again and she followed. He moved as though he were very tired. There was no flame in him, no vital mood, only the cold, indifferent will. He passed his father's door and went on up to the front first-floor room. They entered. It was furnished in the Victorian rococo style. It smelt unlived-in, and was dusty, faded and colourless. It had two glass doors leading to a balcony.

He said: 'This was my mother's drawing-room.' He moved round looking at the photographs massed on the numerous little tables. She wondered if he had been fond of his mother and if he had left home at her death. She said: 'It was your father that irritated you?'

He understood what she was asking and answered her without hesitation. 'No. It was chiefly my mother. She thought of me as a sort of invalid. She devoted her life to me. She kept telling me that she was sacrificing every moment of her life for me, and I couldn't bear it. The burden of her sacrifice was terrible. I had to throw it off and run away. One evening when she was out, I packed my clothes and books and left the house and didn't come back. When she found I was gone and would not come back, she had a stroke. She was paralysed down one side from head to foot. I went to see her. I remember how she smiled on one side of her face only and lifted only one hand. It was as though one half of her were dead. She said she couldn't live without me — but I would not go back. If I had gone back I believe she would have forced herself to get up and drag about doing things for me. I believe she would have lived. But it was either her life or mine. I would not go back. So she died six weeks after I left.'

She shuddered a little as she felt in him the inexorable, egotistical will. She felt a sort of fear of him that heightened her desire for him and, in some way, heightened her sense of a pathos in him. She shuddered and then was touched deeply by a vibrant pity and lust to caress him.

'She left me her money,' he said. 'He holds it in trust until I come of age.'

'Can't you live with your father?'

'No.'

He crossed the room and dropped into an armchair. Elizabeth, standing near the door, watched his movements. He lowered his head slowly to the cushion and the pewter-coloured light from the window moulded his face. It lit the height of his forehead and the oblique lines of his brow; his prominent nose with its wide, dramatic nostrils and his heavy lips. His features had something of the sardonic intelligence of those strange faces in the paintings of the Italian players. He looked a tragic and bitterly intelligent comedian. She knew, if he lived, he would develop in the end all his father's malicious mockery without his humour. Yet, as she watched him, her heart contracted in consciousness of him. He lay still with a sort of death in his stillness, his eyes closed. He was withdrawn as though she were not there.

Suddenly she crossed to him and knelt beside him and put her arms round his waist. She held to him in a fierce agony of passion. She desired him poignantly. He opened his eyes and smiled at her, but he did not move. He smiled as though he were secure from her and beyond her reach. In fury she threw herself upon him and kissed his mouth. She kissed him with a violence of cruelty, trying to hurt him, but he neither moved nor spoke until she released him. He waited until her strength was exhausted, then he rose from her arms and went to the window. He looked out at the tender green of the trees in the square hovering through the curtain of the rain. He spoke as though she had not touched him:

'Do you like my father?'

Rebuffed, she knelt by the chair and did not reply.

'He has a sort of lust for life,' he continued quietly. 'He tried to sap the life from all of us. Only David was stronger than he was. David burnt with an inner fire of belief in himself that my father hated and could not quench. It was not Finnigan who betrayed him to the English, and, if I am betrayed, it will not be Finnigan who will betray me,' his voice was little more than a penetrative whisper. 'But Herbert and Villiers, my other brothers, could not withstand him. He sapped their confidence and sapped the will in them so they sickened and died here. I escaped because my mother shielded me. She stood between my father and me so he could get no hold on me. She hated him. She was a cold puritan of a woman. She despised and hated and feared him, but, because she loved me and had set herself to protect me, she was stronger than he was. But when I went her strength failed. She was afraid when I was not there to require her strength. She died of fear of him and he said I killed her.'

She scarcely listened to him. She sat with her lips bitten in, pale and strained in her hurt resentment. She was filled with a sense of injury. He had struck her cruelly in her tender, vulnerable pride. She moved away from the chair and sat a yard or two away on a stool in the shadow.

The rain was chilling the air with gloom. Everything looked ponderous, old, drear, yet shifting and intangible. His figure hovered unsubstantially against the glass door. He looked unreal as though within another dimension. Her will was lapsed before the egotistical individuality of his will. She sat in helpless and injured quiet.

He returned to his chair.

The door was ajar. A large, black, Persian cat came in and jumped on to his knees. It turned round and round and plucked his trousers with spread claws before it settled into his lap. Then, with little voluptuous movements, it crept up his body until it lay aslant his chest. Its purr thudded through the room. It was quite unaware of the doom hanging in the sombre air. He started to stroke it and speak to it meaninglessly as to an infant and its purr grew vibrant as an organ stop. It fastened and unfastened its claws into his clothes and rubbed its throat against his tie. She watched all its movements with resentment.

His hand fell from the cat to the chair-arm and lay there dully. He began to speak out of the dreary air:

'Four cats have adopted us at different times. The first one came a few days before David was executed. The second one before Herbert died and the third one the week before Villiers died. And here is the fourth one! I wonder what will happen this time!'

She did not believe he was speaking the truth, but the morbid diligence of his self-torturing imagination troubled her so she shivered afraid. It had become cold with the rain. The cold and dust-bleakened room was sinister with unreality. And Sean, become stranger, sat apart in mocking indifference. She watched him as though she watched a ghost that might at any moment disappear. She watched him as though he were already lost to her.

In the solitude to which, for all her angry unwilling, she seemed always forced to return, she felt out of touch with reality. She shuddered in terror of the unreality always beside her and alert to absorb her. It was unbearable. She shuddered darkly. Then her will tautened. She would not let him sink away from her like this. She rose and went and stood over him. She put her hands on the arms of his chair and hung over him in taut anger.

She said: 'You're willing yourself to death in order to have an escape from failure.'

He considered her accusation with a slight smile. 'Perhaps so,' he said. 'I have not Arion's brain or indifference.'

She was furious at his dispassionate interest, his quiet, uncaring consideration of her accusation: 'You won't die.'

He shrugged his shoulders. Her fury stirred through her whole body and her tone was command: 'I tell you, you won't die.'

He moved a little impatiently and when he spoke his voice had become dully reasonable: 'If I fail, what have I to live for?'

She winced at his slight, bitter smile: 'If you die, I shall kill myself.'

He laughed at her.

She clung to his chair in agonized anger; in an agony of need of him. She wanted to strike his mouth. She lifted her hand but she could not touch him as he lay looking up and laughing at her.

She said quietly: 'I love you.'

He stopped laughing and looked down. He turned his head aside and frowned painfully.

'Why do you love me? Why do you trouble me with your love?' She knew he was thinking of Arion. She could see his thoughts as clearly as if he spoke them. He said: 'I do not want anyone to love me. I do not want to belong to anyone or have anyone belong to me. There are two ways of loving and neither repays you for the pain. Either there is a great passion which burns itself out and is dust in your mouth in a little while, or else there is the little, long-lasting affection meted out so slightly — God save us, there's no taste in it and not worth having at all.'

She felt him incapable of response.

He watched her as she moved away and he saw her face drawn stupidly with suffering. Yet he could not realize she was hurt. He could not believe in her suffering or suppose it possible that anyone could suffer because of him. He only could be hurt and tormented, he alone suffered truly. With others it was self pity and pretence. He really had no patience with it.

She felt his thoughts. She said: 'You don't believe in me, do you?'

He said: 'Why should I believe in you?'

'You believe in Arion?'

He paused a moment before he said with a sudden force of conviction: 'Yes. Yes, I believe in Arion.'

'Arion cannot save you from dying.'

'He can save me from failure.'

'But I can make you indifferent to failure. I can make you want life instead of the illusion of success.'

He spoke fiercely, turning the cat roughly off his knees and rising as he spoke: 'Exactly. That's why I don't want you. I don't want to be made to want life. Do you think all the willing in the world will keep me

154

alive when my lungs are gone? If you made me want to live and I said: "No, I will not die," then I would only be deceiving myself and you. I will die.' Suddenly the calm of his face broke and his eyes glittered spitefully: 'And I'm glad. The only thing that can make life bearable for me is success and power. The only thing that can make the thought of death bearable is the success that will make me remembered. If I cannot have it, then I don't care if I live or die. I often wish I'd never lived or, if I had to live, had lived two thousand years ago and now was long dead and long forgotten.'

She said: 'You talk like a fool.'

She looked at him as he stood there difficult, complex, dying. She knew the inevitable end of her desire of him, yet, in her fury, her will rose against its end. She would combat fate and her own habit of dropping things that were too difficult.

He said: 'Love is the last trick of life to imprison you. I will not be caught in the panic to live that comes when one is in love.'

She was jealous that he knew that panic. She said: 'You have loved someone?'

He said: 'I don't know. But I have been so happy that I resented death.'

She could not make him resent death. All she could do was repeat: 'If you die, I will kill myself.'

He shook his head: 'You won't. It's not as easy to die as all that. You'll live to forget me.'

'I wish I'd never known you.'

'I wish so, too.'

Slowly, helplessly, she started to sob. No one else

could make her cry, but this was the second time Sean had done so. She raised her face and the unchecked tears streamed down her cheeks. Her hands lay, palms upwards, forgotten on her lap.

He said: 'You're always crying.'

She jumped to her feet in a sudden reaction of anger: 'And you're always talking about yourself. How we bore one another!' She looked out of the window. The rain was stopping. They stood in a silence of hatred whilst the last of the rain dribbled itself out. The air began to lighten. The temporary dusk was over. Colour and life returned to the room. They went down the stairs again. Sean first. He was without courtesy.

She looked at the back of his neck and felt a revulsion from him. Really, she was sick of him and hated him. She was angry, but dead and weary within.

When they came out the blue of the sky was reflected on the drenched pavements. The air seemed suddenly filled with the chatter of birds. Listen to them! she thought, the damned, silly birds!

Sean got a cloth out of a pocket in the door and carefully dried the seats of the car. Surprised, she watched him. That was the sort of thing she would not have thought of doing herself. She might have flicked off the rain without much thought, but to rub the seats until one side of the duster was saturated and then to turn it and rub again with the dry side until the leather was polished to a shine! It would never have entered her head to do it. And all so carefully and thoroughly! She remembered how, in Galway, he had cleared out the petrol tank. He could apply his attention like a good workman. Fundamentally he was practical and in the world as she was not. Had he been forced to earn his living, had circumstances given him responsibilities and no time to think of himself, he might have been happy. But she, slatternly and baseless creature, would be discontented anywhere.

She thought: 'He is fundamentally a human being, yet I cannot touch his humanity. For me no one is a human being. Why?'

He said: 'Do you want to go home?'

She said: 'Aren't you coming to see Arion?'

He said: 'No. I don't want to see him.'

She would not let him drive her back. She walked through Nassau Street to the main road and bought herself some eggs and sausages. In case Arion was in, she went quietly past his door that he might not know she was returned. She did not want to see him. She did not want to see anyone. Yet she felt no sufficiency within herself. She was filled with a shabby sort of discomfort of discontent. She was sick of everything.

She entered her room and looked at her canvases standing against the wall. Drab, dull, worthless, waste of time, waste of paint!

Oh, God! She set to frying the sausages and an egg.

Eat and sleep! They were the only things worth doing in this world where everyone, save yourself, was hard and implacable, gifted and capable, could make money and enjoy themselves. Damn them all, anyway!

As Arion left the telephone box, someone called him by his name. A young Black and Tan officer, immaculate and debonair, with his tam-o'-shanter cocked over one eye and his cane held stiffly under one arm, barred his way.

'What on earth are you doing here?' asked the soldier.

Arion stood with his hands in his pockets, his shoulders thrust back, his head a little forward, and watched the young man with a smile at once quizzical, gentle and disarming.

'Am I breaking the law?'

'For you there is no law, my dear Arion,' replied the young man with a sort of hesitant and self-conscious affectation. He blushed a little, like a young boy, and gave a nervous laugh. 'I meant — what has brought you to this disconsolate island?'

'I was sent by the *Planet*. I have just been phoning my editor the details of the latest murders, executions, pillages, rapes, lootings, assassinations and similar atrocities. I always exaggerate scandalously those committed by the Black and Tans. And how did you get here?'

'Influence. Nothing but influence. As you know, Arion, I was born to be a soldier. In my childhood I dreamt of nothing but soldiering. I used to play truant from school and go out on to the moors and arrange all the big grey stones amongst the heather into battalions and fight tremendous battles. I would have given anything to have been able to go through Sandhurst and into the regular army. It was the only thing I wanted to do. I wouldn't have cared what I'd been deprived of, if only I could have had that. But I couldn't have it. It was almost the only thing I couldn't have. . . .' He spoke quickly as though it had preyed so frequently and for so long on his mind, once started he must tell all of it and gain a momentary peace. 'Then the war came as a god-send. I really saw it as a sort of gift from God, a compensation for everything. For four years I was gloriously happy, and now I'm trying to prolong my happiness. But it's too much to hope that things can go on like this indefinitely. Something is certain to happen — a truce or something.'

Arion nodded. He considered, with a sort of despondent pleasure of anticipation, the possibility of a truce and how completely it would release him and frustrate Sean. He stared reflectively over Wheeler's shoulder at the passing traffic until the young man, grown in his lifetime acutely and painfully perceptive, caught his arm and asked eagerly: 'You don't know anything, do you, Arion? You haven't got wind of anything going on, anything they're up to?' His affectation was forgotten in his urgent seriousness. 'You know, you civilians find out things weeks before they leak through to us, and if there was anything you could tell me it might make all the difference in the world to me. You know what I mean? A special promotion or a decoration, and they might keep me on as indispensable.' He spoke rapidly, lifting his face as he did so, so Arion glimpsed beneath the cap's curve a staring, china eye. He felt the old pang of pity with which this boy, a child still for all his thirty years, had so often troubled him in the past. He looked away, smiling and shaking his head.

'My English accent doesn't invite confidences,' he said.

'As though a mere English accent could render Arion innocuous!'

'Well! Even if they overlooked it and were induced to confide in me, I would think it safer to respect their confidence. This is a dangerous city, Wheeler. Is it safe for you to be out alone like this, and in uniform?'

Wheeler smiled, showing his neat row of white teeth. 'No one has ever taken a pot at me. The Irish regard me as a sort of Jonah to the English. You know why? They call me "One-eyed Wheeler" and they believe that as long as I'm alive and well the English don't stand an earthly.' He spoke with his mouth distended all the time in an artificial smile that was wry in spite of himself. He changed the subject quickly. 'I've something I'd like to show you — a sorrel filly, a little beauty.' Arion was interested. 'I picked her up cheap off one of the Clayton-Keithleys who was burnt out a few weeks ago at Foxrock. He's selling all he has left and is leaving this Godforsaken country for good. Would you like to see her?'

'Very much. Where do you keep her?'

'At Monkstown. Some friends of the Keithleys have a house there and they let me use their stable. The son exercises her for me. I've got a two-seater outside. Let's go along now and have a look at the old girl!'

Arion followed him as he led the way across the road to a long, swift-looking racing-car parked against the opposite pavement. They climbed in and drove with reckless confidence out of the city.

'You drive well,' said Arion admiringly, knowing exactly what compliments were required of him.

'I have to,' said Wheeler. 'I have to do everything better than other people can do it. I remember when it first happened to me — I was a kid and just out of the nursing home where I'd shrieked my head off for a week with fury and hate and desire for revenge against everything — and they said to me: "You'll have to face it, sonny, that you'll never be able to play cricket or soccer or fire a gun as well as other chaps can!" And I thought: "I'll show you if I can't!" I hadn't cared twopence about cricket or soccer or rugger before that, but within a couple of years I was one of the crack players in my house. I joined the O.T.C., which I'd thought rather a fool business, until then, and I . . .'

Arion recalled having heard all this before. He had almost forgotten what Wheeler was like, but now that he was remembering, he realized there was no change in him. No change, no hint of maturity in the severely classical profile with its good left eye staring out of the wind-screen. He was still pretending to be very businesslike and practical; still living in the nervous strain of having to do everything to the best of his ability because he could not afford to scamp anything or give anyone an opportunity to refer to his half-blindness.

'I haven't seen you since that garden-party my people gave in July, 1914. That seems a hundred years ago. What did you do during the war?'

'I had a job in the War Office.'

'I only got pushed through by influence,' said Wheeler, taking it for granted that Arion had failed the medical examination. 'My old O.T.C. colonel gave me such a recommendation, even the crowd of fools that examined me realized they'd be mad to turn me down. Mad! Why, I'm twice as fit as any of them. I could shoot straighter than any man in my company.' When he spoke, he barked fiercely and ridiculously towards the windscreen, never turning. The world passed for him on one side of his face only.

He was unchanged. Arion remembered how tiring Wheeler could be, and the difficulty of him that was like the difficulty of handling something at once heavy and very fragile. For some reason he had always felt for Wheeler a pity that he was unable to feel for Sean or any other human being. Because he was so tedious, so blunderingly gauche and yet imaginative and self-aware and proud, he had felt for him a worry of compassion that demanded he should do for him whatever was in his power to do. It troubled him like the irritating disquietude of conscience. He could not help wishing he had not met Wheeler. His own problems were worry enough without being beset now by the problem of Wheeler which, to Wheeler, was all of existence. But he could not escape now, and so . . . He shrugged his shoulders and smiled to himself a little.

He sat back in his seat and looked around at the wide stretches of Dublin Bay revealed as the road skirted the sea. To the west a spectacular sunset was preparing itself after the rain. The persimmon colour, reflected in the east, was washed brightly over the flat and motionless stretch of the waters and the flat sands. The pavements were drying, but the pools left on the old, uneven flags flamed with light. A band of orange ran before the car along the centre of the wet road.

The light had grown richer with a sort of depressing autumn lustre when they at last drew up in front of the house. It was a square, ivy-darkened house set fifty yards back from the road at Monkstown. They went round behind it. Arion walked on the right of Wheeler until Wheeler dodged round him and made him walk on his left.

'I forgot,' said Arion. 'I'm sorry.'

'You know,' explained Wheeler apologetically, 'I can't bear people to walk on that side of me. I can't bear it. I can feel them there but can't see them, and it irritates me so I want to strike out at them the same as you would if you felt someone near you in the dark.' He tried to assume an unconcern that heightened his embarrassing difficulty. 'The funny thing is,' he laughed '(and it really is funny), when people see there's something the matter with your body, they seem to think there must be something the matter with your mind, too. They don't realize you have an ordinary human brain and sensibilities. Damned funny!' His attempt to be casual was agonizing. 'They think you're something different – strange and to be pitied.' He added sharply, almost accusingly, 'You don't pity me, do you?'

'Why should I? One doesn't pity the best runner because he is handicapped in a race.'

Wheeler laughed and glanced shyly at Arion. 'You're just the same,' he said with gratitude as though he supposed Arion had remained 'just the same' for eight years against the possibility of again meeting Wheeler and finding him still in need of comfort when in imagination his vanity was hurt.

Yes, tedious.

The stables were in a little valley at the foot of the lawn's slope. Beyond rose a hill that hid Killiney Bay. The light was growing deep and rich. The very long, tall, strong garden wall, built when labour was cheap during the famine years, glowed as though red-hot. A band of terra-cotta lined the vast, classical sweep of the hillside and enhanced its ebony simplicity. The air was flooded with dense, biblical colouring and an atmosphere of Old Testament flame and awe.

The men walked in silence. Wheeler was thinking of the good fortune that had brought him in touch with Arion again. Arion was thinking of nothing in particular. That morning he had taken his arm out of its sling. The graze was healed, but when he moved his arm he could still feel numb twinges of pain glancing down to his finger tips and up to his shoulder. The muscles were stiff. It gave him pleasure to squeeze them and move them about and feel his nerves protest. As he walked down the grass he pressed his elbow and pushed down his forearm, quite intent on the sensation it produced and forgetful of his companion. He was even unaware of the curious display of the light. But when Wheeler emerged from the dark interior of the stable leading the pony, he was tricked, of an instant, back into his old deep and sensuous appreciation of all living beauty.

He saw the slender, delicately stepping beast glint as it stirred through the twilight. He watched it with his naïve concentration of interest, deeply conscious of it, deeply and exquisitely conscious of the reaction of all his senses.

One wall of the stable was mottled with a dark-flowered honeysuckle that filled the air with a luxuriant sweetness. A clump of white weed at his feet gave off a heavy night scent that mingled with the honeysuckle smell and the warm smell of the stable. He could feel, like an inflection of his nerves, the quality of the evening — the fading, terra-cotta light and the coming dusk through wh ch the filly moved the auburn incandescence of her flanks. There was in the silence a mystical quality that beset the fancy as significant.

Even Wheeler was silent, standing there at the mare's head, looking at Arion who leaned a little forward, lost in contemplation.

'What do you think of her?' the young man had to ask at last.

Arion crossed and stood beside him and laid his hand on the soft muzzle of the pony. She stood motionless whilst he held his hand there, not caressingly but with a sort of comprehension. He looked into the great dark eyes of the filly and would not say anything.

'Don't you think she was a bargain?'

Arion nodded slowly: 'I'll have to be getting back,' he said, 'I want to get some work done before I go to bed.'

And Wheeler, quick to take offence, was not offended. He led his pony back to the stable and, after a few minutes, emerged and closed the door.

They walked back to the car. For a long time they did not speak. There was an ease of silence between them, almost a curious sort of sympathy grown strangely from his compassion for Wheeler and Wheeler's wondering delight of him. To Arion, his compassion for this young man that seemed, in some strange way, an obligation to him, was peculiar in that it was almost incomprehensible. It was one of the few things that he had preferred to evade rather than dissect and understand.

Because of this perverse sort of sympathy, he could not help glancing at Wheeler with dislike. Wheeler was walking with his head lifted, staring up with difficulty from under the absurd angle of the cap, and at once Arion was hurt and remorseful. He laughed sharply and said: 'Of what are you thinking? War, death, famine and pestilence?'

'No.' Wheeler swung his head right round to look straight at him and avoid showing the traitorous three-quarter face. 'For me war is no more than an excuse for exercising the perfection of discipline and the beauty of well-drilled men.'

They came to the car and stood still for a moment beside it. No one came from the house or seemed to have seen them arrive. They stood quite alone in the dim drive with the dark, blind house behind them. The last of the strange light had given the country-side an unfamiliar and unearthly air. Wheeler glanced around and said in an excited whisper: 'Arion, when you look round at the hills now, what do you think of?'

Arion, looking round, saw the black hills tangled with briars through which there was a purplish movement. The last of the light slit the sky with a bloody streak like a sword gash. After a moment he answered: 'The country in which Dante found himself before the Inferno was disclosed to him.'

'That's because you are a writer,' said Wheeler.

'If you were a painter you would think of something else.'

'Yes. Doré's illustrations to the Inferno perhaps, or one of those dark Brueghel landscapes, or perhaps . . .'

Wheeler nodded and interrupted impatiently, not really wanting to listen but to talk: 'And I see it as a soldier would see it — as a subject for fortification or attack. There is your battle-field! Now plan your campaign. What possibilities? If you must retreat — what disadvantages?' He paused, then said in a strained voice: 'You believe I want to enter one of the services only because they are the only professions closed to me. You think that from perversity I am walking against my fate. But I am a soldier and if I cannot become one, then I am nothing.' He stood there very pale and young and hopeless, all his defiance and affectations forgotten. He said: 'I am nothing, Arion.'

'I know,' said Arion. He took his seat in the car. But Wheeler still stood beside it and stared across the hill. Suddenly he said as though the memory were amusing: 'I can see that penknife now, just as I saw it when I was looking at it with two eyes. They gave me the football and said: "Blow up the bladder for us, there's a good chap!" It was a bitterly cold day and my fingers were frozen and I couldn't get the knot untied. The others — they were big chaps, prefects, and I was awfully proud that they'd asked me to do something for them — they were changing and I was afraid they'd come back and find I hadn't blown it up for them. At last I got out the penknife to cut the leather string. I can see the playground and the grey sky and the blade of the knife shining as it jerked up because the string was rotten and I'd put too much force into cutting it.'

He stood still and Arion said nothing. After a few minutes he got into the car without speaking again, switched on the headlights and started the engine with a roar.

They returned to the coast road. A great sweep of lights marked the line of the bay. It was night already.

Arion said good-bye to the soldier and gave him his address, then he went to his room. He sat at his desk writing for two hours before he realized the tremulous restlessness that was overwhelming his concentration. He closed his desk and undressed and walked round the room in his dressing-gown. He felt his body like an exposed nerve. He felt with a shuddering acuteness the movement of silk against his flesh. He went to his door and opened it and stood for a moment in the draught, hesitant yet compelled, before he left his room and went up to Elizabeth's room.

She was lying awake. He came into the room silently yet she felt he was there and turned to see him.

She had not drawn the blinds and the room was lit vaguely by a reflected street-lamp. She watched him as he crossed to her bed and stood there beside her. It seemed to her that weeks had passed since they were last in physical contact and, in that time, they had separated and become strangers. She looked at him with curiosity, half repelled and afraid, as though he were coming to her for the first time. Some sympathy between them was lost, yet she moved instinctively to make room for him beside her.

He slipped off his black dressing-gown and stood naked. In the half light his body looked very white and delicately modelled; it looked un-human and almost intangible. She put out her hand to him and he lay down. He lay in silence, not touching her. He felt the chill of restraint in her and hung back, afraid of repulse. But against her will she was drawn to him. She cupped her hand over the curve of his side and smoothed him down to his loins. She pressed her hand deeply into the hard sculptured line of his body until he raised himself and leaned over her. As he leaned over her he seemed to her to have the thoughtful and æsthetic beauty of some early ivory. It was the intellectual quality in his body that made him so desirable to her. She could not resist the desire to pull his body down into her flesh and so extinguish the aloof meditation of his face and limbs.

Yes, he was more desirable than Sean. Sean's humanity and weakness were patent in all his youth and vanity. But Arion's could be disclosed only through his sensuality. To the pleasure of communion with him was added a savour of perversity, a hint of the ancient consciousness of evil almost lost to her generation. It was suspicion of that, that had roused Murtough's curiosity. A flavour of immorality, the Gothic intoxicant, the more intoxicating to one reared on the flavourless Classic unmorality and the shadowless simplicity that could irk one beyond bearing. With Arion there came shadow that was consciousness of evil.

When they separated and lay loosely-held, half sleeping, she whispered: 'Did you wonder what had become of me?'

He smiled without answering or opening his eyes and turned his face into the pillow and slept. His hand fell laxly from her. After a little while she rose and went to the open window. She folded her arms on the sill and lent out towards the deserted street. She felt as though something were pulling her out towards the sky. If she could only raise her feet from the ground she might float out and away. To where?

Arion lay sleeping in her bed. She remembered how small he had seemed in her arms after she had held the width of Sean's shoulders. This Arion had come and roused her from apathy only to leave her again restless and dissatisfied.

Am I of the company of those who, ill-wished by heaven, must needs create for themselves lovers of air?

The house was silent; the street silent and deserted. Arion slept quietly. She returned to her bed and went to sleep beside him.

THURSDAY

When Elizabeth awoke it was late. Arion had gone. She got up and went to the window. Another fine morning. She washed and dressed and boiled herself an egg; then took her bathing costume and went out. It was nearly noon. The sun flooded both pavements. The traffic moved through a haze of heat.

She caught a bus that took her to Howth.

There were some holiday-makers with their picnic baskets on the beach. She climbed over the boulders to avoid them, and walked round beneath the overhang of the cliffs until she was out of sight of everybody. The cliffs were scooped out with shallow caves. But she hated the dank smell of caves. She preferred to undress out in the open on the grey stretches of flat stone that were riddled with little pools and spotted with limpets.

She swam out to the rocks and took off her bathing dress and threw it up to a projection. It hung and flashed in the sunlight its kingfisher blue.

Now she could swim nakedly through the sea. That was what she had wanted to do. She felt a depth of satisfaction in her own nakedness, and in the movement of her muscles and the soft lap of the water along her body. Through the delicate green of the water she could see her limbs drifting lifelessly pallid. They looked like the white marble limbs of an antique statue. She felt a delight in the beauty of her own body, a contentment in it for its own sake that set her apart from need of Arion or Sean or any other man. The sun-dappled sea, on a level with her chin, stretched out of sight. She moved through it lazily, tranquillized by her own self-sufficiency into a sort of waking dream. This was the mood she had deliberately sought. Deliberately, she was setting out to try and cure herself of her reliance on others for the will to live.

She had a nervous hatred of sea-weed and jelly-fish and anything else that might touch her naked body in the water. But to-day the water was clear. It was motionless and uninhabited like a dead sea. She had wanted it so. She was pleased with it and contented. It seemed to her it was her will that had achieved the perfection into which the will can sometimes force circumstances, and she had passed beyond memory of human inadequacy.

She made her way quietly in a wide circle back to her rock. As she approached it she saw a man pull himself up to its highest point and stand a yard from her costume with his hands under his armpits. He stood shaking his wet, curling hair. She swam round and round waiting for him to go. She swam quickly and impatiently now as though to accelerate his going. But he sat down in the sunlight as though he had no intention of going for hours. At last she approached and shouted: 'Hi! Throw me my costume.' He turned and she saw it was Daly.

'I thought it was a stranger,' she said, 'but as it's only you . . .' She climbed up to the rock beside him and stood wet and glittering in the sunlight. Daly looked at her with an artist's appreciation and indifference. He was too lazy to feel any other interest just then.

'Won't you sit down?' he said. She sat and stretched out her legs and watched the water forming rivulets and trickling off her firm, white thighs. She stretched her arms and yawned and smiled.

'Elizabeth Dearborn,' said Daly, 'you are as immodest as ever.'

She hugged herself luxuriantly: 'Modesty,' she said, 'is only a fear of doing something we think others do not want us to do. We're not ashamed of being naked when alone. I'm only modest when I see that somebody I want to attract expects me to be. But I don't care a damn about you and if you don't like me like this, you can get off my rock. It is mine. I found it first. That's my bathing costume.'

He laughed good-naturedly and lay full length at her feet: 'Nothing would induce me to go,' he said. 'Besides, I have something to tell you.'

'Really!' she said, caring about nothing.

'Yes, about Arion.'

'Oh!'

'I saw him last night.'

'So did I.'

'I saw him talking to a Black and Tan officer, and I saw them get into a car and drive away together.'

She kept her head lowered and hid her expression from him. She said: 'He's English. It's quite probable he might know one of them.'

'Yes, very probable. More than one. I've always suspected him.'

'I didn't think even you were such a fool!'

'I'm not a fool. Why should he be interested in our cause? Why should he care a damn for us? He's English and everyone knows the treachery of the English!'

She swung on him, interrupting him angrily: 'What about Finnigan? If I distrusted anyone it would be he. Murtough said yesterday he believed Finnigan would betray Sean, and I wouldn't be surprised if he did. Sean believes in him because he seems to believe in the lot of you — God help him! — but one of you should have the sense to see that Finnigan's not throwing his money away for nothing.'

Daly laughed in the angry delight of an argument: 'Why! Be quiet, do! Don't you know that Finnigan's believed to be Sean's father?'

'What rubbish!'

'It's not rubbish at all! Finnigan was engaged to Sean's mother and Murtough got her to go off with him. Her people had to make him marry her in the end and you can believe that or not, but it's the truth I'm telling you. They were pushing Murtough about in that chair a couple of years before Sean was born and Mrs. Murtough was going about everywhere with Finnigan. It was a great scandal at the time. A great scandal!' Daly grew excited in the recital of it and intoxicated to further revelations by Elizabeth's attempts to interrupt. 'Everyone knew about it and Murtough, too, you can be sure. If anyone does Sean an injury it will be Murtough that will do it.'

'But Sean is the image of Murtough,' she managed to say when Daly paused for breath.

'I can't imagine two people less alike,' said Daly.

'Oh!' she affected a yawn and turned over on to her belly. 'You always were and always will be an old gossip under the guise of innocent peacemaker. I remember how you used to gloat over all the scandal at school.'

'I'm only proving to you that we've nothing to fear from Finnigan. He's got his own reasons for helping Sean. It's Arion that's the dangerous one.'

'Why should Arion want to injure Sean?'

'Why shouldn't he? Do you know anything about him?'

'Only this — that he doesn't care enough about you to betray you. And he doesn't care enough about the English to betray you to them.' She rose, snatched up her costume and put it on as she spoke. 'It's a fool you are, Edmund Daly,' she dived into the water, 'and it's a fool you always will be.'

She heard him splash into the water after her and she lashed her way furiously to the shore. His clothes were lying in a neat heap a few yards from her own. They sat and dressed in silence.

'Will you not come up and have something to eat?'

'No. I will not.'

'Och! Come on!'

Well! After all it would be one way of saving money. 'All right,' she said. They climbed up the cliff steps to a garden with weathered tables and rickety chairs. They sat down. The table was frosted with spiders' webs. The grass and weeds grew rankly round their feet. The little, angular garden, open on one side to the sea, was heavy with untended foliage but no flowers.

'And what I would like to know,' said Daly, 'is this. How did he get that injury to his wrist?'

'A sniper in Merrion Square.'

'But why should they shoot at him?'

'Why not at him any more than at the hundreds of other civilians who've been injured. I wouldn't be surprised if you or O'Rorke put someone up to do it.'

'Is it likely?'

'It is.'

'It is not. I bet you he got it going into the Castle. There's not an armoured car goes in there but is shot at from all sides.'

'You talk to hear yourself,' said Elizabeth.

A big slatternly woman with pendulous breasts and a red face came out of the house. She took their order but did not go. She stood with one fist resting on the table and the other on her hip, talking to Daly. She wanted to hear the latest news from the city and Daly supplied it willingly with exaggerations. She shook her head as she listened and exclaimed: 'Deary me! Deary, deary me! It's a fine state the country's in to be sure!' she said. 'But I hear young Mr. Murtough's going to bring Riordan back and then . . .'

'For God's sake!' cried Daly. 'Who told you a thing like that?'

'My sons told me. Isn't it the common talk amongst the boys?'

'And you telling everyone. You'll get the lot of us shot.'

'Not at all. Not at all. I wouldn't tell a soul.'

'Haven't you just told me?'

'Sure, but I knew at a glance you were one of us.'

'You can't be certain of anyone. I might be a secret service agent. I might be an Orangeman. I might be an informer.'

'You might indeed,' agreed the woman.

'Don't be a fool! You know I'm not.'

'Wasn't that what I said. I knew you weren't.'

'I want to get back to Dublin this afternoon.' Elizabeth's cold, small voice distracted them. The flustered woman disappeared into the house and Daly sat back in a nervous flurry of exasperation.

'It's all over Dublin,' he said.

'Of course. Isn't everything you think all over Dublin even before you've thought of it. It's nothing to worry about. The police never hear of anything until it gets in the papers.'

'They do if someone makes a point of telling them.'

'Who would?'

'Arion.'

'Oh, shut up.'

Her self-sufficiency was failing. She was beginning to feel uneasy, thinking of Sean. She was beginning to suppose he would come and see her. If he found her out there was no knowing when he would come again. She would not go to him. Nothing would induce her to go and see him after he had repudiated her. And yet she wanted to see him. She wanted to be back in Dublin, in her room in case he should come. Daly and his talk was intolerable. Why had she let herself in for this? In a moment she would go. . . .

But the woman came with their meal of bread and butter and prawns. The thick slices of fluffy, white bread and the great, pink, whiskery prawns were on willow pattern plates of crude blue. The tea was to be poured into half-pint cups of the same pattern, very dirty and very cracked.

'Everything's dirty,' said Elizabeth peevishly.

'What does it matter? The food is good,' said Daly. He ate in enormous mouthfuls, his exasperation forgotten. But Elizabeth would not talk. She was filled with unease as though something were happening, or about to happen, from which she was closed out. She could scarcely eat anything.

'I must get back to Dublin,' she said.

'What's the hurry?' asked Daly. He talked about the school and the new students that had come into his class. When he paused she said again: 'I must get back to Dublin.'

The woman came out with a bag of Victoria plums and offered them to her.

'No. I haven't time to eat one.'

'Take one to eat in the bus.'

She took one and hurried away, leaving Daly to settle the bill. She ran for the bus as it was moving and caught it. Looking out of the back window, she laughed with malicious pleasure at Daly running and gesticulating ridiculously after them. Thank God, she was moving; she was returning to Dublin as quickly as was possible and leaving Daly behind.

She started eating the plum. It broke from the stone in stiff, sweet flakes. She took out the clean stone and held the half plum that was beautifully cupped in the centre. It was delicious. One might want it to last for ever, yet she hurried to finish it, hurried to get it eaten and done with.

The bus kept jerking to a standstill at points along the road. Stiff and frowning with impatience, she watched people enter and leave unhurryingly. Fools! They crawled on and off like snails! And the bus stopping! She wished she could get off and push it.

It left her at last at O'Connell Bridge and she ran all the way to the house. She ran up the stairs to her room. But no one had been there. She knew no one had been there. The air had not been disturbed. No one had breathed here since she left. She started tidying the place quickly as though he might come any minute. She made the bed and threw all her shoes beneath it. Her clothes lay about the room. She picked them up in her arms and flung them into a cupboard and locked the door on them. She chose the canvas she thought least unsatisfactory and stood it on the easel in the light.

When all was finished she felt relieved. Now he could come. And she wanted him to come at once. She looked into the street, expecting to find him at the door. But the street was empty. It lay in the rich afternoon sunlight quite empty and unpromising. She got out her drawing board and tried to make herself work. She pretended she was concentrating upon her drawing and nothing else. But all the while her impatience was like a knot being pulled each instant more taut and tight inside her, somewhere between her belly and her chest.

She was working on a set of illustrations to some imaginary poems which she had started a long time ago. When she had started them, she had felt very excited about them, and had built on them a dream of making enough money by them to escape abroad. But when Arion came she neglected them. Now she found them again and set herself to complete one that was unfinished. As she worked, her drawing took on a strange quality, unreal and almost frightening so it did not seem her own work. This new quality, though alien and unsaleable, made all her other drawings look fatuous, so, in a sudden rage, she tore them up and sat with her head between her hands, hating him.

She willed him to come and was on edge expecting at any moment to hear his step on the stairs, yet she did not really believe he would come. In an attempt to curb her disturbing anticipation, she tried to convince herself he would not come, but for all her disbelief, she remained unconvinced. Every few minutes she had to rise and go to the window and look down into the street. The street remained silent and unpopulated. Once a dog, dark with blood-stained dust, came yelping past from a fight. Nothing more all the afternoon.

This would be one of those motionless summer evenings when there came most fully upon her a sense of detachment and of loss. At such a time it seemed to her she had no hold on life.

She moved about restlessly in increasing need of him, but the hours passed and he did not come. She pinned a new sheet of paper to her board and sat down before it. She had no clear vision as a model in her fancy. Her pencil moved about aimlessly, drawing faces and hands and pieces of drapery. She wrote in small, clear letters: 'Sean.' And again: 'Sean.' Then: 'Sean. Sean. Sean.'

She paused and caught her breath. Someone was coming up the stairs. Hers was the only room occupied on this floor. Someone was coming to see her. The footsteps approached her door. In the elongated instant of their approach she became a void through which her heart thundered in an agony.

Sean threw open her door. He stood and stared at her angrily. 'Where is Arion?' he asked.

She shrugged her shoulders. She sat calmly erasing his name from her drawing paper as though his entry were unimportant. And somehow, as he opened the door, it had become less important.

'I can't find him,' said Sean. 'I haven't seen him since Tuesday morning. Perhaps something has happened to him.'

'I don't think so. I saw him last night and he was perfectly well then.'

'Did he say why he didn't come to the meeting?'

'No.'

'Did he mention me?'

'No.'

'Oh!' Sean stood in the doorway, pathetically silenced.

'Won't you come in,' said Elizabeth now she had rubbed out his name. 'I expect he'll be in soon. He has an article to write to-night.'

'No,' said Sean vaguely. 'I won't come in,' but he entered and closed the door. 'There is a telegram for him on the hall table.'

'He often receives telegrams from his paper. They are not particularly important,' said Elizabeth, the well-informed mistress, and Sean stood and looked at her with dislike.

She smiled. She thought she was suddenly become quite indifferent to him, but, when she glanced at her pencil, she saw her hand was trembling and then she dropped her pencil and put her hands in her lap and became self-conscious.

He crossed to the window and stood there looking out for Arion as she had looked out for him. She moved in her seat and saw the dark line of his body against the purple and gold evening light. His shoulders drooped a little. He had a forlorn, deserted air as he gazed down the sheer house side into the empty street. She felt a sudden stab of fear as she realized her own need of him. In a sort of mazed indignation and fear she rose and stood looking at him. Hearing her movement, he looked round as though afraid of something coming upon him from behind, and she saw him with puckered face, grieved, bewildered and lost.

At once her indignation was forgotten. She lifted her hands impulsively and caught his shoulders. He tried to move from her but she held to him so that he had to stand still. He looked at her in a sort of startled and desperate revolt.

'I don't want you,' he said. 'I want Arion.'

'But Arion doesn't want you . . . or me, either. He doesn't want anyone or need anyone. But you must have someone. You cannot live without someone's confidence behind you.'

He did not want her. He held himself aloof in revolt against her hold. But he could not break away from her. She held him by the force of her animal magnetism that was stronger than his revolt or his physical strength. There was a knowledge between

them so that he could no longer look at her with indifference — instead he looked at her with a sort of hate.

He said: 'Arion couldn't desert me now — not now
when I'll soon be needing him more than ever.'

She said: 'Arion couldn't desert you because he
has never been with you. He has never cared about
you. It was only your pride that made you think he
did. If you cease to interest him he will forget you in a
moment. He doesn't care if you succeed or fail. I
think if you bored him he would betray you just to
get rid of you.'

She had expected him to contradict her with fury,
but instead he stared at her in a sort of dazed terror.
She led him across the room to the bed and pulled
him down beside her. They sat close together on the
bed. He did not try to resist her as she held him and
leaned against him, but he said with a sort of petulant
helplessness: 'I don't want you. I want Arion and
you've taken him from me.'

She did not listen to him or answer him. She held
to him and bore him backwards with her weight so he
lay beneath her. He held his mouth from her and said
with a sort of half sob: 'I have been years learning the
trick of dying. You cannot make me want to live.'

'But you won't die.' She covered his mouth with
her lips. So he couldn't answer. She held him tautly
with her will and her body, in complete possession,
until he relaxed wearily, then she curled into the line
of his side so he instinctively roused himself over her
and held her beneath his arms.

He whispered: 'Why do you want me here with
you like this?'

She smiled against his face so he could feel the rising curve of his cheek. She said: 'I don't know. I only know that when I lie with you I feel contented.'

Why seek to question into complexity so rare a simplicity? She felt him about to open his mouth and ask her some other stupid thing, so she pulled his face down into the soft warmth of her neck and he could not speak. They lay in a passionless tranquillity of quiet, abandoned to physical content.

When Arion opened the door they were startled. They had heard nothing until he was in the room and then they lay looking at him, forgetting to move. He was holding the telegram in his hand and he stood in the doorway looking back at them with a sort of curious interest but without surprise. It was Sean who moved first. He suddenly sat upright as though guilty. He ran his fingers through his hair and straightened his tie.

Arion stood still for a few moments. He seemed strangely distant from them and indifferent to them. He showed only a ghost of an amused smile. Elizabeth, feeling his not caring, was suddenly angry with him. She knew how he thought: 'There is so much of me you cannot see. So much you will never understand.' She thought: 'Don't you know that if someone is obviously trying to hide something from you, the politest thing to do is for you to pretend you haven't seen it?'

Sean stood up and walked a little unsteadily round the bed. His face was terrible.

Arion moved towards the window saying something about having met O'Rorke that morning. Neither could remember afterwards what he had said. They could only remember the distant cold of his voice from which all the gentleness and charm was gone. In his complete indifference to them, they saw him naked of charm and felt suddenly chilled and cast out into darkness.

Sean stood steadying himself with one hand on the end of the bed. His face was livid. Arion looked at him as though he didn't see him and, in a moment, before they had had time to speak, he was gone.

They felt as though he had washed his hands of them. At last they had wearied him beyond endurance — the fretful children. He was weary of them and was gone and would not come back again.

In a wave of panic Elizabeth thought: 'But this is ridiculous. Of course I will see him again. He lives in the same house. I can't help seeing him and, when I do, it will all be as though this hadn't happened.'

Sean said in a difficult voice: 'Why did he come in?'

'He wanted to tell me something, but he's gone without saying what it was.' She spoke as though she were out of breath. 'Probably he wouldn't tell me because you were here.' She wanted to accuse him. She felt angry with him and frustrated by him as though he had deprived her of something.

'What would he have to tell you that he couldn't tell me?' He turned on her with an agonized expression that silenced her. Suddenly he ran to the door, but, as he opened it, there came the sound of the front door closing. He ran to the window and peered out and saw Arion moving through the first indecision of the twilight as though through water. He seemed to drift out of sight.

Elizabeth watched Sean at the window in a com-
plication of pity and irritation. She felt towards him as
though he had deprived her of Arion, but her reason
acknowledged that this was not so. Arion was outside
the range of the influence of others. But Sean, she
knew, would not know that. He would not realize that
Arion could choose to leave him. He must believe that,
if Arion left him, some influence must have alienated
him. And whose? Whose but the fiend Elizabeth's?

He moved from the window. He moved about, dim
and wretched in the darkening room. He said with a
sort of dread: 'And it's on Saturday I have to meet
Riordan.'

'That's the day after to-morrow. You'll see plenty
of Arion before that.' Against her own uneasy hurt
and her irritation with Sean, her instinct was to hold
to him. What good in losing everything? She felt
she must behave as though nothing had disturbed
them.

But Sean would not play up to her pretence. He
seemed physically to droop, despairing that Arion was
gone. Nothing else mattered.

'What was it Arion said about O'Rorke?' she asked.

He did not trouble to answer. He sat down on the
other side of the bed away from her. They sat for a
long time in the shadow. The sense of loss was like a
hollow in her, yet she had almost ceased to think of
Arion. She watched Sean, wondering how she
should act to regain his attention. She felt in him
fear and uncertainty and thought perhaps she had
only to put her will on him to take him wholly now.
She wasn't really sure, and yet she was determined.

She watched him and waited for the necessary moment of strength to act. Suddenly, she lay across the bed and, with her head against his thighs, girdled his waist with her arms.

'Why are you afraid like this?' she asked. 'I know you cannot fail.'

He had become aloof and maliciously smiling as he looked down at her: 'And I know that I can,' he said. 'And when we fail, what will they do to us? We'll be shot at dawn and then we'll become martyrs, and men will speak of us in the streets as they speak of Pearse and Macdonagh. Surely success could bring us no more!'

He sat unresponding above her, smiling maliciously. She felt helpless and angry as she had felt before when brought up hardly against his perverse and stubborn will. She said things she did not want to say.

She said: 'Don't you love me at all?'

He answered lightly: 'Perhaps I do — sometimes. But more often I don't.'

'But I love you and you could be happy with me.'

His face gleamed strangely with a sort of spite. He said: 'I don't want to be happy. What's the good of happiness when you're ill and know you'll never get better? That happiness makes the thought of death unbearable. The immortality of achievement is the only comfort that will reconcile me with it.'

She took her arms from about him and said: 'Your self-pity serves you for achievement. If you fail you can always feel sorry for yourself.'

But he only laughed.

'You refuse to live because you are afraid of the

responsibility of yourself. You remind me of the dog
my head mistress had at school. She was trying to train
it always to go to the back gate because it scratched the
paintwork at the front. She used to drive it round to
the back and it would crawl round, looking behind and
sideways for an escape — any escape from the way before it. When it saw a doorway or any little cul-de-sac
it would dodge in and sit there looking thoroughly
miserable and sorry for itself. It would have sat there
all night, perhaps for ever, rather than go out by the
back, if someone hadn't taken it by the collar and pulled
it out and pushed it on its way.'

After a pause he said: 'Do you hope to pull me out
by the collar and force me to use the back gate?'

She couldn't think of a safe answer and so was silent.
He said at last, quite quietly: 'If I cannot go the way
I want to go, then I won't go any way. I don't mind
going to hell if I can go my own way. But I won't be
forced out into the common stream like a dog out of the
back gate.'

She said: 'So you suppose death will conveniently
save you from ignominy. You think if you fail they
will be obliging enough to shoot you. Don't be so
sure. Why should they bother to shoot you for a little
abortive rising?'

'You think they won't?' he smiled. 'Riordan is
already under sentence of death. They're afraid of him.
The English in a panic will shoot anyone. We've seen
that often enough during the last two years.'

She knew that was true, and suddenly she was
flooded with anxious tenderness: 'Why don't you leave
it all alone? Leave it whilst you're still safe. Why will

you throw yourself against difficulties? I could stand
between you and the hardness of things.'

'But I don't want you to. I don't want you to make
things easy for me. I like to feel the hardness of things.
I like to be up against difficulties and unsympathetic
people. They make me hard and brilliantly inhuman
like themselves. But you would weaken me. I won't
be weakened. I want something to strengthen my
teeth on, not you always turning everything into bread
and milk for me.'

'And what did Arion do for you?' she asked, hating
him yet bound to pursue him.

'He made nothing easy for me. He gave me confidence to face difficulties. But they remained difficulties
just the same.'

Oh! This Sean was a fool, a stubborn fool! If he
were attainable she would not want him at any price.

She said: 'He flattered you into attempting the
impossible and now he has deserted you.'

'So I must curse Arion and die?' he smiled; he was
laughing at her cruelly. 'And when I'm dead,' he
dropped his voice in mocking terror, 'I will come at
night and cry outside your window. I'll cry: "Let me
in, let me in out of the cold and dark loneliness of
death." And you will be powerless to help me, I will
cry and cry and you will be powerless because whatever
you do I shall be dead and intangible and the universe
will be between us.'

As he mocked her she looked at him coldly and
thought: 'Utter fool! He really does believe that I'm
in love with him and he is torturing me.'

Suddenly he rose and the fire died in him. Something caught at him so he said in a strained, unhappy voice: 'If only one could set out on a crusade or a pilgrimage or something not knowing when one would arrive and not knowing when one would return or if one would return at all! I'd go and explore Atlantis or hunt Unicorn or find the reason why we are born.' His voice had changed as he spoke.

She said: 'You are being affected and ridiculous. None of those things exist.'

'What difference does that make?'

'How could you look for something you know doesn't exist?' She was stubbornly matter-of-fact in the face of his affectation.

He was pleased with his own restoring cynicism: 'The things that don't exist are the only things worth looking for. How boring to hunt for something that does exist! You might find it!'

She lay on the bed and looked at him with disgust: 'God! How *fin de siècle*! Quite the little Oscar Wilde!'

They looked at one another with a stringent glitter of hate. She knew he was only hanging about now in case Arion should return and, in case Arion should return, she wanted him to go.

'Why don't you go?' she said, cross, empty and irritable; crudely impatient and sick of him.

But for a long time he would not go. He hung about the room in his perverse and acid obstinacy and in the slight hope that suddenly Arion would reappear and things would be restored again. Elizabeth sat on the bed and said nothing. She was really angry now. She was furious with Sean that now he should stay unwanted in her room in the hope of seeing Arion again.

She willed him to go, but when he suddenly turned and swung out of the room, leaving the door open and clattering down the stairs to the street, she wished he had stayed.

She felt dismally alone.

She went on sitting on the bed. She did not think to get up. It was almost dark and the dark air seemed to sweep about her in great electric swirls that, for some reason, increased her sense of desolation.

Why didn't Arion return?

The house and street were very quiet. The whole day had seemed to her empty and deathly quiet and its slight event unpresaging. It was strange to think that on that day some men and women had been born and others had died; that for some it had been the fatal day, the first, the last, the day of new and all-changing influence, whilst for her it had passed like a dream, unprofitably wished away.

She climbed slowly off the bed and went dizzily to the door. On the landing the dark house assailed her with a strange insistence upon its desertion. She felt her way noiselessly down the stars to Arion's room and entered, knowing he was not there. She closed the door after her and tiptoed round through the dimness peering at things. Everything had an innocent, unprotected air so she felt like a trespasser and thief. Yet she felt safe, instinctively knowing Arion would not return and surprise her there. As she moved round in the uncertain, ghostly twilight, she lifted things and touched them and replaced them. The writing-desk was open and, when she came to it, she bent over it and peered into its pigeon holes and drawers. They were full of letters. Slowly she grew hot and her pulse quickened. She put out her hand; then paused, afraid. Anyway, it was too dark to read anything.

She turned her back on the desk and went into the small room that was his bedroom. . . . Of course she could switch on the reading-lamp over the desk, but if Arion were to return and, looking up at his window, see the light, he would know she was there. She knew he would not return, yet she was afraid.

The bedroom faced the east and was very dark. She looked out into the small back yard and up at the irregularly placed house-sides. The roofs were black and sharp against the enamelled brilliance of the sky. Two of the windows in the house-sides were dimly lit by gas-light. Through one she could see a young girl brushing her hair. The girl's hair was dark. As the long brush-strokes struck through it, it sifted round her in a sheenless cloud. Her arms were very thin but white and tender-looking. They rose and fell, making the black cloud of her hair waver like black smoke.

Through the other window Elizabeth could see the hump shape of a big woman in bed. The woman had pulled the covers up over her eyes to close out the light. A man sat on the edge of the bed and read a book. He was half-undressed. It was as though whilst taking off his clothes, he had picked up the book and opened it and then sat down with it forgetting everything else.

As Elizabeth stood and watched them, she thought how she would paint a house with lighted windows and, above the roofs, great stars in a sky the colour of verdigris. Suddenly, as she thought again of the letters in Arion's desk, she burnt with a nervous excitement. At last it became unbearable so she had to return, in a sort of purposeful daze, to the front room and switch on the lamp.

The first letters at which she looked were from publishers and agents; the second from friends of Arion whom she did not know and who wrote of things of which she had not heard. She pushed them back into the pigeon holes in jealousy of his unknown past. Beside them she found S an's letters. When she looked at his signature she was filled with a frigid determination. She drew up a chair and sat down and placed the letters on the blotting-pad before her. Calmly and purposefully she started to read them one by one.

In the first she read: 'I have been ill and got depressed. I expected you to come and see me, but you didn't come. I began to think I could never succeed in anything and I sat by the window thinking I would fail until I couldn't stand it any longer. I went and turned the gas-fire on and didn't light it. I lay down in front of it and waited and was quite glad, thinking this is as good an end as any other. I went unconscious quite easily and quickly, but the gas ran out in the meter and I woke up again. It was the middle of the night. For a long time I wasn't conscious of myself, but I knew I was a something. It was so dark and silent, I thought I was something that was deaf and blind, and I didn't know I could move. Then things cleared a little and I began to feel sick. The sense of sickness became terrible. It was worse than any sort of pain I have known. I sat up, but I couldn't stand. I was terribly dizzy and sick and the most frightful depression came down on me. I can't describe it. It was frightful

— to wake up there in the silence and darkness in the middle of the night, alone. . . .'

She put down the letter without finishing it, but she sat and looked at the page she had read with a sort of bewildered distaste. She felt there was in Sean, and in his adoration of Arion, some quality beyond her understanding and acceptance. It was, she admitted to herself, outside her experience, yet she would not admit that, whilst it remained so, it must always place Sean, himself, outside the range of her experience. She turned over the remaining letters, reading sentences from them, in an attempt rather to extinguish this sense of a strangeness in Sean than to understand it.

She read: 'What do you want me to think? That you have been hurt so much yourself you have lost the sense of obligation towards others? Why should you expect me to tolerate from you cruelty I would not tolerate from any other person?'

The letters were without the conventional beginnings and endings. Each began without warning, abrupt outbursts of complaint, hate, adoration or accusation. They were like the letters of an unhappy lover. They were all written in Dublin. She could not understand why they had been written at all. Surely he must have seen Arion almost every day before he left for Connemara! Why write? She doubted if Arion had ever replied.

'You said that if you had hurt me you were sorry. I don't believe it. I don't believe you are capable of being sorry about anything. You are inhuman. And if you were sorry it was only a perverse exaggeration of your feelings. You will not admit to the common emotions, but let one of them catch you unawares and, to spite yourself or, perhaps, to cure yourself, you'll rub your own nose in it with morose satisfaction.'

That letter surprised her. She did not see Arion like that and could not understand Sean's doing so. But, even then, it did not enter her head to think that Sean might not be attempting to express what he believed, but merely seeking outlet for the furious accusations of his outraged will.

'You think I am absorbed by you, that I cannot do anything without you! You are mistaken. There is nothing I cannot do if I want to do it. Oh, but I hate you. Arion, I hate you. . . .'

This was embarrassing. She pushed the letters back into their pigeon holes. Abruptly she switched off the light and rose and went to the windows overlooking the street.

The letters had disturbed her in a strange way that had lifted the upper bitterness from her own sense of desolation. She felt receded into herself and yet disturbed. For some reason she would not put her thought to the mystery of this disturbance. She wanted to avoid it.

She leaned out into the street and stared down towards the main road. All was inactive and silent. A figure appeared in the distance. She thought it was Arion and, in sudden excitement, she forgot Sean. The figure approached. It was not Arion. Only some stray Dubliner hurrying to cover. She began to doubt if Arion would return that night. He hated to be out after curfew. Because his permit gave him almost complete freedom of action, he would do nothing that would entail his taking advantage of privileges others had not got.

Because she could not think where he might be,

because he was now outside the range of her imagination, she was jealously troubled and restless.

As she moved about the dim room she whispered: 'I want ... I want ...'

But she did not know what she wanted. She felt a weary uncaring as she thought of the confusion of Sean's despair. That was not what she wanted and yet she knew it was that she was always doomed to find. Her instinct, turning her always towards the transient, had doomed her from the first to change and profitless uncertainty. She thought back over the countless procession of men who had felt her attraction. By some unaccountable instinct to avoid certainty, she had chosen those naturally fickle. She knew she had had no reality for any of them. She accepted them because for a time they were necessary to her and then it was ended because of a sudden the necessity was gone. No steadfast thing ever.

When, rarely, she was thrown into contact with the steadfast thing, it had repudiated her. What have I to do with you? And what she always wanted, more than any other thing, was a certainty of love, secure beyond the trivialities of jealousy and mood and change. The sweet comfort of the ever-to-be relied upon certainty. To that she could give everything. She knew she could love so well, but always circumstances had forced on her restraint and a false show of indifference.

Inevitably, against her will, she thought of Arion. If he had not held himself from her, perversely, it seemed now, mockingly and with cruelty, and so forced her to hold herself from him, might they not each have seen in the other his own face?

She went into the bedroom and threw herself on to his bed. She listened for him, alert for his return. Again and again she seemed to hear the front door open and footsteps ascending the stairs, but they never materialized. At last she slept.

When, at midnight, she awoke shivering with cold, she thought someone was standing by the bed. She whispered: 'Arion.' But there was no answer. When she put out her hand and touched only the empty air, she bent her head in a vehemence of tears.

The last train left the station. The backs of houses slid past; then fields; then close-mown grassland set with occasional great trees like a park. In the last gilding of the evening light, golfers moved with a stiff, clean-cut Grecian air like sensate statuary. Colours darkened. Blue displaced red. On a dim edged hill a tree rushed up like a black rocket to enhance the sky's height and brilliance. When it was a little darker, the train suddenly jerked to a standstill.

No one took much notice at first but it became evident that something was the matter and people put their heads out of the little old yellow wooden carriages, dimly gas-lit, and shouted down towards the engine. Soon someone jumped out on to the line and walked along the track. Others followed. Arion sat still until his patience was exhausted, then, in the chill of impatience, he sprang out of the carriage. The deep, soft Prussian blue of the twilight smeared the outline of the group before the engine. Only the glow of the tender outlined here and there a head or back or a gesticulating hand.

Arion, quiet, unobtrusive, frozen in the furious anguish of his impatience, moved round the crowd until a gap showed him the cause of the delay.

Two masked men with revolvers were trying to prevent the driver, stoker and guard from moving a tree trunk they had placed across the line. As Arion came up they were arguing in a friendly, humorous way because the driver was something of a Sinn Feiner himself.

Arion stood and listened to them. At another time he knew he would have been entertained by the adventure and stored it up for recounter, but now he heard them with a disinterested dispassion that he felt might at any moment rise into a furious, shouting demand that the tree trunk be moved at once and the driver return to his post and the train get on its way. . . . At once, at once!

He knew he had time and to spare. The Liverpool boat would not get in before dawn and when he got to Belfast, he would have to go to an hotel or walk the streets half the night. They could waste three or four hours here and he would still be in time, yet he trembled in the tormenting need to go on.

One of the wreckers suggested that the driver should go with them and get a drink in some village a mile away. The guard and stoker thought it a fine idea. Why shouldn't they all go together? As they started moving off, the crowd, that had been half-laughing before, began to protest. Arion, small, pale, dark-clad, unobtrusive, urged on their protest with silent fury but he could not speak himself. He could not say anything.

The men shouted replies over their shoulders to the

crowd but continued into the darkness. They started climbing over the fence into the field. They were going.

Suddenly the woman standing beside Arion called to them to come back for the sake of Christ and all the saints. Her son was lying in the prison hospital at Belfast with a bullet in his lungs. He'd been arrested for shooting an accursed Orangeman....

The driver paused.

... She'd been sent for because he was dying. He wouldn't last the night, they said. Maybe now he was calling for her and her stranded here whilst they went off a mile to get a drink — and him dying in prison for shooting a Protestant!

The wreckers and the stoker and guard came back out of the darkness into the light and the crowd cried shame on them that they could let the poor boy die without a last sight of his mother. In a guilty, foolish way the men set to clearing the line whilst the guard, suddenly officious, ordered the passengers back to their seats. Arion turned, and the woman went beside him. She said laughingly: 'I've got no son at all, but if them lot had been off for a drink it's all night we'd have been sitting here and longer.'

Arion felt grateful and friendly towards her, yet he could not speak. His relief had set a nerve galloping in his chest, but the strain remained. He was not arrived yet. His impatience returned when the train stopped at Drogheda and later at Dundalk. He peered out at the stale, foggy-looking stations and his toes twitched in his shoes. When they arrived at last he made straight for the docks and inquired the time the

Liverpool steamer was due to berth. He had six hours to wait.

The streets were foggy and lit by dirty yellow lights. The cobble stones gleamed damply. There was a film of damp over the black brickwork of the houses. It was a foreign town to him. He seemed to move through an unvarying labyrinth of cobbled streets skirted by works and offices and dead-eyed houses. The street lamps shone on the black window panes. Surely there was no human life behind them? As he turned a corner he came with surprise upon a group of three civilians, holding lanterns, and a policeman silently watching a man half-way up a ladder who was covering a house-side with great brushfuls of paint. Five paint pots, with a brush in each, stood on the ground near the wall. As Arion approached to watch, the men eyed him suspiciously. His impatience was now sufficiently exhausted to allow him to feel here hostility where in the South he would have met friendly interest.

What did he want? They looked at him steadily and he stood as though unaware of them. One of the men held a revolver turned towards him; he pretended not to notice it and stood with his hands in his pockets, watching the painter on the ladder. These hours of waiting mattered so little, living in them he was beyond danger. They had no real significance. They were merely to be lived through and got rid of.

The man on the ladder was painting a picture of King William crossing the Boyne on a white horse. He had drawn the horse well. It was a living beast, stepping daintily out of the blue and white ripples of the water. But the king, outstretching his sword, had a wooden

look. The satisfied artist, the most difficult part done,
was now slashing on the sky from a pot marked
'Celestial Blue'.

The audience kept its attention on Arion. It was
not only possible but probable that he was a Fenian
and would shoot their artist the moment they glanced
aside and gave him a chance to draw a gun. Arion
stood imperturbable. Time was passing. Nothing else
mattered.

The man on the ladder called over his shoulder:
'What shall I write on top?'

The policeman said: 'Write "To Hell with the
Pope." ' And he glared defiantly at Arion. To the
amazement of them all Arion started to speak. He
spoke in his quiet, beautiful voice:

'In the Middle Ages and in the land war days, the
Pope was the chief bulwark of British rule in Ireland.'

The man on the ladder looked round in indignation
and amazement. The others stared for a whole minute
before any of them could find breath to say: 'It's a lie.'

'No. The truth — I assure you,' continued Arion
quite seriously. 'In 1154 Adrian IV gave Henry permission to go on a sort of crusade into Ireland and
subject the people to laws.'

'It's a bloody lie,' said the man with the revolver.

Arion, smiling, gave a little amused shake of his head.

'You're English!' someone accused him. Arion
agreed.

'The English want to sell us to the South,' said the
man on the ladder. Again Arion shook his head, smiling,
scarcely a movement and yet undeniable denial.

The man with the revolver said: 'It was Carson himself that said so. He said we were basely betrayed, faith! and so we were. And when the traitor came to Belfast, me and my mates were standing on the bridge and we said: "Throw him into the Lagan." And we crowded round the car and his face went white. He knew we would do it, too. But his wife was with him and she was frightened, so we let him go.'

Arion smiled his interest. He was safely here and time was passing. Let anything happen if only it passed the time. The others were beginning to feel his attraction. They were moving towards him, on the point of speaking, when suddenly the policeman, feeling himself overlooked, said authoritatively: 'Come on now, boys, hurry up.'

The man up the ladder scrawled across the top of his painting: 'To Hell with the Pope'. Then he climbed down and they all stood in a row on the kerb and admired the completed picture. It had a curious sort of untutored beauty, naïve and decorative as a primitive. The man was something of an artist and conscious of it.

'Well! What do you think of it?' He turned on Arion and ignored the others.

'The horse is good,' said Arion.

'You're one that knows all about painting?' queried the man anxiously.

'Something,' smiled Arion, 'not all.'

'Perhaps you come from London?'

'Yes, I come from London.'

'Then you must have been to some of the great art galleries there, sure? I've heard there's some fine art galleries in London, but there's a fine one in Belfast, too.'

'There is that,' said the man with the revolver, 'and with some fine pictures in it.' He gave his head a half twist of grave relish. 'I haven't been myself,' he added, 'but I'm always meaning to go one day.'

'Come along, come along,' interrupted the impatient policeman, 'there's not one of you should be out at this hour, much less painting house-sides and carrying fire-arms. If you don't lift up your paint pots, Dick MacNeil, I'll take the lot of them to the station and you with them.' He ignored Arion.

The artist started unhurriedly to collect together his pots. Arion helped him. The man with the revolver and the third man, who had not spoken, took the ladder between them. The policeman, on the very edge of the kerb, stood with his back taut. Only the very slightest inclination of his head acknowledged the reward the artist slipped to him. As the men, Arion with them, moved away, he turned his back on them and sauntered with ponderous steps in the opposite direction.

Arion carried three of the paint pots. They all walked in silence to the end of the road where the two carrying the ladder departed with mysterious signs and nods.

'How far have you to go?' Arion asked the painter.

'I live out of the town on the Holywood road.' The man held out his hand for his pots. 'It's a good step from here.'

'Can I come with you?'

'If you like,' laughed the man. He was twice the size of Arion and felt no need to fear him.

'Aren't you afraid I might have a revolver in my pocket?'

'No. I'm not afraid of anything,' replied the man.

'Then let us go,' said Arion. They turned the corner into a long and dreary street of small houses. The street terminated its parallel lines of grimed brick and broken-down iron railings in the black void of a railway arch.

The man started talking, trying to convince Arion that he had been wrong about the Pope. The man talked steadily, but Arion did not listen to him. His own thoughts were more interesting.

'... and I've got a tumbler at home with a picture of Carson on it and underneath is written: "It seems to us as clear as glass the Home Rule Bill will never pass." And Carson's always right, isn't he?'

'Invariably. That is what you want me to say, isn't it?'

'And the Home Rule Bill never will pass. You can take my word for it. They've been fighting a losing battle right from the start. Why? The English can go on indefinitely. They can go on until every shot in the South is fired and every rebel dead and still have men and shots to spare. The Fenians might just as well try and drink up the sea. If they did they'd only burst their bellies in the doing of it and the sea would still be there none the shallower.'

They came up to the black mouth of the railway arch. The iron Victorian structure hung ponderously above their heads doubling the darkness. Their footsteps clanged against the girders. Arion glanced at his companion to see if he would step aside from him in this darkness as from an enemy. But the man was too ab-

sorbed by his own talk to remember the first suspicion
of Arion. He started to plead his own cause now
instead of damning his enemy's:

'And are we not in the right?' he asked. 'Are we not
in the right?'

'Of course,' nodded Arion. 'But what difference
does that make?'

'We want to remain loyal to England.'

'But why, when England wants to betray you so
basely?'

The man started involved explanation skirting with
difficulty the one truth — their hatred of the Catholic
South. Arion did not really listen. He did not want to
know why they wanted to remain loyal to England; he
did not care. He was in a trance of uncaring about
anything but the passing of time. The man's voice,
earnest, swift, insistent, rose and fell beside him with
a certain conviction, but Arion remained detached and
unexalted.

He was beginning to wish himself alone. It seemed
to him that this man's voice interrupted the flow of
time. It was as though the fine, black line of time,
quiveringly sensitive, deeper than the abyss, was scoured
out of alignment by the past-brushing flight of the
Milky Way.

Can we say that this is Arion? This unresponding
shell? No. Arion walked the waters where they broke
in froth against the Isle of Man. Out from the escarp-
ment the light's eye is directed, nerveless as a search-
light, to rest an instant on the tiny ship looped from
bows to stern with its girdle of portholes. Though one
pluck at the ship with a million threads of thought,

though one's whole will become a cable to draw it to its berth, the ship moves not a jot faster.

Tortoise-cautious, steadily, steadily, it crawls without a quiver of its girdle of blond beads. And it is better so. There is no knowing what evil an undue haste might accomplish. Cautiously, then, avoid the Siren's rocks, with all care navigate that you strike not Scylla or descend Charybdis. Cautiously. I fear to breathe lest my will disturb the cosmos and all be lost.

'. . . and they took out the father and the two sons and they stood them in a row at the foot of the garden and shot each one of them in the stomach. They were six hours dying in agony and all that time the Fenians made the mother and daughter stand there and watch. And they lay there amongst the cabbages and currant bushes all the time. . . .'

Five hours separate us. If they were five miles I could traverse them; if I went slowly I could lengthen them and if I ran I could shorten them. But, alas, they are five hours and all my effort can dock no inch of them. I could sit down here by the roadside or run myself exhausted, they would remain uninfluenced and only the hands of my watch can traverse them.

The ship is at the end of a rope five hours long and, though I distract the air with my impatience, it can only be wound into me as swiftly or as slowly as move the hands of my watch. Round and round move the hands of my watch, a capstan winding in the five-hour long cable. . . .

The rain began to fall in a powdery fine shower. Arion noted it petulantly. 'Rain,' he said. 'It's always raining in this country.' When he was a child he had been delicate and had lived most of his life in Italy. He still looked delicate, always more ill than well, and the wet air gave his face a greyish tinge.

But the Irishman would see no fault in his country: 'What would you have?' he asked. 'The sun all day without a blink, like an electric light?'

Arion looked at his watch — not five hours now, only four and a half. Ah! Control your nerves into tranquillity!

Speech is easy enough. For these hours I can occupy myself only by wishing them away. Count sixty and there's a minute gone.

Think! When you come to die you'll beg for the hours you are wishing away.

I don't care.

'This is where I live,' said the man. There was a light in the hall illuminating the coloured glass of the front door. 'Won't you come in now for a cup of tea? My wife will be waiting up and she'll fry us some bacon and potato bread.'

'No. No, thank you,' Arion refused vaguely.

The man, mistaking his vagueness for polite hesitation, urged him to come. Arion was surprised by his persistence. Can't you see I am not here in time, but perched beyond reach on a black peak of eternity watching the hours like bubbles approach, each in turn, swell into sight, encompass me with senses, then pass out of memory.

'Come in until the rain stops, anyway.'

'Where does this road lead?' asked Arion. 'Will it take me to the sea?'

'Any of these turnings on the left will take you down

to the Lough, but if you want the sea proper, it's a good way.'

'I have plenty of time.'

'This road will lead you to Carrickmoy. That's where the Lough meets the sea. But it's a good hour's walk or more. If you want to pass the time you'd be better inside and you could get a sleep on the sofa.'

Arion shuddered at the danger of being tempted into sleep and not waking in time. He moved from the man, bearing his protests only because they were prelude to escape.

And at last he was away, walking out of sight of the town and under the cloudy foliage. Here the summer was retarded by the winds; the branches swayed in a mist of tiny leaves. It was still spring. The intermittent rain drifted about in the air, sometimes clouding the sky with a mist that parted to reveal a spangling of stars.

The way was still lined with houses, separately set in gardens back from the road. It was not until he passed through a village of old houses that he came at length to the complete darkness of the country. Then he felt free to think. The wet air was full of the scent of gorse and earth. He breathed it eagerly and, as though with the intoxication of oxygen, his thought broke free like a parachute, opening and cupping the air and holding him suspended above earth.

In his survey he sought the calmly ploughing little steamer. Perhaps another half an hour was gone and only four were left. That proves if you can but wait long enough, even time passes.

Was she sleeping now? Or was she reading —

propped up on one elbow as he had so often seen her before, the ribbon of her night-gown slipped over her shoulder, her white shoulder and breast leaving him untroubled. Strange, that for all his restless desire for her when parted from her, he could see her so, untroubled, almost with tranquillity, where another woman — Elizabeth, say, or some other such — would entice him almost beyond bearing.

She'd be no more asleep than he was. She would be sitting up with the first book he had given her. In it he had written: 'Now you are new enough to excite me so I am pleased and pleasing. But were you to live with me, then you would see me as I suppose I am; or, rather, as I am not but circumstances can make me seem — disagreeable, perverse, mocking, spiteful, morose, priggish, silent, self-pitying, scornful, refusing to understand. You would have to accept me in all those masks.'

But even then he had known that, with her, he would wear none of them.

At first, could he have said anything that would have made her turn from him, he would have said it, or tried to say it. He had felt a desperate nervousness after their meeting. Living before it wholly of himself, working slowly and with difficulty towards an independent fulfilment, he had hesitated at this sudden promise of a complete and unlabouring fulfilment. Disqualifying as it did, his difficult achievement, he hesitated. As the sentiment of small savings, painfully acquired, can, when threatened by absorption in some vast inheritance, display a disproportionate value, so his achievement held him an instant in a vague nervousness of regret.

An instant. The habit of wealth is rapidly acquired.

But nothing he could have said would have troubled her immediate acceptance of him. At once she had accepted in him his unusually delicate sensibility; and his kindliness given readily when required, never refused, and yet, when unrequested, withheld carefully that it might not, even for a moment, intrude. She had disclosed his perfection without comment. It was himself, and no more than she had expected. There need be no thought to protect from her the perfection of his essential self.

It was not that she had changed him. She had known that he was so. And he was so. Disregarding all his protective masks, she had acknowledged at once his perfection so there was between them no possibility of doubt, but the complete gentleness and generosity of trust.

Who could be content to be less than perfect? What is there to be sought but that freedom to be perfect that is the freedom to remain unirritated and unresenting?

A relationship beyond accusation or the need to accuse. A vindication. But a dependency. So he had fled it, like a fool.

Incredible folly!

And now, supposing the boat were to sink! A storm. No need even for that. A shifting of cargo and then the list growing until, suddenly, the heel over, and she trapped in a cabin.

She was not a strong woman. He brooded over her physical frailty. So small a thing can bring the heart to a sudden standstill. He saw her fall and carried to some desolate Liverpool hospital.

Always this haunting of possible loss, this not to be borne loss that insisted its possibility, its inevitability, so darkly in the night and the early, bitter and sleepless morning hours!

Now there remained in him no frigid wisdom counselling flight from her. Only this need to fly to her and reassure himself that she was still living, tangible and unharmed.

Had she known this when she had wired to him? Did she, knowing so much, know why he had left England?

Three-quarters of an hour gone now, at least. No, nearly an hour, for he was descending into a town. Street lamps were appearing. He could see over the tiered houses down to a black pool that must be the sea.

The street lamps showed the houses were a northern grey, built strongly against the wind. This must be Carrickmoy. He had never heard of it before. Elizabeth had never spoken of it to him. It was strange and without interest for him or associations. He hurried down between the houses to the release of the sea. He came at last to the broad sea wall and, leaning over, stared down at the movement of the black waters. An arm of rock curved round the bay, beyond was the gaping Lough mouth. The steamer would pass here on its way up to Belfast.

Do you remember when we drove out of London one summer evening and stopped near a village in Hertfordshire and looked at a house to let? Do you remember it? — with its white Georgian portico and the great waxen-leafed magnolia threaded between the rows of flat windows? The brick was a deep, Pompeian red, flecked all over with tiny green lichen. For some reason we could not tell, we had liked it better than any other house we knew. Going over it we had played a game — Supposing, when we were young and unmarried, we had met and married one another and come to live here! We would have furnished this room in this way; that room in that way. . . . Here we would have done this, here that. . . . Here we would have slept, here sat, here dined, here played with our children. We had gone laughing from room to room until, in the long, sunlit library with its glass doors opening on to the lawn, you had said: 'And when I died you would not bury me out there in the graveyard, but here in the garden where those white poppies are growing.' And I had said: 'And in the winter when the nights came early, when the wind and the snow came, I would sit by the fire here and think of you until at last I would have to rise and go to the window and look out at your grave alone there in the cold darkness and the winter rain.'

It was then it had overwhelmed me unbearably — the possibility of losing you. I had caught my breath, stunned as though I had bitten in the crown of a tooth.

You looked at me as though I had frightened you and touched my arm and said in a bewildered way: 'What is the matter?'

At once I had shaken you off and said: 'Don't touch me. I can't bear contacts.' And you were not hurt and did not give a thought to your pride. We had just locked the place up and returned the keys to the caretaker without saying anything more about it. It was soon after that I disappeared. . . .

He moved slowly along by the wall. The big sand-
stone squares of the wall were weathered with hollows
in which sea-water and rain-water collected. On the
other side of the road were the tall, flat-fronted houses,
grey, solid and upright against the gales. The shops
had the casual, rather forsaken air of seaside shops. He
thought it a dreary place. He stood beneath a lamp-
post and looked at his watch. Only two more hours.
He could soon begin walking back again.

An inner wall of excitement sustained him so he had
forgotten he could feel fatigue. He crossed a few yards
of bald grass in which was set a shelter and a small iron
bandstand, and came to an old pier. It stretched out
darkly into the dark waters. A tramp steamer rocked
beside it. He could see from it another pier, new and
white, and, between the two, lay a small, square harbour
of sluggish water and ebony sand. He followed the
wall to where the wild rocks were outflung like plough-
shares furrowing the sea. The smell of the wrack was
strong and harsh. He looked back at the houses piled
up round the coast curve like the steps of an amphi-
theatre. They stared out over his head to the sea. In
this town he had seen no living thing — not even a
policeman or a marauding cat. The houses might all
be empty and the inhabitants dead for all the sign they
gave. He was glad of that. It enhanced the unreality
of these hours that he was willing away.

He stopped and looked at his watch again. Only an
hour and a half. He began to walk back quickly. Yes,
that was the danger when you had too much time to
spare; you usually wasted it so damned effectively you
ended by being late after all.

He made his way up the slope of the main street and heard ringingly through the silence the steady approach of feet from a side road. Oh God, now he was going to be challenged! He began at once to take out his permit that his delay might be the less. But the footsteps turned on their traces and he went on unhindered. The return journey seemed interminable. Whenever there was light enough he looked at his watch and renewed his speed.

The sky began to pale as he approached the city again. The light came, throwing upon the skyline, as upon a white screen, the monstrous shapes of the shipping yards. The rain had stopped. The wet, cobbled streets had a bleached and strange, foreign air in the dawn. They were portentous now there was no time to waste.

He came to the quayside as the steamer approached her berth at a majestic crawl, lazily throwing to either side a long, sleek, oily ripple. She came alongside. Ropes were thrown ashore to lasso the bollards. They tautened and creaked with the strain, but held. The ship's side grated against the quay. In the half-light the dim, infernal figures of the sailors moved about and shouted to one another. The main mast swayed a little against a delicate sky before it stilled. The gangways were thrown out and the steerage passengers, who had been up all night and were blue with cold and sleeplessness, filed ashore.

He thought: 'She's still asleep. She won't come yet.' He walked to the end of the quay and sat down on some packing cases and buried his face in his hands. He felt sick and a little apprehensive now.

After a few minutes he heard someone coming towards him and pause in front of him. He jerked up his head. She put out her hand and he caught hold of it. They stood smiling and looking at one another. Then she sat down and he sat beside her. She said: 'How is your wife?'

He said: 'Quite well. She has taken a house in Majorca.'

'And the children?'

'Well, too. How is your husband?'

'Just the same. You will see him. He is meeting me here at eight o'clock.'

'What is he doing here?'

'Some political business. I will stay the day with an aunt I have here and then go back with him to-night.'

There was very little to be said. They sat in silence that was like a sort of tranquil oblivion.

After a while she said: 'Were you surprised when you got my wire?'

'Not a bit. I knew it was coming. I knew I would soon see you again.'

'Are you coming back to London?'

'Yes.'

They sat quite still and silent with their hands touching. It seemed to Arion only a few minutes had passed since their meeting, when she arose and said: 'Eight o'clock is striking. We must walk along to the gangway as though we had just come off the ship.'

They had scarcely reached the gangway when a tall, overbearingly handsome man appeared and greeted Arion jovially: 'My dear fellow! What are you doing here? I thought you were in Dublin.'

'I had some business in Liverpool last night. I'm off now to catch my train back.'

'We'll see you to it.'

Arion walked between them as they crossed the cobbled streets to the station. The husband talked all the time. He was a Member of Parliament and here on some important concern.

'... that I cannot disclose at the moment, old chap. But you'll hear all about it in a day or two. I spent a couple of hours with Carson last night. I think we can all hope for an amicable agreement soon.' He had the declamatory confidence and optimistic air of the practised public speaker. Arion and the woman, both small of stature, quiet and unobtrusive in manner, seemed dwarfed beneath the dominion of his voice. They glanced at one another with an amused smile.

Arion's train was in. He found a compartment, then looked out of the window at the woman and the large, impressive man who attracted attention wherever he went.

'When are you coming back to London?' asked the man.

'Soon,' smiled Arion. 'Soon, soon.'

'Give us a ring the evening you arrive and come round and have dinner.'

'I should like to.'

'Yes, do.'

'Good-bye.'

'Good-bye.'

The woman had not spoken. She waved, smiling. The station slid out of sight. Arion turned back to the compartment to find two other people had got into it from the corridor whilst his back was turned. He brushed past them to find a compartment in which he could be alone. He went up and down the length of the train and it seemed to him men and women were talking in every compartment. He was sick of the Irish and their incessant talk.

He stood in the corridor and looked out of the window. The tranquillity into which she had eased him was failing before these assailing voices. He was tired of the Irish as he had been so often tired of the English and of all humanity. He had no love for his father's people — the English — nor for his mother's — the Scotch. There was French and Hungarian blood in his family. Hybrid, cosmopolitan, over-intelligent, untroubled by patriotism, he had all his life been conscious that he was alien in all the countries through which he had spent his youth travelling. Each place in turn had wearied him so he was still unclaimed.

He stood in a maze of troubled thought. He began to think of his wife. He had never for a moment questioned why he had married her. He had known from the beginning that nature, with her plebeian adoration of the average and her disregard of individuals, was tricking him into misery for her own ends. Of all the women he might have married, he had married the one who had with him no thought in common, no common interest, nothing that would bear them through middle-age when passion was spent. He had married, knowing the marriage must end in severance or wretchedness; but before that its purpose was accomplished. The children were begotten, sustaining in their qualities — a mixture of his and her's — the desired equilibrium.

That was all that mattered and, accomplished, the instruments could cut one another's throats for all nature cared.

He realized the trick of physical attraction, yet knew that, were he young again and desire the strongest force in him, he would marry again for it. For without it, all other perfections offered no more than dust, but with it, all imperfections were, for the time, acceptable.

But desire was no longer the strongest force in him.

He thought wearily of his obligation to help Sean; of Elizabeth whom he could never refuse whilst she was at hand to be accepted. He did not give a thought to having found them together. They were children playing and meant nothing to him.

Now that the first amusement was gone, he thought wearily of having still to take part in the game. If only someone would throw over the board so the moves were lost. . . .

But he had no hope of escaping so easily. He could only hope that Riordan would fail to appear or the truce, of which there was so much talk, be declared at once and get them all out of the wretched muddle.

He stared unappeased out at the beautiful turn of the dark blue clouds over the Mountains of Mourne. All he wanted now was to return to his flat in Hampstead and the familiar streets in which he could meet her shopping or with her children. He felt an impatience with all the things that held him here.

He started walking up and down the corridor again and found an empty carriage he had overlooked before. Making himself comfortable in a corner, he fell asleep. He slept until Dublin was reached.

As he came down the road from the station an armoured car drew up at the kerb and an English voice hailed him:

'Arion.'

Arion stopped. A familiar profile, proud, clear-cut and intelligent, was held towards him whilst the eye strained back to see him.

'Have you paid a visit to the Castle yet?' asked Wheeler.

'No, nor have I tried to commit suicide,' smiled Arion, his charm suddenly returned.

'Jump in,' said Wheeler. 'I'll give you something to write about.'

Arion jumped in. The armoured door closed on him.

In a few minutes they came to the barrier of steel plates and barbed wire entanglements that fenced the Castle. The gate opened, and, as they entered, a hail of bullets, from the watchful gunmen, struck the steel encasing them.

FRIDAY

As Sean made to cross Little Ship Street he was obliged
to pause and let an armoured car pass. He looked
through its windscreen and saw Arion seated between
the driver and a young, laughing and talking Black and
Tan officer. After an instant's shocked, involuntary
pause, he started to run after it and so was scarcely a
hundred yards from it when it passed through the
Castle gates. He heard the twang of the assailing
bullets and the swift close-to of the gates. They shut.

He stood in the middle of the road staring at them.
After a few minutes a cyclist, ringing furiously, skidded
round him and swore at him. He stared about him,
dazed, then crossed to the pavement. He had forgotten
where he had been going when the car appeared. He
began slowly to retrace his steps towards Bride Street.
Some of the people he passed turned and stared after
him, but he was unaware that he passed anyone. Without surprise he found himself back on the quay from
which he had started half an hour before. He walked
beside the river to O'Connell Bridge, then crossed to
the other side and stopped at a bookshop. Someone
caught his arm. He half-turned. It was Daly.

'I thought it was you,' said Daly.

Sean stared at him vaguely.

'You're not looking yourself at all? Is anything the
matter?'

'No. I'm perfectly well,' replied Sean.

'It's to-morrow you go?'

Sean stared at him without answering.

'Look here!' exclaimed Daly, concerned. 'If you don't feel like going, sure one of us could go instead.'

'I am going,' said Sean.

'Well, of course, if you've made up your mind! What time do you leave?'

'To-morrow morning. I'm going by train.'

'But I thought you were going in Arion's car.'

'I've changed my mind.'

'Why? Is anything the matter?'

'No. Nothing.'

Daly looked at him queerly for a moment then turned aside his head. 'It would be better if you took the car,' he said, 'someone might recognize Riordan in the train. Your bringing him back by car was the whole point of your meeting him there at all.'

'I know what I'm doing,' said Sean.

'You've no right to take risks that might mean the end of all of us.'

'I must take unavoidable risks,' said Sean in a curiously dull and even voice.

'Has Arion refused to lend you the car?'

'No.'

'Then why is your travelling by train unavoidable?'

Sean stood for a full minute looking over Daly's shoulder at a string of barges laden with barrels that were sliding down the river. 'Because the car has broken down,' he said at last.

Daly twisted his lip in frank unbelief: 'Can't something be done to it before to-morrow?'

'No.'

'Take it round to my brother's garage and I'll bet you anything you like he'll take the whole inside out and put in a new one if you want it, by to-morrow.'

Sean turned on him an agonized look, so Daly was silenced. He put out his hand to grip Sean's elbow, but Sean moved slightly and was out of reach.

'What's the matter, Sean?' asked Daly in a changed voice.

'Nothing. Nothing.'

'Oh, very well!' Daly shrugged his shoulders and moved off.

Sean watched him pushing past the loiterers at the bookstall, knowing he was off to find O'Rorke and Finnigan and Sharp and rouse them to anger at the change of plans.

'Daly.'

Daly paused. Sean hurried to him: 'I want to tell you I'm meeting Riordan at the Pier at Costello, near Galway.'

'Why are you telling me that now?'

'I thought you ought to know. I want you to tell all of them.' Yes, they must all know so there might be no certainty who was betrayer if they were betrayed.

'They all know.'

'But how did they find out!'

'Arion met Sharp one day and told him and Sharp told everyone.'

'But Arion must have known it was best not to let them all know.'

'What makes you think he would see any reason for keeping it a secret? Why should he see any reason for keeping anything a secret? It's all without significance for him. It's just a game.'

'That's nonsense,' interrupted Sean, suddenly angry. 'He knows this isn't a game. He knows we're deadly serious.'

'Everything's a game to the English, but they're children and take games seriously. Arion's a rare sort of thing. He's a grown-up Englishman, so he doesn't take anything seriously.'

'I'm grown-up and I take this seriously.'

'It isn't a game to you.'

'Nor to Arion.'

'Wait until he tires of it and then see.'

Sean stood so long without speaking that Daly turned and left him.

Men and girls rounding the corner for a walk by the quay in their luncheon hour, jostled Sean until he was obliged to move. He started walking about the streets again. He saw a tram-car and boarded it and went and sat on the top in the hope of escaping humanity. But the conductor followed him up and demanded a fare. He gave him twopence without asking where it would take him and then, alone again, relaxed into a dream of unthinking. He felt a thin whistle of air on his cheek and saw in the pane beside him a bullet hole no bigger than a threepenny bit rayed with cracks round which a circle had been drawn with a diamond. It gave him a curious, shrill stab of pleasure, a relief to imagine that he had been sitting here when the shot was fired and it had lodged in his brain. He was dead though staying here a little while until he had gathered strength to go forth boldly into freedom.

At the next stop three revolting little girls came stamping up the stairs and settled themselves restlessly a few seats from him. They were chewing sweets. They chewed loudly, opening and shutting their lips with wide, smacking movements. They kept sniffing and giggling and turning round to stare at him.

He stared steadily from them in disgust, hating them. He hated children. He hated it when, at a party, a child was brought into the room and attracted the attention from him; and all children, feeling his resentment, responded instantly with distrust. And he hated adolescents with their affectations. And he hated these half-grown, giggling, snuffling, chewing, smelly, dirty, little girls.

But he would not let them drive him off the tram. He sat still, pretending not to see them until at last, with squawking agitation, they all tumbled over one another down the steps, staring at him with open mouth and eyes until the floor hid him from their sight.

Thank God! He relaxed again. But the tram-car did not move. The conductor came up the stairs and shouted at him suspiciously: 'Where do you want to go?'

He descended, too angry to speak, and found himself opposite the entrance to the Zoological Gardens. Out of sheer purposelessness, he paid his money and passed through the turnstile. When he was inside he saw, to his horror, that the three wretched, unforgivable, female brats had preceded him in. They still gaped at him. He felt they were hanging round waiting to see which way he would go, so they could follow him. To be followed would be unendurable.

He stood in frozen anger looking across the grass to the river with its water-fowls and grasses, until the children were obliged by sheer boredom to seek out a more animate and less hostile creature for their contemplation. When they trailed off, the anger, that had tautened all his nerves, released him and he stepped forward, freed from it as from an iron cage.

He stood at the water's edge and looked at the little gathering of birds that were watching him intently, supposing he had come to feed them.

The black swan, with its rose-coloured beak and a golden glint between the feathers of its delicately arched neck, rode like a galleon at anchor, pretending indifference, yet cautiously watching, alert to be the first to snap if anything edible appeared. Around him, without any pretence, quivered the anxious ducks, whiter than snow, suède white and flawless, quivering and quacking, always hungry.

'I'm sorry,' he said. He really was sorry. He felt guilty and ungenerous, standing there looking and giving nothing.

As though they had understood him, the ducks began to move off, one behind the other, each drawing after it from either side of its breast a long ripple of water. Each duck with its ripples formed an arrow-head in the water. The water was full of arrow heads.

From behind a clump of greyish grasses came a fleet of some sort of birds he could not recognize. They had a Chinese look with their neatly placed feathers of a brilliant ginger-brown. Each wore a white collar dividing the ginger feathers from the black and glistening head feathers. For all their exotic look, they waggled their tails as invitingly as the everyday ducks. After them came the little black coots . . .

'I'm sorry,' said Sean.

. . . and after them came edging round the hard, yellow stems of the grasses a chunk of waterlogged bread.

'There!' cried Sean, pointing to it. 'Look!' But they would not look. Only one of the coots glanced at it and back again as though wondering why he had been asked to look.

'Here, silly ducks!' The bread, with its pale, swollen crust, looked pathetic. It would be happier eaten. 'Look, bread!'

He knelt down and made waves with his hand and washed the bread out into the open. Before any of the others saw it, the swan bent languidly forward and swallowed it at a gulp. Seeing one beak filled, the others perked up with renewed hope and eagerness.

Some sea-gulls from the river walked about the grass at his feet and raised their thin, curved beaks to him in anticipation. Three white swans appeared and started crowding the poor little bald-headed coots into the background.

'No. Nothing, nothing, nothing.' Sean turned and ran from them like a felon, conscious of the disappointment he was leaving behind.

He passed the monkey-house. He could not bear monkeys with their self-conscious antics and one eye always turned for applause. He went to the cage of the great, white, beautiful bears. The day was sultry and the discomforted beasts in their heavy coats lay wearily in the water. He stood for a long time watching and they did not give him a glance. That pleased him. He was pleased he had come. He went to the lion house. It was in an uproar. In the end cage a lioness marched backwards and forwards in a terrifying exultation of rage. Her roars filled the house and agitated the other lions. Only the long, silken panther lay indifferently like a pool of glimmering, tropical shadow. He cared nothing for the suffering of the lioness, and the lioness cared for nothing and no one. Her fury was beyond restraint.

'Have you taken away her cubs?' he asked a keeper.

At first the man would not reply, and then he said grudgingly: 'Yes.'

'Could I see them?'

After a long pause the man grunted: 'It's impossible.'

'My name is Murtough. My father is one of the Fellows.'

After another pause, the man felt in his pockets for his keys and then unwillingly, with a sullen silence of one that is coerced, led Sean to a door. Inside were the six lion cubs huddled together in a corner of a great cage, separated by a partition from their outraged mother. The thuds of the lioness shook the partition. The cubs took no notice, but stared out with round eyes at Sean and the keeper. And Sean leant against the bar and looked at them, absorbed by them.

Birds and beasts had for him a more intense reality than human beings. Their silent and involute self-sufficiency satisfied him in a peculiar way. They did not irritate him or seek to impose on him, and when he wished to turn his back on them they would not weary him with their importunings. With them he felt, within himself, a vindicated independence. They were; and he was; and he wanted nothing from them. But with men there was no sure peace. He felt impelled by the force of his consciousness of their critical intelligence to impress himself upon them. He must be eternally portraying his possibilities. Sean, the this, the that . . . ! And then they had to try and impress themselves on him and his impatience of them became unendurable.

Unendurable.

It was only with such a rare one as Arion who accepted all with understanding and required no like acceptance in payment, that he was completely happy. What could he not do, charmed so, and no longer required to fight against exclusion?

He wished Arion were here with him now and wondered where he was.

It was with a sudden stab of remembrance that he jerked upright. He gave the keeper the half-crown he had meant to spend on his luncheon and went out into the fresh air. He still saw before him the six little flower faces of the wondering cubs, but he was thinking of Arion. His thought faded the cub faces and he saw Arion smiling with his old charm as he glanced at the young officer beside him.

Sean felt again the sick spasm of jealousy and suspicion that had distracted him. He felt hollow as though some dreadful experience lay before him.

He thought that to-morrow he must start for Galway in order to meet Riordan at Costello on Sunday morning. But that was not the thing he feared. It was as though his sub-conscious, seeking into the future, vouchsafed him not knowledge but only the dread of what it saw. Arion he knew had deserted him. He must go on now without Arion. But not for a moment would he admit fear that Arion had betrayed him. It was not possible. It was not a thing that Arion could do.

And yet might not a clever man mislead him — Sean — with flattery to bring about Riordan's destruction?

Riordan, the last of the Easter Week leaders, all of whom were revered as saints by the people; as gods, almost; as the ones who saw clearly Ireland's need was action when everyone else talked only! What hope for England were Riordan returned?

And you can find him, Sean, if no one else can. And now you have found him — no, don't tell me where he is (cunning that!) — but you will meet him on Sunday morning at Costello Pier!

And who on Sunday morning might await Riordan there?

'I will be there,' said Sean.

But the possibility of such betrayal was not a part of Arion. He knew that. Arion might tire of it all; it might be unreal for him and he turn his back on it, but he must know that Riordan's danger was a reality and all their faith in Riordan a reality!

If Arion were weary of it now and gone back to his own people, if he would help no longer, well! he, Sean, would go alone and carry it through without Arion.

Quite suddenly he was resolved.

He felt an amazing pleasure of relief. He had made up his own mind without influence. But, behind it, was the thought that when he succeeded Arion would hear of it and know that at the last he had succeeded alone. Arion would know. For no matter how short a time, Arion's whole attention would be once again concentrated upon him.

He began to feel almost happy and a little excited. He had a shilling left. He must get something to eat with it. He left the zoo and walked across the park.

The dreary morning had become a bright afternoon. The deer lay under the trees, congregated in the shade, avoiding the heat of the light-spangled grasses. Sean crept up behind them, but always as he came within a certain distance of them they rose cautiously one after the other, and all faced him. If he persisted in his advance, they would spring away with a sudden light movement as though bouncing on little, rubber feet. Then they stood still again, watching.

'No, don't run away.' Sean held out his hand. 'Don't run away,' he whispered seductively, encroaching warily under cover of the hypnotism of his voice. This time the foremost let him come to within a foot of its head before it made to leap aside. But it made to leap too late; with as sudden and as swift a movement, Sean caught its antler. It dipped its head and tried to back free, but Sean held it until it quietened into submission and stood with nervous and rather pathetic unwilling, avoiding Sean's eyes.

'I will not hurt you,' whispered Sean. 'Will not, will not, will not.'

He laid his hand on the beast's neck and felt, beneath the brittle and dry, warm hair, the fluttering and apprehensive nerves. In this exultant and vindicated mood he felt with hyper-sensitive appreciation the quality of the unknown individual in things. A wave of almost unbearable compassion swept out from him towards the captive deer, and those others grouped behind, converging as he lifted his eyes, and watching in unaiding timidity.

'To-morrow,' he whispered, 'I am going by train to Galway. And I don't want his help. Before the moment comes, you fear things, you are lost and without resolution, you would rather step back into inactivity than move forward an inch alone, you rely on the strength of another — and then, suddenly and without warning, the moment comes and all your fears fade into meaninglessness. You comprehend things so they are dangerless and you, by reason of your comprehension, are dominant and invulnerable. This is the truth — that you need fear nothing. You may do and say what you wish for whatever you do, whatever you say, you can but go on living till you die.'

He laid his cheek against the head of the deer and felt against his skin the short, sharp, sun-heated hairs. The deer did not struggle or move from him. The nerves had subsided beneath his hand. He released it. It stood still beside him.

So I go to-morrow. And I will do what I planned to do alone and without help. And when it is all accomplished I will come and see you again. Until then: Good-bye.

The deer stood and watched him go. Good-bye. Good-bye. He swung over the grass with a curiously exultant pleasure in everything.

One of the chestnut trees was still in flower. It was

covered so closely with flowers it seemed, at a distance, a toy tree carved in pink sugar. Beneath it lay six more deer. Towards them a man and a girl on horseback undulated in a slow, easy canter. Watching them, out of sound of them, it seemed to Sean they moved with the effortless silence of fish through water. The dappled deer lifted their faces, then rose and took to their heels as the riders advanced. For a while they kept ahead, so the scene seemed a hunt drawn with the ordered pageantry of a primitive frieze. Then the apprehensive deer divided and scattered; the riders, unheeding, passed on. The deer slowed and came to a standstill, looking stupid and a little ashamed.

Suddenly Sean started to run. In pleasure of his mind's liberty, he sped with long strides over the grass until he was brought up short by a fit of coughing. He had to stand and cough until it was over, then, sobered, he went on slowly.

He began to think of the days he had spent in his search in Connemara with no more to help him than the long-studied portraits of Riordan and a sort of inspired determination to find him. There was not even the certainty that Riordan was still in the West, or even that he was still in Ireland. It was only known that he had been left in the Connemara hills after his escape from Dublin and the west was the safest place for a penniless, hunted man to hide.

Arion, to help Sean, knowing his nervous and imaginative diffidence, had motored him to Clifden. He had said: 'I'll make a point of being in every evening after eight o'clock so you can telephone me if you need help or money, or, if you like, you can wire me.'

Arion would have left him the car had he wanted it, but he knew his search would not keep him to the roads and he would be freer on foot.

So, even when left alone there, Sean had felt Arion no more than a step behind him, always there to be turned to. He need only cry 'Help me', and help would come. Because of that he felt no desire to cry it. It was as though an amazing confidence had excited all his capabilities so success was inevitable.

He had intended going north to Donegal and then to the south, but first, after he had searched the likely hills, some instinct had led him to cross to the islands. He had scarcely stepped from the steamer before he was questioning the islanders on the quay: 'Is there a tall man living here; a stranger to the place; pale, with curling auburn hair?'

They had looked at one another and at once he had cried with furious, impatient excitement: 'I am a friend of his. I have been looking for him. I have got news for him.'

Someone had taken him to Riordan, whom they called O'Reilley. He remembered, as he might remember a miracle, the wonder of his success. He had swept like a wave upon Riordan to overwhelm him, to swirl round him, to catch him up into his excitement with the rapidly described details of the scheme.

This is our plan. This, this, this. We will bring you back to Dublin, keep you there secretly, then let one or two know, gradually let more know so you become a rumour and people are wondering and anticipating; keep them waiting until any hesitation they might have had is lost in impatience, then you appear to be acclaimed, to lead them, to liberate all of us. . . . You will come, of course? Of course.

He scarcely noticed then, it was afterwards he remembered with a sudden uncertainty, that Riordan had not immediately reflected his excitement, but had looked at him for a few moments with blank eyes and answered then quietly and slowly: 'Yes, I will come when you need me.'

By that time the steamer had gone back and was not due again until Wednesday. It was unthinkable that he should stay on the island a moment longer than was necessary. Was there a telephone on the island? Yes, at the post office in the village there was one — only used in matters of great urgency.

At once to telephone Arion and when at last, after maddening delay, he heard Arion's voice: 'Arion, Arion, I have succeeded. You must come for me in the car. I haven't enough money to get back to Dublin. I can't wait for you to send some. To-morrow is Sunday. There would be no end of waiting. You must come for me. If you start at once you will be in Galway in the morning. You must meet me at Costello Pier.'

Arion had said quietly, without protest or questioning: 'Very well, I will meet you there.'

And then he must get to Costello Pier — nearly three hours' row from the island. How was it to be arranged? Transported by success, he could not suppose that anything he wanted could not be arranged.

Riordan said: 'I will row you across in the morning.'

But no. He did not want Riordan to meet Arion. At least, not yet. . . . He did not know why. But he was determined Riordan should not row him across.

Riordan was indifferent. Then, if Sean wished, he could take the dinghy and row himself. If he made fast the dinghy to the pier one of the fishermen would bring it back some time next day.

Yes.

He wanted to start there and then, but was prevailed upon to wait until daylight. Riordan lived with an island family and Sean was put into their spare bedroom. But he could not sleep. He tossed restlessly, wide awake, until his agitation became unbearable. At last he went into Riordan's room.

Something about Riordan lying there with the moonlight on his face, his mouth half-open, had paused him, so he stood and stared at him, puzzled a little, not knowing what was the matter or what chilled him. Then Riordan had moved in his sleep and Sean had wakened him. He sat up sleepily.

'I'm going now,' said Sean.

Riordan yawned and got up with dull movement. 'I'll come to the shore with you.'

Out on the moon-lit road Riordan had trudged along beside him. Sean, for all the intoxication of the light and the strange hour, had felt a sort of disappointment. He wanted only to get away.

Riordan, very strong and with a ponderous sort of capability, had pulled the black dinghy down the white sand to the water and pushed Sean off. He waved good-bye.

'Next Sunday morning at daybreak at the pier.'

Sean had rowed well once but not for some years. At first he was awkward with the oars, but soon enough it became easy. He pulled away until Riordan was out

of sight and he could revert from worried consciousness of him to thought of Arion approaching Costello
as he was approaching it. Not for a moment did he
fear that Arion would fail to come.

A mist had covered the sea at dawn, so he lost his
way and, for all his early start, was late at the pier.
And when at last he had found it and called to Arion,
who had he seen but that girl, that Elizabeth Dearborn
who had, in some mysterious way, got a hold on Arion
during his absence! It seemed to him it was from the
moment of her appearance that morning that things
had started to go wrong.

He thought of her in a sullen, resentful way; and of
her ineffable physical attraction to which, at times,
even he had half succumbed. He was suspicious of her
and of it. He could not honestly suppose she had been
instrumental in getting Arion to go with an English
officer to the Castle — but there was no knowing. She
had come from the North and was probably a Protestant.
If so, he felt her capable of anything.

Now he was out of the park and between streets
again. He was very hungry, but it was getting late and
the public-house where he ate his meals would be
closed. He could never eat the food in the cheap eating
houses. He went to a restaurant in Grafton Street
where women congregated to take tea in the after-
noons and he had sometimes gone with his mother.

It was too late for luncheon. He had to content
himself with buttered toast and tea. At another time
he would have hated being in this place, but now he did
not mind. It was, after all, quite a good place. For
once he was not irritated by the unceasing talk of the

women. Why should they not talk if they wished? He felt an easy amusement at his own tolerance. He poured out more tea. At another time he would have shut out their chatter in fury of it, but now, when he had eaten, he lit a cigarette and leant back in his chair in sympathetic willingness to listen to anything that might impinge itself upon his ears.

'... so we started quarrelling again and he said "This life is unbearable, I'll go and drown myself in the river", and I said "Sure there's not much point in doing that whilst you've still got a shilling for a seat at the cinema, it's just a waste of money ..."'

'... My father was eighty-five yesterday. It's a great age, isn't it? The other day he sat and stared at me until I said, "What are you staring at, Da?" and he said in a funny sort of way: "I was just thinking to myself: You're my daughter and you're an old woman." There now, what do you think of that?' 'Och away, woman, you're not old at all. He was blethering. Not a bit of ye's old.' 'But it's true, Anna, I'm not so young as I was.' 'Well, what of it anyway? It's a relief to be getting on in years and not to have to worry all the time about your figure or your skin. If I feel like having a slab of chocolate cream now, I just have it ...'

'... It was last winter I got them, and he said: "You're not to sleep with them in all night. You're to take them out and give the gums a rest." So I put them in a glass of water and next morning when I woke up the water was frozen solid and there they were looking beautiful and I couldn't get near them ...'

'... During the war she went to Cork for her holidays and she met a navy man there. And you know what young girls are! She said: "I don't know if I like him or not." "Mary," I said, "if you've the chance of a navy man, snap at it, for their widows get a pension and they're good dead or alive." "You're so unromantic," she said. "When you're my age," I said, "you'll know that romance is nothing more than the bit of tissue paper the toffee's wrapped up in. Just a make-weight. It's his money that counts." ' 'And did she marry him?' 'No, the little fool! And what do you think? He was blown up on the *Sapphire* six months later. If she'd only taken him she'd have had a good sitting down for the rest of her natural life and no husband to bother her. Hundreds of girls would have been only too glad to have had the opportunity.' 'But she wasn't to know he was going to get killed.' 'Well, no, that's true enough. But you've got to take a chance with everything. . . .'

After all, they were real and they had a right to be alive. He felt his realization of their reality and their right like a curious enlightenment. He felt his admission of them to be adventurous. He was amused.

As he left, he passed through a lounge furnished with a pseudo-luxurious air of heavy Persian rugs and antique furniture. Two young men whom he had known at Trinity were sitting in a corner. He passed them without looking at them, but as he stood at the pay-desk he remembered having heard that last year they had gone to Galway.

Whilst the girl counted out his change, he watched them as though afraid they might escape him. Feeling his eyes on them, they both looked up at the same time and recognized him and nodded coldly. Sean gathered up his change and moved across to speak to them whilst they watched him unsmilingly, with half-hostile, half-curious eyes.

They were dressed in trousers of hand-woven tweed and expensive-looking jerseys made to look like fishermen's jerseys. They chewed their unlit pipes and watched him. Sean remembered how much he had disliked them when, at lectures, they had asked clever questions in their languidly affected English voices.

'Haven't seen you for a long time,' said Sean.

'No,' they agreed discouragingly. They thought him queer, fanatic, in with all this wretched rebellion business and mixed up with a very doubtful crowd. Not only that, he was notoriously unsociable, conceited as the devil and ill-mannered, and they regarded this sudden friendliness with the darkest suspicion. What did he want?

'What are you doing now?' asked Sean.

'Still in London,' the elder replied grudgingly yet unable to resist the opportunity to insist their superiority. 'I'm still at the Royal Academy of Dramatic Art and Kenneth's studying architecture. And you?' They were the sons of an English doctor who had bought a fashionable practice in Dublin. Their mother belonged to a very wealthy Anglo-Irish family.

Sean shrugged his shoulders in answer to their question: 'Nothing much.'

That was exactly what they had expected him to answer, but they raised their eyes in disapproval of an Irish loafer whether of the educated or the uneducated classes. He was impossible. They glanced at one another as he sat down on the seat beside them.

'You went to Connemara last year, didn't you?'

'Yes.'

'A friend of mine over from England was thinking of going there, or to Killarney. He hasn't time to do both and asked me which I advised. I only know Killarney. I was wondering what you thought of Connemara?'

'Oh!' Realizing he wanted nothing more than information, their manner changed.

'The sanitation is disgusting,' said the younger.

'Really?' said Sean. He could not remember having noticed it.

'It's an amazing thing that the whole population hasn't been wiped out by typhus long ago. The people are disgustingly dirty and lazy.'

'Aren't the mountains supposed to be rather fine?'

'Well, yes. They're quite good if you have the stomach for them after some of those privies.'

They were still talking in spite of themselves, still in need of encouragement.

'How did you go? By train, of course? Did you go to Clifden? Or how?'

'By train to Galway, then took a bus to Clifden.'

'Yes?' They did not continue, so: 'The trains are pretty awful, I suppose?'

'God, yes.' They looked at one another and laughed and Sean knew it would not be many moments now before they started talking voluntarily. He kept a humble yet eager silence.

'Will you ever forget the Galway express?' the elder asked the younger with a spurt of laughter. The younger laughed, too, and shook his head. They were forgetting their restraint. Sean watched them, determined that they should tell him about the journey and so make it familiar and bearable for him.

'The carriages!' said the younger, the architect.

'You see,' the elder became a little confidential, 'until last year we had taken all our holidays abroad so travelling in Ireland was quite a novelty. We'd never before seen anything like those carriages.' He had an impressive voice and, as he spoke, he kept glancing round to see if anyone else in the lounge could hear him. 'The carriages seemed to be made of plywood with bits of stair-carpet tacked on the seats.'

'But did you go third class?' asked Sean with surprise.

'Yes, just for the fun of it. Mother said it simply wasn't done to travel third class in Ireland, so, of course, we had to do it.'

Sean could not see the force of this argument, but he nodded and smiled as though he did: 'Of course, and much more fun!'

'We were quite early and got good corner seats and thought we'd done rather well for ourselves when along came an old woman who said: "Am I right for Sligo?" and a man answered: "If you're not then we're all wrong," and we couldn't help hoping they were all wrong. "But doesn't the train go to Galway?" we asked. "Not this carriage," they said, "only the next carriage." Apparently every carriage went to a different place. Very continental, wasn't it? Then another woman said to please us: "Sure, and we go to Galway before we go to Sligo," and this upset everyone else. At last a porter came along and said: "Next carriage for Galway," and out we had to get!' The elder made an elaborate gesture of shooting himself and his luggage on to the platform. It was evident this story had become part of his repertoire and he had made quite a little play out of it. The younger did not interrupt. He merely led the appreciative audience.

'By the time we got to the next carriage half of Dublin was already in it. It had rows of seats like an American Pullman, although it apparently dated prior to the discovery of America. We made a couple of chaps push up so we could sit opposite one another, then there was only one seat left that someone had put a hat on. A young girl came in and tried to sit on it. Opposite there was a dreary looking priest who lifted a long, red, pointed nose from a Latin bible and said in a furry voice: "That seat is reserved for a Christian Brother." At once the unhappy girl, conscious of her sacrilege, leapt to her feet and clutched her backside as though it were burnt . . .' Another gesture here — very clever, very clever indeed — and all the while the younger brother watched the elder and half said with his lips what came next and smiled at the jokes before they were made. 'She sat down on the arm of the seat and the priest replaced his nose and the horrified carriage relaxed. A long time after, when we were well on the way, people began to realize no Christian Brother had appeared. There the poor girl was still on the arm of the seat and falling off whenever the train lurched! The priest said he thought the C.B. must be doing penance by offering up prayers in the water-closet.'

'And what a penance!' murmured the architect.

'But suddenly someone found C.B. comfortably

asleep in the seat in front, and the priest, very unwillingly as though it went against his conscience to do
it, had to lift his hat and let the girl sit down.'

'The carriage was all muffled up like a Victorian
drawing-room,' said the younger.

'Yes. It was amazing. And it had stained-glass
panels in the roof. No one came to light the gas until
it was quite dark.'

Suddenly and vividly, Sean saw the carriage with the
pale ovals of faces glimmering in the blue darkness and,
between the heavy, uplooped and tasselled curtains,
the evening country through which he had passed
with Arion and Elizabeth scarcely a week before. He
saw the wide and lofty sky with its few pulled clouds
of a faded magenta rimmed with yellow mother-of-
pearl. And the jewel-green fields scattered with heaps
of light, fawn hay. He felt a nervous tremor of
pleasurable excitement. He must go in the evening,
not in the morning. Now the evening journey existed
for him.

'What time did you arrive in Galway?'

'We should have arrived at eleven o'clock, but we
lost the staff.'

'The what?'

They laughed together helplessly: 'The staff. We
lost the staff.'

'But what staff?'

'It's a sort of iron rod or something that the driver
picks up at one station and hands in at the next one.
Our driver picked one up at Mullingar or somewhere,
and before we got to Athlone he found he'd lost it and
he couldn't go into the station without it. The train

drew up and, after about half an hour of doing nothing, people began to lean out of the windows and shout out: "What's the matter?" The guard came along with a lantern, grinning as though they'd done something clever: "We've lost the staff," he said, "and the driver and the fireman are away looking for it." They couldn't find it and they had to 'phone to the station and get permission to go in without it. This would have been a serious business in England, but when the station-master at Athlone came round to look at the tickets, he thought the whole affair was a great joke.'

'The Irish are a scream,' said the younger.

'Really!' said Sean.

They gave him a quick look, remembering that he was Irish. They began to think of the curious things that were said about him and they looked down uncomfortably at the smoke of their cigarettes. Before either of them could speak again, the shop door opened and their mother came in. She was a tall, handsome woman who went to London for her clothes. She was charming to Sean because she had not heard about him and asked him to come into the café and have tea with them.

'I'm not hungry,' said Sean.

'Does that matter?' smiled the charming woman. 'Isn't it a privilege of civilization to eat when one is not hungry?'

'I have just finished eating,' said Sean.

Now that he had got all he wanted from the Englishmen, he reverted at once to his usual manner towards people for whom he cared nothing. The Englishmen, looking at him, saw him uncouth and conceited. Whilst it had pleased him that they should, they had forgotten

244

he was like that. They were annoyed at themselves for having let themselves go with him to such an extent. They turned their backs and drew their mother away.

They could go. He had no further use for them. He brushed past them and went out without speaking.

As he had risen to his feet to meet the woman, he had become suddenly conscious of the pain in his chest. It was always there — a gentle and intimate ache — but now it was as though something had struck him a blow and the ache had leapt at once into a poignancy of pain. He walked with difficulty towards the river, feeling on fire with the effort. He started coughing very carefully. He was terrified that he was about to have a haemorrhage and would not be able to go to-morrow. To be at the last frustrated by physical weakness was the least forgivable of frustrations.

He walked slowly and cautiously, like an old man, down the quay to his door. The danger lay in sudden shock or effort. He moved up the stairs. One by one. At last he was at the top. He had to pause there and lean against the wall. He felt as though he were going to faint. The stairs opened and shut like the sticks of a fan and any moment he might topple over the edge. But he held himself taut and at last was able to go on to his room. There he laid himself very quietly and very gently on his bed. He lay quite still in a thankful quiet, feeling his nerves subside into a sort of coma.

Slowly, with the long, plangent and widening revolutions of sleep, he circled downwards out of light and caring and the hold of sickness.

Elizabeth, cold and stiff, awoke on Arion's bed. He had not returned. She felt no anxiety about him. When he had entered her room the night before she had known that something had happened to him. She had felt him to be transported from the visible world. He had had a divested air as though he were about to go upon a journey, as though already he were away. She was filled with a rebellious resentment that one step could take him beyond her reach.

But where have you gone? She touched his brushes and the bottles on his dressing-table. He had taken nothing with him. Not even his toothbrush. Something had said to him: 'Come', and at once and without pausing to put in his pocket this or that, he had walked out of the house.

But first he had gone up to tell her something? What? And she wondered why! What was it that he would not also tell Sean? Perhaps he had nothing to tell either of them. Perhaps he had merely wandered up to her room in the exaltation of the moment. Merely to say, 'I am going away . . .' Not for long, without a toothbrush or hairbrushes.

How strange if he never returned again. How strange if his belongings remained here unclaimed until the landlord packed them up and sold them in lieu of rent. She felt it was in him to disappear so unaccountably. Hadn't he as unaccountably appeared in Dublin at a time when the majority of Englishmen were keeping wisely away?

She brushed her hair with his brushes. They were too soft for her. They could not reach to the roots of her thick hair. She stood for a long time examining the

246

silken texture of the ivory and rubbing the inset gold
of the initials. She went to the desk and saw it disturbed
as she had left it the night before. She packed all the
letters neatly back again. She now felt no desire to
look at them, no interest in them. She scarcely gave
them a glance as she shuffled them together and pushed
them back into their pigeon holes. She did not really
care what he wrote or what was written to him. No.
She didn't care.

She went and had a bath, then made her breakfast.
What was she going to do to-day?

Now for five years, since she had left the activity
and comradeship of the art school, the days had been
passing in anticipation of the ultimate day that would
give meaning to all of them. But the ultimate day
seemed to come no nearer. She met people. They
liked her, but she laid no hold on them. She let them
slip away. Her emotional attachments always failed
in the end and always she was relieved by their failure.
There had been a flaw in all of them and what she
sought must be flawless. She would make no effort.
Even with Arion — no effort. Even with Sean.

She felt the fault was in herself that all her time and
undertakings went down profitlessly into the past. She
knew it was from sheer lassitude she had let her art
slip from her. Her hope was no longer in it. She
dropped it at once for an easier excitement and resumed
it wearily like a penance. The joy of it was gone. If
she married there'd be an end of art. She was tired of
its difficulty. She wished she might marry to escape
the responsibility of these accusing and empty days.
But whom had she ever met that she could marry? Who

had been sufficient to absorb her completely from boredom and a looking aside at the new, the beckoning interest? All those who were past had faded too completely from her thought to glimmer even with the ghost of the possibility they had once seemed to have.

Arion — but she could not marry him, so why think of him?

Sean . . .

She could marry Sean. Yes. No doubting it. The country of Sean, still unconquered and unexplored, had its fascination. Until its limitations were discovered the possibilities were unlimited.

She felt as though she had made a discovery. Her marriage to Sean seemed of a sudden a part of fate, the preformulated and inescapable destiny. Of a sudden she was quite happy. She dressed and went out. Now she had forgotten Arion.

She went to Sean's door on the quay and up to his room. His bedroom door was open and she saw at once that he was out. His bed was made, the room tidied, the dishes washed. So he must have risen in a gay mood as he had risen on Tuesday morning. He must have set himself to clean the place and then gone out thinking that to-morrow he would be off with Arion to meet Riordan. To-morrow the adventure would begin.

He could not know that Arion was gone and maybe would not return again. She felt an envy that he had gone out gaily in anticipation of recovering his beloved Arion the next day. She wished she had been here that she might have said to him: 'Where is Arion? He did

not return last night. I hope nothing has happened
to him.'

That would have brought Sean's gaiety to a pause.
What! Has Arion deserted you at the last minute?
'He has already been shot at once. I do hope . . .'
But, no. That would distract Sean, not only beyond
the reach of gaiety, but beyond her own reach. No,
suggest nothing more than that he had absented himself
willingly, absented himself for some good reason!
What folly to rely on Arion who needs and cares for
no one! Now, were you to place your hope in me. . . .

In me, Elizabeth Dearborn . . .

But no, there wasn't much wisdom in it all. If she
were to say all this and then Arion returned, Sean
would but double his regard of him in penance for his
doubt.

It was just as well that Sean was out and she could
say nothing to him. She never knew the wisest thing
to say, or do either. She was a fool. When would she
gain the power of silence and inaction?

She leant out of the window and saw the river
glimmering palely beneath the white Venetian curves
of the bridges. Everything was light coloured and
shadowless in the morning sunlight. In the distance
there was a clatter of rifle fire followed by an echo.
When that died there was a long silence, curious after
the incessant vibration of the war, and the city lay
motionless. The shattered Four Courts and surrounding houses seemed poised uneasily expectant for
the fray's return. It came renewed and nearer. When
she looked down towards O'Connell Bridge she could
see people running but was not near enough to tell

whether they were soldiers or irregulars or merely nervous civilians unwillingly mixed up in a shooting. After another silence a single revolver shot rang out through the clear air.

Supposing that shot had killed Sean or Arion, or perhaps Daly with whom she had been talking yesterday, or someone she had known well at the art school or a person she passed frequently in the street or a shopkeeper with whom she dealt and whose face had grown familiar as a friend's! She stared towards the bridge. Only three figures stood on it, although there was a crowd at either end. After a few moments there came the urgent ringing of an ambulance bell. The crowd parted. The ambulance swung on to the bridge and stopped by the three waiting men. Something was lifted in. The ambulance went off, ringing its bell all the time. Out of the way, out of the way, out of the way . . . The barriers were lifted. People could cross the bridge again.

The pause of climax — the lifted baton, the curiously intent and restricted movement of hyper-pertinent consciousness! Then — ah! breathe again. It is all over. Forgotten, too, in a little while. But the shots continued in the background.

Out on the landing she brushed against Sean's overcoat. The pocket swung heavily. She put her hand in and brought out a book. It was a thick, black-covered manuscript book half full of writing: 'The Life of Riordan' by Sean Murtough. Putting it under her arm, she took it with her to Stephen's Green and, lying on the grass beneath a tree, read it until the afternoon.

'Well! What do you think of it?' asked Arion as he

stepped over the low railing from the path and stood with his shadow falling over her page.

She looked up, startled, and stared at him, screwing up her eyes against the sun. At once she knew something had happened to him. There was in him a subtle and almost indescribable change. She could feel only that something had set his existence in motion. Before it had seemed still and imperturbable, now it was like a disk that moves so swiftly it appears to be at rest. The difference was a thing discernible rather by instinct than by sense. She watched him without answering him.

He laughed at her and sat down on the grass beside her. He leaned towards her in an intimate, almost affectionate way, and looked at the book and asked again: 'What do you think of it?'

She knew he was completely out of her reach. She lowered her head and stared at the writing on the page. 'I don't know,' she said. 'I can't really understand . . .' She paused.

'What?' asked Arion.

She pulled herself together with a sudden, quick effort: 'I can't understand how Sean discovered so much about Riordan. Most of this must have been written before he even met him.'

'All of it. I am sure he hasn't written a word since he returned from Costello.'

'You mean that this is not written about a reality, but a sort of dream, and the reality has destroyed the dream?'

Arion laughed: 'It is written about a dream, as you call it — a dream aspect of me that Sean has used as a basis for a dream aspect of Riordan. It is an unreality based on an unreality. It portrays nothing but Sean's image of me.'

'Yes,' she nodded slowly, then added abruptly: 'Poor Sean!'

She put the book on the ground and, leaning away from Arion on her elbow, started turning the pages over idly. She could not think of anything pertinent to say. She said: 'He hasn't told you anything about Riordan? What he is really like, I mean?'

'No, he has scarcely mentioned him.'

'Why is that, do you think?'

He shrugged his shoulders a little. After a moment he yawned and shook his head and smiled: 'When Riordan arrives you'll see him.'

'Are you going with Sean to-morrow?'

He did not move or cease to smile as he replied: 'No. I don't think I will go. Sean can take the car. When he has Riordan he will not need me any more.'

She looked at him, bewildered and half-angry. She felt there were a lot of things she might say, but she could not think of anything. She said rather stupidly: 'But do you think Riordan will absorb him as much as that?'

'Why not? Isn't Riordan the leader, the power and cause behind it all? I have merely been a sort of dilettant conspirator.'

She was appalled by the casual righteousness of his desertion. And yet she could see no vulnerable point in him at which to aim a blow. She said at last: 'You were away last night?'

'Yes. I went to Belfast.'

'To Belfast? Why?'

'I went to meet a friend who arrived there on the steamer this morning.'

'Oh!'

'I caught a fast train back and was in Dublin again before eleven this morning.'

'You did not see much of your friend, then.'

'No.'

He did not look at her. She looked at him with a frown of dark suffering: 'Have you seen Sean this morning?'

'No. Not this morning.'

But she did not care if he had seen Sean or not. What did she really care about Sean? She said: 'I went to see him but he was out.'

Arion yawned again without speaking.

She said: 'I expect he is excited about going to-morrow.'

'Yes. To-morrow is the beginning of everything for him. If he succeeds he may become a great man in Ireland, but even if he fails his name will never be forgotten.' He spoke without much thought as though Sean's success or failure were of equally little importance to him.

'Do you think he will succeed?'

'It rests with Riordan now.'

He was not thinking of her. He was staring into the distance with a reflective and gentle smile about his lips. She knew that nothing she could say would interest him. He was finished with everything here.

Even then she thought that perhaps he was not irrevocably lost. Perhaps even then if she could but make the effort . . . But she could not make it. She knew that always the last, the achieving effort would be beyond her power. Rather than have to attempt to make it, she would let it all fall at last from her hands. She felt an exhausted weariness as she looked at him.

After a moment she felt irritated. She thought: 'What does it matter, anyway. At his best he does no more than whet the appetite. What has he ever given anyone but dissatisfaction.'

Yet she felt in some way slighted at the thought of his going. Unreasonably, knowing he had found her with Sean the night before, she felt that by going he was deserting her, too, and unfairly.

She wanted to hurt him: 'Why are you afraid to meet Riordan?' she asked.

He sat and smiled without answering.

'Are you afraid that he'll see through you?'

His smile widened into a laugh. For a moment he seemed to try and hold it back, then it broke out aloud, thoroughly amused. 'Perhaps,' he replied.

She knew he was laughing at her. He did not care what she might think or surmise. He did not care what anyone might think, or what construction anyone might place upon his actions. And that rendered him unscrupulous and uninfluenceable. It was infuriating. Really, she could hate Arion!

She got to her feet: 'I'm hungry. I've had nothing to eat since breakfast.'

'Come and have something.' He took her to an hotel opposite the park.

They talked politely, like strangers. She felt like an abyss between them the depth of their separation. At

moments he had approached her so closely she felt
that, had he allowed it, they might have merged into
one consciousness; but always he had held himself a
little beyond; a hair's-breadth held him to freedom and
now the earth's width was between them. She had
felt him alert always to go when the moment came for
going. And now he was going.

Well! Let him go.

She moved back into herself and watched him. He
was a little man with a pale, contemplative face, seeming
shrunken into a corner of the heavy Victorian chair in
the hotel lounge. The crimson walls and looming
decor of the place overhung the air with ponderous
gloom. In the gloom, above the darkness of his clothes
and against the black leather of the chair, hung the
narrow, pale triangle of his face set with its large,
heavily-lidded, unbetraying eyes. He let his head fall
back and yawned: 'I'm half asleep,' he said.

'I suppose you did not get much sleep last night?'

'No. None.'

There were quite a lot of things she might have
said about Belfast, but, after all, why bother to say
them? And he had nothing to say.

She drank her tea and ate buttered toast and cakes.
And he lay back with his eyes closed, the razor-thin
line of his face lifted so she saw his long, narrow
nostrils, and the wide, closely-closed restraint of his
lips. She looked at him, knowing that she knew him no
better now than she had done when she first met him.
Indeed she knew him less, for his approach had merely
displaced her instinctive conception of him and he
had given her nothing with which to replace it.

She thought: 'People are in three layers. The top and bottom layers are the same. It's the middle one that throws you out of your reckoning.' Now she could define him only by her first thought of him, that he was indefinable.

Even the physical contact had produced no understanding. His hands, lying on the broad leather chair-arms, were the hands of a stranger. It was difficult to realize they had caressed the intimate warmth of her body. It was difficult to realize she had ever been physically nearer to him than they were at that moment. She knew that when he left Ireland she would not see him or hear from him again. Though she would not forget him, his face would fade from her memory and the memory of their pleasure would fade. It would all be lost and forgotten. She felt a despairing anger that it should be forgotten and lost so.

It was as though a never-to-be-regained possibility had been held towards her and yet withheld from her. She had recognized its possibility and yet, somehow, had been powerless. And now it was gone. As though the fault had been hers, she was troubled by regret.

She thought bitterly that a woman was always dependent for her happiness upon someone else. She could not go out and seize it as her inalienable right. She must wait until it was handed to her and then be so careful, so cautious, so circumspect for fear of losing it by a false move. 'That is,' thought Elizabeth, 'if happiness is the knowledge that you are desired.' But she could think of no other.

She spoke and her voice sounded cold and sharp in

the big, empty lounge: 'Suppose Sean cannot succeed without you?'

Arion opened his eyes sleepily and, in an exhausted voice, answered without moving his head: 'He must learn to succeed without me. If I stayed he would merely become a sort of disciple of mine. Any individual can have disciples. I don't want them. It is easier to be a disciple than an individual. It is easier to adopt another's thoughts than to think for yourself. But I cannot let Sean be wasted that way.'

She said: 'But he may merely attach himself to Riordan.'

'No. I don't think he will do that. I will tell him that I am going because he must rely on himself.'

She interrupted him angrily: 'You are only going because you want to go. How can you pretend about it? How can you be so smug? I wouldn't have thought you were capable of that.'

He looked at her for a moment with hurt surprise before he said slowly: 'I suppose it always surprises us when we discover how completely our actions can be misunderstood.'

Her hostility wavered. She felt that she really had misunderstood him, and yet . . . She didn't know what to say. She did not really know what to think. Was he unfathomable? Or was he no more than the sky-reflecting mirror on which you struck your head whenever you tried to plunge into its apparent depths?

He said in an uneasy, self-conscious way that was strange for him: 'When things become necessary to us they become stronger than we are. They deprive us of

257

our dependence and individuality and that freedom
that is self-sufficiency.'

She interrupted him with a sort of painful eagerness:
'But if oneself is not sufficient?'

'Individuality is self-sufficient. It is the completion
within oneself. If you are an individual the crowd will
have none of you. Instinctively it rejects you. You
must be content with the completion of yourself, not
for ever running round the fringe of humanity crying:
'Accept me.' It will never accept you. And even if it
were to, you would never be content with its acceptance.'

She wondered what he was trying to tell her, or if
he were trying to tell her anything. She felt his remoteness like a barrier over which he talked with effort and
difficulty, not really wishing to talk, uncaring and
thinking of some other thing.

She wondered if he were talking out of a sense of
duty to her, because he felt there was something he
should say although he had no interest in the saying of
it. Strangely, now, for all his remoteness, he seemed
more human than she had known him before.

She said: 'Are you self-sufficient?'

He looked at her with a little frown that was not so
much at the intrusion of her question as of surprise as
he realized she was there listening with her brain,
judging and questioning.

He said: 'No,' then added: 'But failure is often
necessary, like a pause in which to gain strength to
make another step towards success.'

'And you will succeed?'

'Of course.'

He had never before told her so much and yet,

because the restraint remained, was more tautly
persistent than before, she could discover nothing. He
spoke, but his words were inapplicable and told her
nothing.

She said: 'But Sean . . .'

He interrupted her quietly and patiently: 'Can't
you see, it is better for Sean that I should go. Whilst I
am here he will try and be myself rather than himself.
If I pushed him always in a wheel-chair he would lose
the use of his legs; if I kept him and fed him as though
he were a child he would lose the keenness of his wits;
if I told him always what to think he would become
nothing more than a parrot.'

'But, for all that, you're not going because it is
better for Sean?'

'No.'

'And the Rising?'

'It is only a sort of toy like a vaulting horse or a set
of parallel bars on which a gymnast develops his
muscles. If he succeeds or fails it does not matter.' He
turned to her, half-smiling. 'Believe me, it does not
matter.'

'But he cannot see it like that.'

'He will.'

'If the things that seem important to us and the
things that seem necessary do not matter, then what
does matter?'

'I don't know. I have known. I have seen it at
moments as you might see for moments the solution of
a problem you still can't work out. I must work it out
to its completion before I can prove it to anyone else.
Have you finished your tea?'

'Yes.' She took a powder-box from her hand-bag and peered into the little convex mirror in its lid.

He rose quietly and stood with his hat in his hand, looking at her: 'Don't think that I am deserting him cruelly, and don't think that, after taking everything, I am leaving you without a thought.'

She snapped the little box closed and got to her feet. Her mouth was set and her face expressionless.

'But you do think so, don't you?' he asked.

'Yes, I do. I think you are deserting Sean and I know that, after all, I am nothing to you. I know that neither Sean nor I have any reality for you. Nothing has any reality for you, but the narrow circle of your self. You are afraid to admit the reality of other things. You were afraid to admit my reality. You excluded me deliberately because you were afraid my reality might get a hold on you. The same with Sean. You flattered him into believing he was something different from what he is so you need not be troubled by what he really is. You flatter people into unreality in order to keep them at a distance. You say: "Amazing and wonderful creature! How amazing and wonderful you are!" So they must keep up the show of being amazing and wonderful and save you from realizing they are really only suffering and bewildered.'

He looked at her for a moment with a curious expression, then smiled a little: 'The funny thing,' he said, 'is that you are quite wrong. You are wrong because you have been looking at me the wrong way. I have not been real to you any more than you have been real to me. There has been no reality between us, so why should we quarrel now over something that has never existed? I want to go and telephone my paper. What are you going to do?'

'I don't know,' she answered vaguely.

Whilst Arion paid the bill she wandered out to the steps of the hotel and saw the sunlight beginning to slant across the square. She felt lost and empty and without purpose. Alone, it was as though she were in a desert. She must have someone, something to which to attach herself and so escape the desert of herself.

Arion came out walking quickly. He had found it was getting late. He had to hurry to the post office. He hurried along beside her, absorbed in the progress of his own life. She went along with him because she had nothing else to do. She felt like a dog that attaches itself to people because it has no purpose of its own. Now she was aimless as a stray dog. She must attach herself to someone. But to whom? Now that Arion was leaving, she thought again of Sean.

Arion went into the telephone box and she stood in the stuffy atmosphere of the post office. People came and went. Arion emerged at last and they returned to the street. The shops were shutting. All the people on the pavements seemed to have somewhere to go. She felt the deadly ennui of her inactivity.

'And soon,' she thought, 'I will be getting old.' At that moment she could have bent her head into her hands and wept in despair.

'I am going to have supper with Murtough,' said Arion. He felt her aimlessness and pitied it. 'Would you like to come?'

'Oh, no.' The thought of going to that house in this mood was unbearable.

'Why don't you go and see Sean.'

'I expect he is out.'

'He may not be.'

'Yes, I will go.'

Arion was released. She watched him make his way between the people on the pavement. She watched him out of sight — the detached and complete stranger — and then she turned towards the river.

In Grafton Street, as she made to cross the road, O'Rorke ran to her and gripped her arm. She turned in surprise.

'We have been arrested — Sharp and I. They went to Merrion Square to try and find Sean, but of course he wasn't there. They want to know where he lives.' O'Rorke spoke rapidly. 'Go and warn him. He must not bring Riordan here.'

There was a shot and he caught his shoulder. His face crumpled up with pain. The soldier from whom he had broken away was striding towards him. In the background, Elizabeth could see Sharp held on either side. The door of his office was lying open behind him.

Without answering O'Rorke, she slipped away between the gathering crowd before anyone thought to detain her. As soon as she was beyond the radius of the crowd she turned into a side street and started running rapidly towards the river. In an instant her depression was gone. She was alert and authoritative. She felt capable of taking the whole thing into her own hands and even yet prevailing over the threatened failure. Now that the project was threatened it had meaning for her. She felt she could force Sean to succeed now.

And, meanwhile, there was something to be done.

He was lying on his bed. He had been started into wakefulness by the noise of her entry.

'Get up quickly,' she said. 'O'Rorke and Sharp have been arrested. The Black and Tans are looking for you. You must get away from here.'

She felt that the sheer force of her energy must make him jump up and obey her until he was in safety, but he did not move. He lay as before with scarcely any change of expression. But he grew very pale. It was as though the fire had burnt itself out in him, the whole flaming structure had collapsed and, of an instant, there remained nothing but a little white ash. He stared at her.

'Sean,' she said, impatiently, 'get up. You must prevent Riordan landing at Costello on Sunday. You are the only one left to warn him.'

He moved slowly until he was resting on his elbow, then said very quietly: 'Did anyone follow you here?'

'I don't think so. O'Rorke ran up to me in Grafton Street and told me. The Black and Tans had got him. I made off as quickly as I could. They were too busy with him to think of me.'

He lay back again and still spoke in an unnaturally quiet voice: 'Even if they haven't followed you, they can always get my address from Arion.'

'Why should Arion tell them? You are being ridiculous. I have only just left him. He was just the same as ever.'

'Did he say why he went to the Castle this morning?'

'Did he go to the Castle?'

263

'Yes. I saw him go in in an armoured car with a Black and Tan officer.'

'But you must have been mistaken. Why should Arion go to the Castle?'

'To inform on us.'

'Don't be a fool. That's not a thing Arion would do.'

'Don't you think so?' he queried apathetically, without cynicism. 'If he didn't, who did?'

'Anyone might have done it. Half Dublin knew you had found Riordan and were going to bring him back. Yesterday, when I was at Howth, a woman mentioned it . . .'

'No one in Dublin would betray me. It means too much to them. But Arion would because it means nothing to him.' He spoke as though now it meant nothing to him, either. Something in his apathetic uncaring weakened the force in her, yet she would not admit it weakened. She bent over him and said angrily: 'Don't you realize that time is precious? It is a matter of Riordan's life or death. Won't you do anything to save him?'

'Perhaps they are only pretending they don't know where I am so, when I go off to Costello, they can follow me. Perhaps he hasn't given Riordan away. It wouldn't be safe for me to go.' He spoke in a rambling way with a hint of complaint in the background of his voice. He sounded like a sick, delirious man. She frowned at him, puzzled, beginning to feel helpless against him. She realized he had no intention of doing anything.

'Wouldn't it be possible to telephone him? You 'phoned Arion from the place where Riordan is.'

He shook his head. 'There is only one telephone on the island and it's a couple of miles from where Riordan lives. Even if we 'phoned through and got them to find him and tell him to 'phone us at your house or at a call box, it wouldn't be safe. It wouldn't be safe for anyone in any way connected with this business to telephone the place where he is. . . .' There was something frightening in the calm reasonableness with which he spoke.

She said: 'Could I go and tell him?'

He said: 'Yes. I suppose you could. You would have to go at once. You'd have to take the steamer from Galway and it leaves early to-morrow morning. It only goes twice a week.'

'Then I'll go. I'll take the car and go at once.'

He did not answer. He lay staring in a fixed and stupid way at the wall before him. She bent over him and saw his cheeks flushed and a strange, pinched, pale look round his nostrils. She felt afraid and said abruptly: 'What is the matter with you?'

He moved a little then, and frowned peevishly: 'I don't know. I think I've caught a cold or something. I've a pain in my chest.' After a pause he added irritably, 'I feel bloody.'

She looked intently at him and he huddled himself up in the bed, avoiding her eyes. She felt in him a fixed and obstinate purpose apart from her. He was deliberated, but she could not think what he would do. Caught as he was, his cause lost and hopeless, she could not think what held him now in calm, apart and indifferent.

'When did you begin to feel ill?'

'I don't know.' He didn't know. He had not

realized he felt really ill until she came. She stood looking at him:

'You must tell me where I can find Riordan.'

He told her. '. . . and he is called O'Reilley there. He lives in the house of a man called Nolan. Anyone will direct you to it. You should go at once before they come for me or it is just possible they will arrest you too.'

But she could not go yet. She could think of nothing to say, yet could not turn and leave him there lying in his extraordinary gloom of indifference that presaged she knew not what. She said at last: 'If you are arrested they can't detain you long. They can prove nothing against you.'

After a pause he said: 'No.'

Still she lingered. She felt him slipped from her and felt that before she went she must, by some definite action, put the seal of her possession on him. Now, she thought, she was too old and wise to let the restraint of atmosphere, the vagaries of mood deprive her of happiness. She'd snatch what she wanted and be damned to all the dallying of uncertainty.

She bent over him: 'As soon as you are free you will come and see me?'

He did not answer, but as she watched him she saw him smile secretly into himself and she caught her breath in a sudden hopelessness of understanding. Quickly a fury of will displaced her fear. She caught his shoulders and shook him.

'Sean,' she said, 'you will come and see me? You will come? I tell you you must come.'

He held his face away from her in obstinate silence.

She bent over him until she half lay across his body. She held him fiercely in an almost ferocious effort of nerve and sinew. She pinned him beneath the weight of her body as though beneath the weight of her will that he might not elude her.

'Answer me,' she said. 'Answer me.'

His calm was broken by her insistence. He started to struggle beneath her. He caught her arms in an effort to throw them off. He tried to push her away and when he spoke his voice had in it a new note of suffering and complaint: 'Go away,' he said. 'Can't you leave me alone even at a time like this? For God's sake go away and leave me to die in peace.'

Ah! She had known it. Now he had given himself away and she was dominant. She gripped his wrists and held them down. She was strong and, in this violence of effort, she was the stronger.

'You will not die,' she said. 'I say that you will not die. If you haven't Arion, you have me, and I am more to you than Arion.'

'You have brought me nothing but defeat.' He strained from her in an agony of exhaustion. He wanted to fling her from him and he could not. He could not bear the insistent, undeniable life in her that, against his will, set his pulse quickening in unwilling response, that dragged him back from the penumbra of his decision into the full light of living. He looked at her, at her broad, pale face and fierce eyes and her dark, out-thrust angry mouth. In sudden panic he struggled, ordering her to release him. She clung to him determinedly until she felt his strength fail beneath her. He began to cough in a weak, painful way. He fumbled for his handkerchief. She gave it to him. He pressed it over his mouth and coughed until his exhaustion exhausted his coughing. His face had been flushed with fever. Now it grew very white. He lay beneath her with closed eyes, helplessly unavailing. She felt her will melt in pity and tenderness, yet she'd have neither of them. She held herself rigidly in possession of him; she would not relax her hold on him, she would not submit.

She said brutally: 'You will not die whilst I am away?'

He shook his head and caught his breath to gain strength to answer her: 'No, I won't die.'

When he had said that she was content. She could go contentedly now. Her tautened muscles subsided against him and she lay as exhausted as he was, in half oblivion.

There was a sound of knocking at the front door. Sean, startled, tried to rise. She lifted her head.

'They've come,' said Sean.

She slipped down from the bed and went to the window. Below she saw in the failing light a dark movement of men at the door. She looked back and nodded to him. He was sitting up with a strangely awakened expression as though it was only at that moment he had realized he was beaten. He said curiously: 'But it doesn't matter so much that we are beaten. What matters is that we have not been allowed to fight.'

She said: 'There are other days for fighting. They can't keep you long and when you are released we'll begin all over again.'

But there was no answering hope in him. He slid

his legs off the bed and sat on the edge with his shoulders sloping and his head down. Now she felt she had overcome him, she scarcely considered him. She must go.

'I must go. I will be back by Sunday. Good-bye.'

He did not reply. She hurried from the room. The men below were opening the door. She went into the bathroom and listened to the heavy clatter of feet come up the uncarpeted stairs. They passed and went into Sean's room. In a few minutes they came out. It seemed to her no words had been spoken; that they had merely entered the room and left it again and now were returning down the stairs.

When they were gone she hurried across the landing. She half expected to find Sean was still there. But the room was empty. He had gone. There was nothing for her to do but go, too.

Out on the landing she noticed his tweed coat and remembered she was still carrying his manuscript book. He had not noticed her with it. She put it back into the pocket and then left the house.

VII

SATURDAY AND SUNDAY

At daybreak Elizabeth was a mile from Galway. She saw, with the wide-eyed intelligence of extreme fatigue, the clarity of the light encroaching shrilly and coldly over the broad fields. Clouds had obscured the moon. She had had to go cautiously through the darkness, all her nerves trained attentively to the road. Now she was arrived and the daylight come and her eyes ached. She was alert with hunger and lack of sleep and had no interest in anything.

Her head tried to nod heavily forward. She ran the car up on to a stretch of gorse land and settled herself into a corner to sleep. For a long time she could not sleep; she could not even keep her eyes closed — then, quite suddenly, she sank into a deep unconsciousness. When she awoke she started up, afraid she had missed the boat. She backed the car to the road and raced the mile to Galway. But when she got into the town she found it was only a little after nine o'clock. Things were only beginning to wake up and she had time to find a garage for the car and have breakfast at the water-front hotel, before making her way down between the old warehouses and the grass-grown, whitewashed walls, to the quay.

The day was brilliant with sunlight.

She could not find the steamer. It was getting late.

She began to worry again. 'Where is the steamer?' she asked some men with a donkey cart.

'There.' They pointed to the other side of the quay. 'That's her funnel over there.'

'Oh!' She ran. Panting, she took her ticket and hurried on board. She was lucky — in another minute it would have gone! In another minute . . . but not a bit of it. Half the passengers were still loitering on the quay. 'When do we go?' she asked. Soon enough. An American visitor had run back to his hotel to get his camera and someone else was expecting a friend to arrive any moment. . . .

She realized how ineffectual was impatience now. Riordan would not leave the island until to-morrow and, however long they took getting there, they must arrive some time to-day.

She went to the gunwale and watched a great family of swans navigating with proprietary indifference the harbour waters. The bright, cool sunlight floated like oil over the surface of the waters. She glanced to the horizon and her eyes dazzled. She turned her back on the sun and looked at the passengers. She saw a few Galway people making the day trip for the fun of it. There was also a young girl dressed in green homespun caught at the neck with a large silver and blue Celtic pin, a few men that looked like school teachers and a group of Americans. She felt aloof and secret from all of them. Quite suddenly she was caught up into the excitement of her errand. There was a purpose in her journey that set her apart from the other passengers. Having found something to do, she felt confident and happy and apart. She did not want to speak to anyone or attach herself to anyone. One of the men eyed her; she looked from him without interest. Her completion was in Sean.

At last they crept out of the harbour into the bay where the sea lay around them in great shallow dimples like sheet isinglass. Looking back at Galway she saw, knife-edged and brilliant against the clear, pale blue of the sky, the white squares of the houses, silver-roofed and interspersed with dark spires. Who would suppose that this was the town they had seen in its wet prison-grey a week before?

'Look! There are the islands!' said someone. They had been journeying an hour or more and at last the islands were appearing, lying like whales across the horizon.

She felt no interest in them. Everyone, even the Galwaymen and natives who must have seen them dozens of times, crowded to the gunwale to look at them. But she did not move or care about them. She was not on holiday. That interest in things for their exciting strangeness was not part of her present. Life was altogether a more serious business for her. She felt surprisingly pleased with herself. She really felt at last protected by being part of something. For once her movements were actuated by something other than the whim of her own will. And it seemed to her a thing of moment sufficient to content and absorb her, and to reconcile her with trivialities so they were no longer an irritant but could be dismissed with amusing contempt.

She required nothing more. Yet it was part of the nature and fascination of the thing that it was to be got over and done with with businesslike celerity. Indeed, that was the source of content in it — that it allowed no time for pausing to observe this or that unaccustomed beauty that might trouble the imagination and pluck the spirit down with thought of necessity's falling short.

When she heard that they were calling first at the two smaller islands to load beasts for the Galway market, she felt only a fury of impatience. She watched with impatience the approach of the little island. It was no more than the very tip of some submerged peak. She looked at it breaking the waters so beautifully there — the wretched little island that was going to absorb so much of the precious time. Yet she could not turn from it — its beauty was exquisite. Against her will, against her furiously resenting will, it touched her and she recoiled at the first return of that nostalgic hyperconsciousness of beauty. It was that that she hated. It was that that was unbearable because unalleviable. . . .

The steamer hove-to a hundred yards from the shore and the curraghs came out to it. Elizabeth was standing by the gunwale. The others crowded behind her to watch. She was held there to watch too.

The island glittered. The grey limestone of its shore, riven into boulders that lay one upon another like coffins on which others were set up like idols, was interrupted by a quarter-of-a-mile-long, frost-white strand scattered over with tiny men and women and beasts, curiously grouped, brilliant and individual like the figures in a primitive painting. Some of the curraghs were being hauled rapidly down the sand,

273

but the majority of them had already started towards the ship and the sea was full of them.

The first curragh arrived. There were pigs in it lying on their backs, winking apprehensive, little eyes, ready to scream whether hurt or not when the crane hoisted them on board.

'Isn't it exciting,' breathed the girl in homespun beside Elizabeth, but Elizabeth kept an unfriendly silence.

The creaking crane jerked a hook down into the curragh. The island men hooked on one of the pigs; the crane creaked the hook up; the pigs, one after another, went with it and protested shamelessly until the safety of the lower deck was reached and they could lie and sob themselves into hysterical grunting, sulky snuffles. After the pigs came creamy coloured sheep that could not be hoisted because of their delicate slender legs. As they were handed over the gunwale they lay like sacrificial lambs subsided into themselves, crumpled and limp with nervous exhaustion. No one was sorry for the hysterical pigs, but everyone cried out: 'Look at the sheep! The poor sheep!' and moved over to look down into the hold and see them lying there like heaps of newly washed fleece. The poor, helpless sheep! The ever-to-be-slaughtered innocents! But one of the men untied their legs and set them on their feet and gave their behinds an encouraging pat and off they trotted none the worse for it all.

Then a little brown calf was hoisted aboard and lay with its soft, wrinkled neck twisted as though broken until steadied upright, when it stumbled off in a dazed way after the sheep.

The first mate, an island man, a tyrant, speaking

English as well as he spoke Gaelic, gave the orders to
the curraghs. The curraghs, black and shining, with
their bows standing up out of the water, waited in
patient rows. The steamer passengers stared down
into them and stared at the waiting men. The men, in
their sleeveless frieze jackets over navy blue jerseys,
kept their heads shyly lowered, but looked up with their
eyes at the down-peering passengers and laughed across
at one another self-consciously.

'Look! The excitement on shore!'

All the tiny, scattered figures were converging to
persuade the cattle into the water. Out came fresh
curraghs, each with a man in the stern gripping the
head of a beast in the water. The beasts swam
frantically, never hoping to arrive alive, never hoping
. . . But they arrived all right and were hoisted by the
ropes round their bellies into the air where they hung
a moment with their legs dangling and the water
pouring from their sides, before coming to the secure,
the blessed deck.

The passengers watched it all intently. They watched
with a raw excitement that was almost silent.

Elizabeth, looking from the immediate activity to
the distant island, felt as though she were sitting at the
back of a theatre gallery watching a play that was
diminished by distance into miniature and dream-like
unreality. She thought: 'I hate it all. I haven't come
here to see this and I don't want to see it.' And yet, as
she watched, she felt amazingly that the aroused
conflict was again resolving itself into content — a
different sort of content as though something of herself
was at home here. Although she watched as she might

watch a play, she was beginning to feel it had for her the curious super-reality of the presaging or symbolical thing. She was gradually forgetting the object of her coming here, in a sort of wondering suspicion that all the devious intricacies of event had but thrust out arms heading her off from this or that path to keep her to the road that had eventually led her here.

The noon sun struck the white sand until its iridescence hurt the eyes. Behind the sand the grey rocks, rising in tiers, were topped with ruins that gave it all a classical air. The surrounding sea, of the emerald purity of thick glass, was stained purple here and there by beds of sea-weed. All the time the steamer had been lying there, a shoal of mackerel fry had been passing beneath it. Millions of fish, silver, black, and swift as infant eels, streamed past and still there were more to come.

Half-way between the shore and the steamer a bullock made a frantic effort to escape; it lost the struggle and when at last it was brought alongside, one of its horns was smashed and the canoe was awash with blood. As it was hoisted, it struggled again and stained the green waters with its brilliant ocre-coloured dung. Last of all came a pregnant cow lying motionless like a drowned cow with a swollen belly.

All was aboard. The curraghs were loaded with cases of tea and sugar and bags of flour. As they returned, they looked back in farewells to the steamer, but the steamer was already cutting a perfect semi-circle of foam as she turned to make for the second island. Everyone turned too, with shameless perfidy; Elizabeth with them.

The first, the tiny crown-like island in a Mediterranean sea, had had a Grecian look, but the sky clouded over and the second island was steel frigid. From the barren rocks a cold wind blew, the curraghs with the lean, red-faced men were already out and waiting. They lay in a row in the terrible Prussian-green sea that was almost black like malachite. The steamer was able to approach much nearer the second island. The people on this shore were almost life-size. They were grouped to gossip. Some, assisted by their busy dogs, were chasing a runaway cow.

It had not the gem-tiny, exquisite beauty of the last scene, nor the fascination. But there was beauty enough. The women, sitting in rows on the rocks, wore full petticoats dyed red with madder. There they looked like a gathering of cardinals, but those that were brought aboard had got themselves into cheap, factory-made dresses from the mainland and looked like clumsy servant-girls.

More pigs; a lamb with a black Astrakhan coat; more cattle unwillingly swimming in the bleak sea. There was a new atmosphere here; a new brutality. When a cow came aboard a man dug his fingers into its nostrils whilst it was released and then the others belaboured it into the black hold. These new arrivals were confident and voluble with no interest in the staring passengers. They talked loudly and their Irish had an excitable sound so it seemed a perpetual squabble was going on. But it was all good-natured banter and when they had cause for annoyance, it ceased. When the mate refused to take on board a tool chest that had been lent to the islanders to help them construct their houses, they towed it back in silence.

On at last to the third island, the biggest, where she was to find Riordan. Elizabeth went down to the little saloon where she was able to buy tea, sandwiches and fruit. When she returned to the deck the sun had come out again, but already it had an evening look. It was nearly five o'clock before the steamer approached the quay. On the quay a crowd stood waiting, all faces turned towards the deck. Beside the steamer, like an escort of welcome, leapt three dolphins.

'The dolphins,' cried the girl with the Gaelic brooch. 'The lovely dolphins!' She spoke again to Elizabeth, but Elizabeth remained uncommunicative.

With her chin propped on her hand, she watched for the flash of the leaping fish — the mother, father and, beside them, the baby dolphin, so tiny and yet as quick as the others, always beside them, never losing an inch. How capture their perfection? Sweep a pencil across paper in an arch and there in the rhythmic, exquisite sweep of line was all you saw of them.

They sank and did not reappear. The steamer was slowing. All the faces on the quay looked curiously at the newcomers on the steamer. The islanders who had rooms to let or jaunting cars for hire were pushing eagerly to the front.

As Elizabeth looked round at the little, grey houses and the plain, rough, brown-faced islanders, she felt a revulsion from it all. At once she became all urgency to finish her journey and be safely on her way back to Dublin. As soon as the gangway was thrown out, she hurried ashore. She had little enough time now. The steamer left again in an hour or so.

'I want to find Nolan's house,' she said to a man with a car.

'Jump up,' he said. 'And I'll take you there myself.'

She climbed up. The man whipped the horse and off they went over the cobbles of the pier. She looked at the grey, naked houses of the little town, wondering in which she would find Riordan. But they left the town behind and followed the uneven lane-small road between the fields of flat, grey and riven limestone. No trees and where there was grass the rock was less than an inch beneath it.

'Maybe it's staying with Nolan you are?' queried the man, turning round on his seat to look at her.

No. No, she wasn't staying with Nolan.

'Maybe you're looking for a place to stay?'

No.

'You're not disappointed with the place now, are you? Everyone when they come for the first are disappointed, but they never want to leave.'

No. She had merely come to see someone, and she was in a hurry. She wanted to return on the steamer to Galway that night.

But he did not hurry. Outside the town he had let the horse slow until now it was walking leisurely.

'Is it O'Reilley you've come to see?'

'Yes,' said Elizabeth. 'Is the house far?'

'A mile or two.'

'Don't you think we could go a little faster?'

'Certainly, certainly.' Off they went again, jolting to left and right, Elizabeth hanging on to the car for fear of being thrown from it. She sat facing the coast,

seeing, beyond the strait, the hills that had been hidden
in the mists last Sunday.

'See!' The man pointed with his whip towards the
waters. 'The gannets! There's mackerel out in the
bay.' She looked and saw the gannets hanging motionless in the air before dropping like stones down upon
the mackerel. 'There go the curraghs.' The black
canoes each with its three or four moving oars, looked,
in the distance, like inverted wood-lice.

'I suppose O'Reilley isn't in one of them.'

'He may be. Yes, indeed, he may be. And if he is he
won't be back before the dawn.'

It was unlikely he would spend a wakeful night on
the water before going to Costello. But another thought
struck her: 'You are sure he wasn't on the quay?'

'No, no, he was not. He keeps well away from the
quay on steamer days.'

Oh! So they knew all about O'Reilley.

'Here's the city now,' said the man as they rounded
a corner and came upon half a dozen whitewashed
houses. They arrived.

'Shall I wait?' asked the man.

'Yes, wait,' she said and ran up the steps to the open
door of the square, whitewashed house. She looked into
the kitchen. A big, ungainly island woman straightened
her back from the pot over the fire and moved forward
in her heavy skirts. She peered towards Elizabeth with
stupidly smiling surprise.

'Welcome to this house,' she said.

'I have come to see Mr. O'Reilley,' said Elizabeth.

The woman could not grasp the sense of Elizabeth's
quickly-spoken English, but she caught the name of

O'Reilley. 'Yes,' she said. 'It is here he lives.' Her English was laboured and muddled. 'Here it is. Yes.'

'I want to see him,' said Elizabeth impatiently.

To see him? Oh! But he was not there and she did not know where he was. He went off by himself as always on steamer days. There was no knowing where he might be — but would she not come in and sit down and O'Reilley would be back in a little while, no doubt.

The woman looked out jealously at the driver and nodded to him without much friendliness. No need to ask him to wait. Her husband had a car and would drive her back to the quay when she wanted to go.

'But I'm afraid of missing the boat,' said Elizabeth, lingering doubtfully on the doorstep.

Oh, no, she wouldn't miss it. The woman spoke as though the boat would wait for Elizabeth, and Elizabeth, feeling there was not much else to do, gave the man half a crown and let him go.

She went into the dimness of the big kitchen. The woman would have her sit on the one wooden chair, but Elizabeth preferred the little stool by the open hearth and, with her elbows on her knees and her head on her hands, sat staring out of the doorway at the shore, the sea and the Connemara hills. She was impatient for Riordan's return.

The woman, moving ponderously about doing nothing in particular, looked at Elizabeth with curiosity and tried to keep up a conversation about her journey and her impression of the islands and her reason for her visit. But Elizabeth was in no mood to unravel the questions, or to simplify her answers to the woman's understanding. They lapsed into silence.

The foremost hills were green streaked and edged with sunlight. Those behind were fogged, and the farthest dissolved as you watched them into the horizon. Elizabeth regarded them peevishly. Make a nice picture postcard! Very pretty with that nice bit of blue sea in the foreground! Confound Riordan! Why didn't he return! She was beginning to fear she might not be back in Dublin by Sunday. She had told Sean she would be back by Sunday and, strangely, she was obsessed by the thought were she a moment longer than the journey required, he would escape her. She held him by her will until Sunday. But after that . . . She crouched in an agony of impatience, frigidly still and silent.

At last the steamer gave a warning hoot. In a moment it would be gone. She heard it hoot again. Too late, too late. It was gone.

The kitchen was almost unfurnished. Two doors opened on to it and a wooden staircase came down into it. Beside the chair, there was a dresser and a table pushed under the stairs, with some wooden forms, like school forms, placed round it. A few disconsolate chickens wandered in at the door and pecked at the bare, hard, earthen floor. The woman shooed them out and they went, squawking, to return the next moment as disconsolate and jerkily pecking as before.

Now the Connemara hills burnt dully purple like old, dusty amethysts set in old pinchbeck. Their dim and dusty colour lay in softly puckered folds and peaks beyond the unruffled sea.

It began to get late. Soon the men who had been down to the quay started coming up the road singly and in couples. Their feet in skin shoes made no noise but their voices impinged curiously shrill and alien upon the quiet air. They came suddenly into hearing and quickly, and as suddenly, passed out of hearing.

The evening was falling. Layer upon layer the insistent shadows heaped up in the corners. The kitchen was becoming dark. The light still hung about in the open air, but it did not penetrate through the doorway. Soon the kitchen was quite dark. The peats burnt slowly with deep, rich warmth and beautiful clarity of colour, but they gave no light. They lay in the black well of the hearth like incandescent bricks, filling the air with their smell and smoke and heat, but no light. The door became a black frame for the slope of the grey rocks to the grey sea. The hills losing force and substance, dissolved to ashen blue, to an ashen-pearl cloud softness in the long decline of the day.

The dusk seemed to muffle things. The men passed more and more silently until the last of them went like a ghost. Even the woman stopped wandering about aimlessly and settled down out of thought in a corner by the table. Now that the steamer was gone and worry and impatience would not help her, she sank back into a sort of unthinking acceptance of the tranquillity of the place. There seemed no reason now why she should not sit for ever watching, through the iron-black rigidity of the doorway, the silver sky and hills and the pale sea. It seemed that nothing had substance now. Even the doorway was rigid only in line and would not withstand the touch. A young girl from one of the neighbouring cottages came up the steps and leaned

softly against it without speaking. Her darkness seemed
to flow into the darkness of the doorway so she was only
a contour against the light. She did not move.

After a few minutes the woman parted from the
shadows and crossed to her. Conscious of Elizabeth,
they whispered together and the girl unobtrusively
slipped some money to the woman. The woman went
into the next room, which was a tiny shop, and returned
with a packet of cigarettes. The girl took them and
moved away as quietly as she had come. The extremely
soft quiet and edgelessness of their movements was
somnambulistic. The air seemed filled with sleep like
a drug. There was a spell of sleep on the place, muting
the senses, so one might remain here for ever
motionless. Time passed. It did not matter.

Then the man of the house arrived and started
noisily to wake things up. He put a match to the lamp
and a dingy light returned everything to the mean and
commonplace. He closed the door. The last sweetness
of the daylight was lost.

Elizabeth straightened her back and looked round
irritably. She did not like this man. He aroused her
hostility. She felt that places accepted her, but the
people in them spoilt everything.

He sat on the chair opposite her. He was shy at
first, but he had had a few drinks and the desire to talk
and show what a fine, clever fellow he was, stirred his
tongue. The woman was simple, slow-moving and
obtuse. But the man was intelligent enough to be
self-conscious.

The islanders were beginning to realize the money
value of their barren, riven, limestone fields and the

innumerable churches, tiny, beautiful things, left from Ireland's saint-ridden days. And the views ... They listened to the exclamations of the visitors and repeated them. They had never actually seen the views, but they could point them all out. And look! The maidenhair fern growing in the depths of the rock crannies! And feel the air slipping like warm silk across your face! And here are the dry-stone fortresses, so old nobody really knows anything about them! And again the churches, and the legends of the innumerable saints, and the fern-fringed holy wells! Money in all of them.

There was great competition to board and bed the profitable visitors. The man saw possibilities in Elizabeth and became garrulous. He sat in his heavy blue jersey and frieze trousers and sleeveless coat. His hands hung between his legs. His face with its long nose was thin, red and lined. He looked humble and shy with a furtive glance, but he had a great opinion of his own cunning.

'You're a pretty girl, God bless you,' he said. 'But pale. It's not very strong you look.' Now this was the place to make a girl fine and strong. And it was a good place to stay because of the great honesty of the people. He had another spare room beside the room he let to Mr. O'Reilley — a fine man, God bless him! — and this would be a fine house to stay in. It was the best house on the island and himself was the most honest of them all. Soon, to enhance his own honesty, he was making the others out to be rogues. But the islands were perfect, he concluded, and indeed the people were perfect enough and lacked nothing but money.

'Why should you want money?' asked Elizabeth.

'There is nothing to spend it on. What would you do with it?'

'If we had money we could go away. We could go to America.'

'What would you do in America?'

'Make more money.' He looked at her sideways out of his large pale eyes, shaped like horses' eyes, and, after a pause, added quickly: 'But money isn't everything. No, it is not indeed. It's a very little thing when we've got everything here that anyone could be wanting. What good is money, anyway?'

'I don't know what good it is,' answered Elizabeth with the frigid honesty of boredom. 'But I don't see why you shouldn't want it the same as everybody else does. You might grow up with views all around you, but you're only human beings for all that.'

Nolan got no more than the gist of this, but it was enough to make him open his eyes in surprised admiration: 'There's a wise lady for you,' he called out to his wife, the ponderous woman looking twenty years his senior.

She smiled and nodded stupidly and echoed him in her muddled English: 'A wise lady! Indeed, yes, I do think. Indeed so.'

'She knows it's the money — indeed, yes, the money! Who wouldn't be wanting it, I'd like to know.' The man laughed and nodded, looking at her admiringly, his eyes nakedly exposing a curious mixture of generosity and naïve greed. He would do anything to inveigle a shilling out of you, but once he got it he would feel a little ashamed and want to give you something in return.

He talked on in a rambling way, flattering Elizabeth.

At first there had been the slight novelty of his transparency, now that that was ceasing to be a novelty, she felt restless with boredom. It was necessary to repeat everything to him so often, to simplify it to the mere bones of its meaning before he understood. And most of the time it was obvious he was merely pretending to understand. It was rather tedious. The wooden stool was beginning to make her behind ache.

She got up and went to the door and opened it. Outside the night was so soft and black, she half expected it to stream in like a black powder through the doorway. There were no lights on the island but the little, piercing lights of the windows. Later, if it remained clear, there would be a moon, but now there was only darkness.

The woman put some mackerel in a pan on the fire. 'You'll be hungry,' she said to Elizabeth.

Yes. Elizabeth realized she was hungry. The table was laid for her in the sitting-room that was very cold, without ventilation and filled with a rancid smell of stale smoke. She said she'd rather eat in the kitchen, but no, she must eat in the sitting-room for she was a guest. Here there was a cast-iron fire-place filled with crinkled paper and a mantelpiece hung with a green plush labrequin, and crowded over with scripture cards and the little delf ornaments one wins at fairs. At the end of the room was a large wardrobe painted yellow and brown. Another small table by the wall held all the household's superior possessions — knives and forks, bought butter in paper, bought jam mixed with flies and wasps in a jar, and four glass candlesticks each moulded in the shape of a crucifix.

As Elizabeth ate her mackerel and home-made bread, she heard someone come into the house. This must be Riordan. She began to feel excited. After all, she might be about to make a discovery. She stopped eating and waited for the door to open.

It opened. He entered the sitting-room. He said: 'Good evening', and then stood looking at her as though there was really nothing else to be said.

She nodded: 'Good evening.' She knew that he knew why she had come, so there seemed no need to start telling him. But she did not know what to say, so said: 'You know why I have come, don't you?'

'Yes,' he smiled a little as though he were inwardly amused at something. 'When you have finished,' he said, 'we will go out.'

He looked at her with polite interest as though he had just been introduced to her in a drawing-room. She met his pleasant, rather tired smile, and he seemed to her like one of those middle-aged men who keep up the pretence that they still have the interests they had in youth. He leant against the wall with his hands in his pockets — very tall and strongly built, wearing corduroy trousers and the heavy, knitted jersey and coloured, woven belt of the islanders. He was very handsome in the classical fashion with dark auburn hair, greying at the temples, that curled over his head in a poetic way. His beauty was the only arresting thing about him. Yes, the only thing. She saw him kindly, charming enough, but quite ineffectual, and she felt the stronger.

'Aren't you going to have anything to eat?' she asked.

'I had supper at the house of a friend.'

She said: 'How can I get back to Galway? I must be in Dublin to-morrow.'

'I will row you back to Costello in the morning. You can get a bus from there to Galway.'

Because she felt the stronger she felt patronizingly towards him and half contemptuous. She said: 'Those glass candlesticks are rather curious.'

He went and picked one up as though he had not seen them before: 'Nolan hires them out to anyone having a wake. They stand two at either end of the corpse.'

'Oh!' She remembered they had been mixed up with the butter and jam and cutlery. She really did not want anything more to eat.

'Nolan brought them from America.'

'Really!' That surprised her so she forgot the corpses and went on eating automatically. 'When did Nolan go to America?'

'When he was a young man. All the Islanders will tell you they have never left the islands, but after you have been talking to them a little while, you discover that most of them have been to America at some time or other. They get the boat at Galway and just cross the Atlantic. That means nothing to them. They put more trust in the sea than in the land and New York is only over the water. On a clear day, when you stand on the cliff, you might almost think you could see it. It's not a journey for them. It would cause them more trepidation to set out for Dublin.'

Yes, he was really quite a charming man; willing to talk; willing to amuse and interest her. But where was Riordan the great leader?

How he must have disappointed Sean! Here was no force to uphold the uncertain Sean against surrender and despair. It was understandable now that Sean had had so little to say of him. What could he say? That Riordan was a pleasant man? When all anticipated the fierce, undefeatable leadership of a great liberator!

She got up from the table: 'I've finished,' she said, 'shall we go now?'

'Yes.' He opened the door for her. In all his speech and movement there was a quality of completion. You felt the man was fulfilled and complete. There was no further development in him. This is the finished product — this! How terribly that must have lamed Sean who drew his sustenance from the inspiration of possibility in people. No unplundered depths or reservations. Here is all displayed — a delightful and satisfactory shop window.

No more?

As they passed through the kitchen, he said to Nolan: 'We are going for a walk.'

'And the young lady?' inquired Nolan in an anxious voice. 'Will she be spending the night here?'

'Yes.' Riordan opened the door.

'Then we will make the spare bed. . . .'

Riordan closed the door and they merged into the soot-dark night. There was no telling earth from sky. The road seemed to glimmer faintly because they knew it was there. Riordan turned to the left, away from the road to the harbour, towards the rising headland of the north.

Elizabeth said: 'Someone must have informed on them. Sean was arrested.'

'I am sorry,' said Riordan, but there was no regret in his tone. Something in his placid acceptance of Sean's failure, in his placid, unthinking acceptance of his own safety, made her want to strike out viciously at him.

'If I had not come,' she said, 'would you have gone to Costello to-morrow morning?'

'Yes, of course,' he said quietly, quite unresentfully.

'Without much enthusiasm?'

He shrugged his shoulders a little and did not reply.

'You have no faith in Sean?' she asked.

He paused a moment before saying in his quiet, unoffending voice: 'It is not that.'

'None in yourself?'

He said nothing, but went to the wall from which the fields fell down in steep slopes to the sea. He looked down and Elizabeth, feeling she was expected to look, too, looked and saw below the slight, pale movement of the huddled sheep. He said: 'The beasts here are left out all night, winter and summer. Even in the lambing season the ewes are left in the fields. There are no frosts. If it were not for the wind anything would grow.' He must talk, he must entertain the visitor that chance had put upon him. She wondered if his silence and then this deviation into politely proffered information, was rebuke to her question, or if, as it seemed, he had not heard her ask it.

For some reason, she felt he had heard her. The change of subject seemed too studied to be other than admonitory. Was he one of those — a dying kind, thank heaven! a discomfort to her and natural enemy — who felt all frankness a discourtesy? Immediately she feared it, she felt muffled. The company of anyone who required her to restrain her tongue irked her beyond endurance. With Arion the restraint was instinctive — a different thing — and their silence had serpent's fangs. With this Riordan her instinct was to jar him out of complacency by the penetration of her questioning. And he was going to reprove her with unanswerable politeness! She felt stifled. He talked. She listened unwillingly, not really listening.

As they walked the eastern sky lightened and the air began to glow with the delicately diffused light of the hidden moon. The road and the fields appeared slowly out of the darkness. Elizabeth saw before her the great sand crescent and motionless waters of a bay.

Suddenly there was a sound of hoofs and of stones falling from a wall and, in an instant, a stallion had leapt down to the road a few yards before them and was galloping wildly to the shore. When it came to the soft, dry sand banked at the top of the beach it lay down and rolled about, throwing up sand clouds that hung in the silver light like great silver-webs.

'What's come over the beast at all?' said Riordan.

They stopped in the roadway and watched it. Its movements, flashing iridescent in the strange light, had a furious vitality as though the beast that during the day was a common stallion cropping grass in a field, at night assumed a centaur strength and the old centaur rule over a world returned to pristine freshness.

Waves of sand curled like spray into the air. The stallion whinnied, then, with a great flourish of mane and tail, leapt to its feet and cantered off. There was a noise in the fields above. Again the wall was broken and down swept a dark horse to follow the white. The white one glanced away as the dark one approached and the dark followed closely like the shadow of the white taken upon itself an individual life in this mystical air. They swerved and, as quickly as they had appeared, disappeared into the shadows beyond the beach.

Elizabeth, watching them, was elated as she had been when, a student, she had felt her increasing ability sufficient excuse for existence. She began to think how she might paint this silver horse with its dark shadow, flourishing its uncut mane and tail through the silver light. She felt the excitement of wanting to paint them.

She stood for a long time looking towards them as they vanished into the distance. At last Riordan moved a little and she turned quickly and found him watching her. She felt distant from him. In some way she felt unsubstantial and diffused, yet curiously aware. She smiled at him, charitable in her superior consciousness.

'They seemed to amuse you,' he said.

'I am a painter,' she said, distant and contemptuous of him.

He nodded: 'The world has another dimension for an artist.'

She did not reply, but followed him as he turned off from the road. They began climbing up slopes covered with coarse, hard grass through which the rocks could be felt like bones. She kept wanting to speak to him and question him now that he had said that, yet, strangely, she could not say anything. They climbed up in silence. They passed a white house. It was so sheltered by the towering headland a fuchsia hedge had been able to grow round it. The little flowers hung blackly all over the hedge. They left the house behind and went on up, crossing one field after another, climbing the walls of loose stone and replacing the stones that fell as they jumped down on the other side.

Elizabeth was conscious of their silence. Every moment she felt on the point of breaking it, yet could not. Her consciousness was divided. The inspired and nervous excitement to which the horses' flight had raised her was now contested by new awareness of Riordan. Might there be in him something to be discovered — and discoverable. She could not leave unprobed the mystery in people.

They came at length to a steep field set all over with jagged stones and above them towered the wall of the great fortress. Riordan started telling her about it — that it had no history because it was older even than the memory of the islanders. The light of the moon was beginning to slope up the grasses. It touched the stones of the wall. They passed through the entrance, a low and narrow archway cut in the great thickness of the wall, and came into the fortress. The walls tiered up on either side of them and they stood in a monstrous grass-covered arena. The wind was so strong, Elizabeth felt she could turn and lean against it. The fall of the cliffs in centuries had broken away an arc in the wall's oval so a horseshoe remained. Riordan crossed the grass and Elizabeth followed him until they came to the cliff's edge. The sea broke ceaselessly against the rocks below. They stood and looked out over the Atlantic Ocean. The sea, hidden by the island from the rising moon, was a black void. The cliff fell sheer

into blackness from their feet. It was as though the
earth were really flat and they had come to the edge of
it and stared out now into space.

Elizabeth threw herself down on to the grass and
felt the reverberation of the earth as the waves' thunder
sipped at the cliff's base. Riordan remained standing.
The moon was higher now. It was lighting the arena,
though the void beneath them remained impenetrably
dark. Riordan became visible from the shadows
standing there staring out at the Atlantic, his hands
hanging at his sides. He was slightly round-shouldered.
She felt his inertia like a numbness in the air — yet he
no longer left her untroubled.

She said: 'Doesn't it matter to you that the rising has
failed?'

He looked round slowly and seeing she was seated,
lowered himself down on to the grass a little way from
her. All his movements had a slightly aged stiffness.
He lay on his side, propped on one elbow and picked
aimlessly at the short, brittle grass.

After a moment, he said: 'If it were Sean's idea, then
I am sorry for his sake,' and added, after a pause,
'But it has not failed. Nothing fails in Ireland. It is
only that the victory is delayed.'

'But you do not want to come?'

'I am quite content here.'

'What have you found to make you contented here?'

He shrugged his shoulders and smiled a little. She
looked across at him, at his surprisingly perfect profile
that, nevertheless, lacked for her the quality of beauty,
and said: 'But what can there be for you here? Are you
working on some great book?'

'No,' he shook his head, 'I don't write now.'

'You were a rebel, but you are so contented here you cannot be a rebel any longer.'

He laughed suddenly and turned to her. 'Vanity will make you one thing and unhappiness make you another — but are you either of those things? Vanity can intoxicate you into believing yourself a writer and you can write when intoxicated by vanity. I wrote well enough — nothing genuine, of course, but it deceived most people. The danger is that something will happen to destroy your vanity and then you must face sobriety.'

'What happened to you?' she asked with the rather insolent abruptness she adopted towards some people.

'A very commonplace thing — I was treated badly by a woman. When I got over it, I found I had become quite cold inside. Nothing could excite my brain any more. I was sober and dead. By that time I had come to regard myself as a writer — and, afterwards, I could not write. It was as though I had no life to draw on. There was nothing inside me but clockwork. I thought it was nerves and would pass off, but it didn't.'

'Haven't you written anything since?'

'Once or twice in a sort of anger I forced myself to write. I worked myself up into a sort of false intoxication of anger — but it was no good. It passed too quickly and I couldn't finish what I had begun. I started dozens of things and couldn't finish them.'

The moon suddenly touched the water. Curiously, in the black depths beyond the cliffs, appeared a wrinkled serpent of silver. Riordan looked down at it, his face dully expressionless. He was not even bitter.

She said, a little jealously: 'She must have been a very remarkable woman.'

'No,' Riordan shook his head with reflective slowness, 'she was very ordinary. It wasn't the woman. It was the idea.'

Elizabeth could not understand that. 'Do you mean ideal?' she asked thinking uncharitably that he would probably mean something like that.

'No. Not ideal. I saw her quite clearly. I knew exactly what she was like. I thought there was a sort of understanding between us, and that it was the sort of understanding that makes you feel you would be at home in eternity. I thought that because I had no illusions about her there was nothing to be destroyed and the perfection of our relationship was indestructible. She was married and separated from her husband who would not divorce her, so we could not marry. One day she met someone she liked better and left me. The strange thing was — she said she had always hated me. She said she had only put up with me because she could not afford to leave me until she had somewhere to go. It was just as though I had injured her in some way.' He looked at Elizabeth with a sort of bewildered smile.

'Did she make you write?'

'No, she was a damned nuisance, really. I often wished I'd never met her. She took the edge off things so I could not feel enough to write well, but I wrote quite smugly and comfortably and prolifically.'

'Yet you never thought of breaking with her?'

'I wouldn't have believed it possible to do so. But she left me. Before that I had pretty straightforward ideas about everything. I knew what I wanted to write and how to write it. It was all clear enough. Being so sure of her, I felt sure of everything else. But afterwards it was as though everything had been broken up and pieced together wrong. I couldn't see anything clearly. What could I write about when everything seemed a pointless muddle? Sometimes I forced myself to write articles for papers as I used. But as soon as I set down one statement, I could see the force of its contradiction and, therefore, it didn't seem much good writing anything. After that it was hell. I used to get in a panic as though I were trapped in a maze. All I wanted then was some sort of explosion to clear the air.'

He still talked in his conversational way, easily and expressionlessly; and, as he talked, he looked away from her towards the sea. She did not say anything. She did not want to interrupt him or remind him that whilst he talked she listened.

'I couldn't bear to go on being conscious of myself — that's why I wanted something violent to happen outside myself to absorb me. It was then I got in with Connolly. His ideas were clear enough. He knew what he wanted and all there was to do was to get it or die in the attempt. I let him absorb me completely. His cause became my whole life; there was nothing else for me. There was nothing I would not say or do on his behalf. I was afraid of nothing because nothing could happen to me worse than had happened. Death seemed to me trivial compared with it. You will find that a good many people are courageous for that reason, and give up their lives only to escape their own bewilderment. We said we would liberate Ireland or die. But I didn't die. Whilst I was lying unconscious in

Stephen's Green, someone put me in a car and got me out of Dublin before the arrests were made. At first I was furious at finding I had failed and yet was still alive. I felt as though a trick had been played on me. I wandered about the Connemara Hills hoping I would die. I did not try to save myself from cold or starvation, yet despite myself, I was saved every time. People were always finding me and helping me. They did not know who I was. I was nothing to them, yet they saved my life merely because life itself was marvellous to them and of value. Life for its own sake had seemed to me not only valueless, but distasteful. I would not be reconciled with the commonplace of existence into which I had been placed unconsulted' (that reminded her of Sean. Strangely, she was hearing Sean speak now). 'I wanted something better than that, and if I couldn't have something better, then I didn't want anything. So I sulked about the hills until, finding that for all my sulks I was still alive and could make no active attempt to kill myself, I suddenly started laughing at myself . . .'

'And so,' said Elizabeth, 'you became reconciled to your own mediocrity.'

'Yes,' he nodded, completely untroubled by her, 'reconciled to my own mediocrity. I realized I was not Riordan the writer or Riordan to whom an extraordinay love had been given, or Riordan the leader. I was only the very ordinary Riordan who now lives on this island. I eat, sleep, fish, cart sea-weed and peats and get drunk with the rest occasionally. One day perhaps I will marry one of the women here and the others will help me to build a house.'

After a pause, Elizabeth said: 'Don't you realize that to the young men of Ireland you are still the great leader who will come again?'

He said: 'They will forget me.'

She said: 'What would you have done if Sean had taken you to Dublin?'

He shrugged his shoulders a little: 'I suppose my reputation would have carried me through. If not, I would have disappointed them all.'

His placidity infuriated her: 'But if Sean comes to you again and asks you . . .'

He interrupted quietly: 'He won't come again.'

'How do you know he won't come again. You said yourself that to the Irish there is no such thing as defeat, only delayed victory. Do you suppose he won't try again?'

'Probably. But you will not let him come to me again.'

'I won't? But . . .'

'Why do you suppose I brought you here and told you so much about myself? You are an intelligent young woman. Can't you see the folly of taking me to Dublin and setting me up as a leader? You would not let Sean attempt anything so foolish again.'

'But why didn't you tell Sean about yourself this time?'

'If you had been me, could you have told him?'

'You are a coward,' said Elizabeth.

'Yes,' he nodded and smiled a little, 'I am a coward amongst other things. I am a coward in the same way as so many ordinary people are. I cannot hurt people or destroy their hope — so I let things go on and trust to luck and muddle through somehow. You should be glad your Rising has failed. I'm afraid it might have failed even more ingloriously if I had come and we had attempted it.'

'Not if Arion had been there.'

'Who is Arion?'

She shook her head without answering and stood up. She had no interest left for Riordan. She only wanted to be on her way back to Dublin. She said: 'Couldn't you row me over to the mainland now?'

He said: 'What would you do when you got there? How would you get from Costello to Galway? There are no buses at this time of night and it would take you till daybreak to walk it.'

She knew this and could not insist further. But she felt angry and frustrated and wanted to accuse him. Her contempt for him made her feel in some way intimate with him and uncaring of what she said or did when with him. She said: 'Then I suppose I must sleep at Nolan's?'

All the time he was very charming and courteous: 'It is the best thing I can suggest.'

She said angrily: 'I wish you hadn't made me miss the steamer back. You should have come to see if anyone were there for you. You might have known it would be possible.'

He shrugged his shoulders and said lamely: 'I did not think of it.'

He exasperated her painfully, the more so because she felt she was behaving badly with him. She was showing him the worst side of herself from sheer indifference to him, and she felt there was something vulgar about doing that. She could not help it. She did not really want to help it.

And, in a way, too, her exasperation was partly of disappointment. She had not been conscious of expecting anything much from him. She had not been conscious of his having for her a possibility from which his reality had deviated, yet she was disappointed. After all, he might have been the divinizer that would give meaning to all things, instead of just another little blind alley like the many she had wasted her days exploring. No revelation here, no hope of mutation.

They passed through the archway and came out to the hillside. The hillside was flooded now with the white light of the moon. The whole vast, rock-broken slope down to the shore and the waters was revealed. The waters and, beyond them, the black and static Twelve Pins. The great arc of the sky was whitened by the light of the moon. The whole scene was inhumanly lit by the limelight of the moon!

They started walking down between the stones of the *chevaux de frise*. Elizabeth was conscious of Riordan moving beside her; she was conscious of the slightly ponderous stiffness of his movements and her exasperation became unbearable. As they climbed over the first wall, she suddenly leapt down and away from him. She ran away from him headlong over the difficult ground in an almost ecstatic relief of escape from him.

The wind was with her. It hastened her progress until she felt rising in her the wild force of excitement that had possessed her so often in adolescence and which she seemed, somehow, to have lost since. She felt a new welling-up in her of the stream of excitement that had once rushed through her, promising so much and which she had let peter away in futile, little *affaires*, in uncertainties and indecisions and futile, little hopes; the stream she had let peter away, almost willed away to escape the depths and heights to which it had carried her, and to escape the nervous suffering of disappointment and the labour of harnessing its power.

She felt as though she had taken wings in flight. She sped over the walls and across the fields down to the shore. The white strand was like a great white stage behind which lay the scenery of sea and hills. Amazingly, there might break through the sky a whirling descent of charioteers — winged chariots, winged horses in the rhythmic flight of ballet. She paused, peopling, in a sort of vision, the white, unbroken stage. Once she had dreamt of being a great decorative artist. She had seemed to possess the elated and dramatic fancy, the unending ideas crowding in so it had seemed she would not have time enough to express them all. And now she had been wasting time for years.

But she would waste no more. Why should she give a damn for anyone when there was so much to be done?

It was like coming to life again. She ran furiously.

She came at last to the great, flat stretches of rocks and leapt over the chasms that struck deeply into them. The rock was striped with veins of white granite lying straight and cleanly marked like the lines of a tennis court. The moonlight glittered over the strand. Everywhere the sand glittered white and frigid like salt. The livid, dazzling light enhanced the silence and desertion of the place. It maddened her. She ran over the sand

and let herself sink and fall into its softness. Tears streamed down her face. She wanted to scream and pommel the sand with her fists. She cried out loudly: 'Oh God, make use of me or I shall go mad.' She covered her face with her hands and sank down in furious tears.

Riordan, who had followed her as closely as he could, fearing she might fall and injure herself, stood and watched her in bewilderment. He came close to her and stood over her and asked quietly: 'What is the matter?'

After a while she shook her head and sobbed bitterly into herself: 'I don't know. I don't know. I don't know what's going to happen to me.'

Bewildered, worried and concerned, he knelt down beside her and asked: 'But what would be likely to happen to you?'

She was abandoned to her nerves, she was quite uncaring of him in her voluptuous abandonment. She spoke half to him, half to herself, with a clear and passionate violence, extraverting the concentrated flood of her unused energy: 'I don't know. Sometimes I feel something terrible is going to happen to me. Yes, something terrible. I don't know what. I don't know.'

He talked soothingly. 'Of course nothing will happen to you. Why should it? Lots of people have had the same sort of dread of something happening and nothing has happened. It's all nerves and imagination. Nothing will happen to you.'

She lifted her face, red and stained with tears, and looked at him impatiently: 'But don't you realize its just that nothing happening that I dread? All my life passing with nothing happening! Year after year of my life, and my youth passing, all my youth and energy being wasted in nothing happening!' Her voice weakened until she broke down altogether and subsided into sobs. 'It's all such a waste. I thought once I could do so much that I'd never have time to do it all, and yet in all these years I've done nothing. It's such a terrible waste . . . a terrible waste.'

Riordan patted her shoulder: 'You're very tired, aren't you?'

She nodded agreement. He went on in a soothing half whisper: 'Very tired. Very tired.' He put his arm gently round her and with a gentle, effortless strength, raised her up. She lent against him, exhausted, as they went back to the road. They walked quietly over the white road. After a while he said in a fatherly, solicitous way: 'You know, you'd be much happier married.'

She said: 'I know,' in a weak, small voice, pleasurably melted into acceptance of his solicitude.

'What about Sean?'

'Oh!' she said. 'He doesn't care about me. He doesn't want me.'

'And this Arion you mentioned?'

'He's married — and I don't mean anything to him, anyway.' As she spoke she realized the truth of what she said. With an amazing clarity, she realized it and admitted it and remained indifferent.

'Then there's no one?'

'No.'

'That's a pity,' he said easily and held her the tighter.

When they came to the house they found it in darkness. The Nolans had gone to bed. The front door was not bolted. They went in and Riordan lit the lamp. The peats were still hot in the open hearth. Mrs. Nolan had left two glasses of milk for them on the table. Riordan still talked.

'She is an extraordinary woman,' he said, 'she always cooks twice as many potatoes as she needs and throws half of them away. I asked her why she didn't keep a pig and she said there was no profit in pigs, but the truth is she'd be too lazy to feed it. Rather than go to the spring for water she washes my glass out with milk and throws the milk out of the door. But they're all alike. I'm not an unnecessarily active man, but I'm regarded as a positive fount of energy here.'

Elizabeth sat and sipped her milk and half listened in a daze of exhaustion. When Riordan showed her to the room that the Nolans preserved for the few visitors they captured, she lay, without undressing, on the bed and fell immediately asleep.

VIII

AND MONDAY

SHE awoke at noon with a headache and, still tired, lay for a long time on the bed, uncomfortable but without energy to move. After the first few hours she had not slept well. She had awakened three times in the night and each time sat up thinking someone had opened the door and entered her room. The second time she found the matches in her handbag, struck one, and looked round in the glimmering of light at the closed door and the bare room. Outside it was very dark and everything was strange.

When she awoke the third time it was dawn. She got up and leaned from the window and watched the light give, with gentle slowness, form and colour to the hills. As though materializing from nothingness, they grew out of the air with the lustre of glass. They darkened as the sky whitened, deepening beneath their light sheen to green and onyx. The sea lay like a mist between them and the island. In the fields running down to the shore, the sea mist billowed round the newly awakened beasts so only their heads and backs were visible. In a little while everything cleared. The colour of sea and sky and fields crept like a dye through the mist, gaining and hardening brilliantly until there was revealed the delicate certainty of water, grass and shell-silver clouds. Everything looked to her new and wonderful as though she were Adam and this the first morning of creation. She felt there was a sufficiency in solitude in this place if she could only overcome her consciousness of people.

She began to yawn. Her head throbbed. She felt completely and stupidly exhausted. She returned to bed and slept until noon.

The sun on the bare, unpainted walls made the room look like a room in an unfinished house. It was big, with the bed, a chair and a washstand all crowded together at one end and nothing at the other end but a large, flowered chamber-pot in the middle of the floor. The window was not more than two foot square and set low in the wall beside the bed. The bedstead was a double, iron bedstead. It was draped with dirty muslin curtains. On to the top rail, where the curtains parted, hung a postcard on which was pasted a red velvet sacred heart. The cotton sheets were wrinkled because they had never been ironed and they had a grey look.

For a long time she lay wondering what was depressing her; then she remembered what she had said to Riordan the night before. She thought of Sean and Arion, and, suddenly, she felt she must get back to Dublin. She was no longer anxious to return to Sean now. She seemed to have lost the illusion of a relationship between them. In the instant of telling Riordan that Sean cared nothing for her, the illusion was past....
And yet, not wholly. She was sick with uncertainty, restless to be back again and gain certainty.

She splashed her face with the cold water in the jug and repaired her appearance with the comb and powder in her handbag.

She found Riordan talking to a group of men in the

road outside the house. She ran out to him: 'I must go now.'

'But you must eat something first.'

'No. I'm not hungry. I really must go.'

'Just one moment, then.' He went towards the house. As he moved away the men called after him, laughingly, in Irish. She followed him in and asked: 'What were they saying?'

He turned to her, laughing, too, and said: 'They wanted to know was I marrying at last.'

'Oh!' She had nothing to say. He went up to his room and came down with a jersey over his shirt. Mrs. Nolan, who had been making his bed, came down with him and was flusteredly determined that Elizabeth should eat before she went. A heap of newly-caught mackerel lay on the table. She set to frying one and Elizabeth had to wait impatiently and eat impatiently when it was fried. But she was glad of it.

Mrs. Nolan waved her away and, at last, she and Riordan were returning to the strand that faced Costello. Two black upturned curraghs lay like long, strange beetles on the sand. Riordan's dinghy was beside them. Whilst he pulled it down to the shore, cutting a deep trench as he went, Elizabeth stood at the water's edge and felt the soft, sweet wind in her face. She glanced back over the grey uprising of land against the blue sky, then round again to the glass-clear water, and was suddenly caught into an enchantment by the place. Without thinking, she said to herself: 'I must come back here', and then shut her lips angrily, feeling as though she had been tricked.

As she sat in the stern, Riordan stared over her

shoulder at the receding shore. He said: 'Do you like my island?'

After a pause she said: 'I feel I must go back to it again.'

He smiled and said: 'If it has caught you, you will come back.'

They said little more than that as they rowed for nearly three hours across the flat, shining sound towards the mainland. The hills grew steadily defined. Houses and trees grew out of indecision. The road, along which she had driven with Sean and Arion the week before, appeared brownish and stony and deserted.

She said: 'Is this the dinghy Sean had last week?'

Yes, it was. 'One of the curraghs brought it back for me.'

'But why didn't you go over with him and bring it back yourself?'

'He wanted to go alone. He said he did not want anyone else to see me until the time came.'

She believed, then, that Sean had suspected Riordan and would not let Arion, with his penetrating criticism, see him and make suspicion certainty.

Riordan avoided Cashla Bay and the pier in case the police were waiting for him there. He rowed along the coast and drew into the shore near Inveran. He said: 'You should get a bus to Galway easily from here. And you will come back again?'

'One day, perhaps.'

He had drawn the boat up into the shingle so she could jump ashore without getting her feet wet. He stood on the shore and held her hand instead of shaking it. 'Why not come back and marry me?' he said.

She was appalled at the idea. And yet, perversely, almost with a sort of perverse pleasure, she considered it seriously. It was just the sort of thing that would happen to her. Yes, she recognized it, appalled: just the sort of thing. As though in spite of herself, she smiled, carefully preserving the idea, careful not to discourage him beyond hope in case she might, one day, want to return and marry him. It was the retention of a sort of despondent insurance against complete loneliness.

She said: 'I might, one day.'

As she went up the stone-littered beach to the turf, she turned twice and smiled good-bye to him. Really, she did not want him at all. Not at all. She couldn't bear him. Couldn't. She was appalled at the idea of marrying him — and, yet, she knew he thought she would return. She felt revolted by the thought of physical intimacy with him, and, yet, curious, wondering how it would rouse him. But of course she would not return.

She hurried to the road and walked along it until a bus came up behind her. She stopped and boarded it and was driven on to Galway. The town was becoming familiar. This remote, western town, to which she had scarcely given even a thought until a week before, was becoming familiar. From henceforth when someone spoke of it, it would be a real place to her with shops and houses and people in the street. And some of the places she would remember very well — the inn where they had had breakfast last week, the bridge over the salmon preserves and the fish in the water, the quay, even the garage where she had left the car. . . .

She found the garage. It was locked and deserted. For God's sake! She knocked on the rickety but un-yielding doors and there was no reply. On either side were dilapidated warehouses — tall and strongly built, bearing, over their doorways, the arms of the Lynchs. Their windows were boarded; grass grew from their whitewashed walls. No one to question in the whole length of the road. She started walking furiously up and down; then, as furiously, pounded on the door with her fists.

At last a man appeared from a tenement house some way down on the other side of the road and stood and watched her with interest. When she saw him she flung over to him and demanded where was the pro-prietor of the garage? He said he didn't really know, but — and he became confidential — the proprietor was a member of the I.R.A., so it was likely enough he'd been called away on duty that day.

But hadn't he an assistant?

Yes, but with the proprietor away it was only to be expected that the assistant would take the day off. The assistant was Dave O'Day — he spoke the name as though it were a famous one — and, maybe, he could be found.

But he must be found. 'My car's in there and I've got to get back to Dublin to-night. Where can I find him?'

'Sure, I'll send one of the youngsters to find him for you.'

After what seemed to Elizabeth an interminable delay for explanations and comments, a small boy was dispatched to go the round of the public houses in search of Dave O'Day. In an hour he had not reappeared, nor in two hours, nor three.

She went to get something to eat and, when she returned, the man had found a bundle of old keys somewhere and was trying them, one after the other, in the padlock on the garage. None fitted. Becoming interested and persevering, he went round the house borrowing likely keys from all the other occupants. Then he went to other houses. A crowd began to collect and the women from the surrounding tenements, touched by Elizabeth's anxiety, came out and presented her with an endless procession of cups of tea. She kept repeating her gratitude, but she hated tea and, suddenly she said before she knew she was going to say it: 'I hate tea', and everyone was aghast. After that there was a strained silence. It began to get dark and she found she was being left alone. She walked up and down, almost demented with worry and boredom, until, at last, the small boy reappeared with a grinning, delighted Dave O'Day.

At last, at last, she was returning. She drove out her fury in an insanely reckless flight through the darkness and then slowed to a steady twenty-five miles an hour. As she tired, she went more slowly until, at dawn, she was no further than Kilcock. At Lucan, she came to the tram lines. They shone blae in the coming light. The air was greyly strange in the silent, unawakened streets. Although she was more asleep than awake when she reached the bridge, she made straight for Sean's rooms. The door opened when she tried it. She went up the stairs and found the bed tossed exactly as he had left it on Saturday night. Everything else was

313

overturned in a search that must have taken place some time after his arrest. Someone had attempted to strip from the walls the pencilled newspaper paragraphs — but they were too tightly stuck.

So he had not been released yet?

She lay down on his bed and went to sleep. When she awoke to the sunlight of midday she was conscious of a curious hush in the air. For a long time she could not account for it, then, suddenly, she realized the firing had ceased. Something had happened. She jumped up and ran downstairs and, as she did so, met O'Rorke coming up. She said: 'So you are released!'

He said: 'Yes, I was released this morning. I have seen Sharp and Daly. I don't think Finnigan was arrested, but I can find nothing out about Sean. Is he here?'

'He is not,' she replied. They went together down to the street: 'What has happened?' she asked.

'A truce,' said O'Rorke, 'they have let all the prisoners out on parole. To think of it! A truce! There's an end for you! But of course it's not the end! We've still Riordan up our sleeve.'

She left him with a sense of dejection. Dusty and stale with travel, she drove back to her lodging house. How amazingly quiet was the air! People walked with a new carelessness. Gunmen and soldiers greeted one another in the street and shook hands and laughed together. Elizabeth, newly returned, dusty and tired, felt outsider and half foolish, like one in church who has gone on singing after the choir has ceased. It was as though she had made a sacrifice and then been told it was not necessary. Flippantly told: 'How foolish of

you! Sacrifices are out of fashion. That's all over now.'
And it was all over and she outsider, fool and loser.
She was dreary with a sense of loss, but she did not
know what she had lost.

After the months of intermittent gunfire the continual silence was unearthly. It was as though some
tension had gone out of the air. The muscles of the
air were relaxed in lassitude that was like a sort of
death.

As she went up the stairs she caught her breath in
apprehension at the thought of entering Arion's room.
She was afraid of finding it empty. But he was there.
He was in the bedroom. His suitcases lay open on his
bed. His wardrobe door stood open. The drawers in
the chest of drawers were all pulled out. Arion, with
careful and precise movements of his small hands, was
lifting out socks and shirts, ties and suits, and, after
folding them carefully, packing them carefully in the
suitcases. She crossed and stood for a few moments
behind him before speaking. He had not seen her enter.
She said: 'Where is Sean?'

He turned quickly and, seeing her, smiled as though
something had hurt him. He said: 'But where have you
been? You have been away, haven't you?'

'Yes,' she nodded without smiling back, 'I went to
warn Riordan. He is safe.'

'That is good,' he answered quietly.

'Where is Sean?'

He looked at her with a sort of reflective suffering
and said: 'He's dead.'

When she did not say anything, he went on in a
hurried voice: 'He died early yesterday morning. He

315

was feverish on Saturday night and they took him to the prison hospital. He was delirious all night and he died yesterday morning. He asked to see me and they would have sent for me but, before they could get permission through, it was too late.'

'But he promised he would not die,' she said vaguely. 'He promised . . .' and then, with a sudden fury: 'People don't die suddenly like that just because they're feverish. It just doesn't happen.'

'I'm afraid it does happen. He had had pneumonia for some days without knowing it and his lungs were affected.' Arion was quiet with the old tender quietness with which he had assailed her when they first became lovers. He lifted up the ivory hair-brushes and tucked them into the suitcase.

She said: 'They must have shot him.'

Arion looked up, a little startled, opened his mouth, then closed it again and looked away. He grew paler. He started packing again with his slow method.

'They shot him,' she said, 'and told you he died because they knew there was to be a truce and they had no right to shoot him.' Her anger struck at him, but he would not look up. He said:

'No, I'm sure they did not shoot him. As a matter of fact, I know . . .'

'How do you know? How can you possibly know?'

He shrugged his shoulders and would not answer and she knew it was useless to question him any more. He closed one of the suitcases. For the first time she thought to ask him: 'Where are you going?'

'To England. To London.'

'Can I come with you?'

'I would prefer you didn't.' He was a stranger, but hadn't he been that all the time?

'When are you going? Now?'

'In a few minutes. I am catching the boat at Kingstown.'

She looked round and saw he had packed all his things. He must have already sent his trunk.

Looking at her, he saw her dull glance round and was irritated by a sort of pity of her. He felt a relief knowing he would never see her again. When he finished with people, he finished with them completely. He left no loose ends trailing by which they could catch and draw him back again. If he met a past friend again there was absolutely no point of contact. He was a stranger, with this difference — his strangeness was an end, not a beginning. There had been only the one relationship he had been unable to terminate with this finality.

She said: 'Were you arrested on Saturday night?'

'No.'

'But the others were — not only Sean, but Sharp, O'Rorke and Daly!'

'I know. I suppose, being English. . . .' He closed another suitcase. She was standing by the window looking down into the street. Her desolation touched and hurt him. Yet, what could he do? He asked himself: 'But what can I do?' He answered himself: 'Nothing,' and went on packing his letters and papers into the last and smallest of the cases, one finely made of crocodile skin.

Looking down into the street she was appalled at the thought of his going and leaving her alone in Dublin.

It seemed to her that all her old acquaintances had been diminished out of knowing by her acquaintance with Arion. She had forgotten them and did not want to know them again. It seemed to her that with Arion gone she would know no one.

She said in her small, desolate voice: 'I shall be quite alone here when you go.'

He said: 'Does that matter?'

She did not answer and, when he glanced up, he saw her leaning against the window-frame staring down into the street with a sort of despairing dread. She irritated him as though she were thrusting a responsibility upon him. For an instant his irritation and a fear that she might, in some way, try to prevent his going or try to force him to take her, wavered his self-control. He said with an angry quiet: 'Can't you ever depend on yourself? Must you always live vicariously off someone stronger than yourself?'

She said, as though she had not heard him: 'What about the car?'

His annoyance was gone at once. He said: 'I am not taking it back. You can have it, if you like.'

'Oh, thank you,' she nodded. 'Would you like me to drive you to Kingstown?'

'That would be very kind of you.' He smiled at her a polite and charming stranger's smile.

The caretaker's husband came up and carried the cases down to the car. Whilst they were waiting for him to bring the last case, Arion said: 'I know several publishers in London. I will let you have their addresses and, if you care to send them some of your work, I'll see what I can do.'

She was sitting at the wheel of the car. She did not answer. He said: 'I think you should send some. It is good, you know! There is something about it. If you liked to give enough time to it, I think you'd make a name for yourself one day.'

She said: 'But I don't want that. What I want — what I have always wanted and never had — is intimacy and understanding with someone I love and who loves me. I have never asked for more than that.'

'You couldn't ask for more,' he said.

'Isn't it what the majority of women get as a matter of course and still aren't contented?' When he did not answer, she went on: 'I'm not unwilling to do my share. I could love very much but, somehow, I've never been allowed to. My grandmother never encouraged me to give very much or expect very much. And with other people I've always just missed it, somehow. Either they haven't wanted all I could give or they've been the sort to whom I couldn't give anything. . . .'

The man appeared with the bag and she was forced to an abrupt silence. They drove away. Arion did not ask her to continue what she was saying, and she would not say anything more unasked.

When they arrived at Kingstown the boat was on the point of leaving. A porter seized Arion's bags and hurried him on board. It seemed to Elizabeth that all in a moment he was gone without having had time to say good-bye to her. When he remembered her and came to the gunwale to wave, she had already turned her back on the ship and was walking slowly down the pier.

She did not know where to go. She did not know

319

what to do. She began walking down the promenade in a slow, aimless way. When she saw a seat, she sat down on it and looked at the sea wrinkling the sunlight into scales. She did not look at Arion's ship that was turning now towards the open sea. She found herself thinking of Riordan in fear that, in the end, she, too, would have to be content with nothing better than living.

A man sat beside her and read 'Notes of the Month'. After a while, a thin little boy with sunken, old-looking eyes, came up to the man. He was holding a jam jar full of water.

'Hasn't anyone come yet?' asked the boy and the man not wishing to be troubled, said: 'No.'

'Haven't you seen them?'

'I haven't been looking.'

'Haven't you heard anyone call out "Victor!"?' persisted the lonely little boy.

The man shook his head and went on reading. The boy stood still without speaking and stared at the ground.

'Go away and play by yourself, can't you?' said the man at last, irritated by the proximity of the boy, hating his standing there alone and miserable.

The little boy went to play by himself and Elizabeth, looking after him, saw in his dragging feet all humanity's injury.

VIRAGO MODERN CLASSICS

The first Virago Modern Classic, *Frost in May* by Antonia White, was published in 1978. It launched a list dedicated to the celebration of women writers and to the rediscovery and reprinting of their works. Its aim was, and is, to demonstrate the existence of a female tradition in fiction which is both enriching and enjoyable. The Leavisite notion of the 'Great Tradition', and the narrow, academic definition of a 'classic', has meant the neglect of a large number of interesting secondary works of fiction. In calling the series 'Modern Classics' we do not necessarily mean 'great' — although this is often the case. Published with new critical and biographical introductions, books are chosen for many reasons: sometimes for their importance in literary history; sometimes because they illuminate particular aspects of womens' lives, both personal and public. They may be classics of comedy or storytelling; their interest can be historical, feminist, political or literary.

Initially the Virago Modern Classics concentrated on English novels and short stories published in the early decades of this century. As the series has grown it has broadened to include works of fiction from different centuries, different countries, cultures and literary traditions. In 1984 the Victorian Classics were launched; there are separate lists of Irish, Scottish, European, American, Australian and other English-speaking countries; there are books written by Black women, by Catholic and Jewish women, and a few relevant novels by men. There is, too, a companion series of Non-Fiction Classics constituting biography, autobiography, travel, journalism, essays, poetry, letters and diaries.

By the end of 1988 over 300 titles will have been published in these two series, many of which have been suggested by our readers.

Other Novels of Interest by Olivia Manning

The Doves of Venus

"She opened her window and gazed down on the window of Margaretta Terrace . . . What lay ahead for her? Would she ever rap on door-knockers with the urgency of important emotions? and run round a corner wearing a fur coat? and, lifting a hand to an approaching taxi, impress some other girl named Ellie and fill her with envy and ambition?"

Red-haired, eighteen-year-old Ellie leaves her home in the provincial seaside town of Eastsea and goes to London in search of independence, employment and experience. She finds a bedsit in Chelsea, a job painting "antique" furniture and a middle-aged lover called Quinton Bellot. Quintin's life is spent under the beady eye of his neurotic ex-wife Petta who haunts King's Road pubs with assorted Bohemians, nurturing virulent feelings towards Quintin's "little girls." And Ellie, having given her heart with the impetuosity of youth, gradually discovers the eternal complications of a love affair with a married man . . .

The Playroom

' "It wasn't just his looks. There was something about him—something. . ." In her effort to define Clarrie Piper's quality, Vicky drew in her breath, then said: "Something savage. He was extraordinary. Beyond dreams" '

Fifteen-year-old Laura lives with her family in the seaside town of Camperlea. It is the Swinging Sixties, and Laura's ambition is to leave home for London and work in a Chelsea boutique. Meanwhile she worships her schoolfriend Vicky Logan who is all Laura longs to be: popular, outrageous, sensual, she lives in a large house on "the right side of town." Vicky knows she can have any man she wants—but she chooses a rough factory worker, Clarrie Piper. She begins to frequent the factory dances and Laura watches in powerless dread and fascination as the teasing game Vicky plays through one feverish summer draws to its inevitable, terrifying conclusion. . .